Stellar Ne

AK Cooper-Elliot

Table of Contents

DEDICATION i

ACKNOWLEDGEMENTS ii

ABOUT THE AUTHOR iii

PROLOGUE iv

CHAPTER 1 1

CHAPTER 2 14

CHAPTER 3 20

CHAPTER 4 28

CHAPTER 5 38

CHAPTER 6 48

CHAPTER 7 60

CHAPTER 8 71

CHAPTER 9 83

CHAPTER 10 95

CHAPTER 11 105

CHAPTER 12 117

CHAPTER 13 139

CHAPTER 14 153

CHAPTER 15 167

CHAPTER 16 191

CHAPTER 17 206

CHAPTER 18 223

CHAPTER 19 256

CHAPTER 20 273

EPILOGUE 327

STELLAR NEBULA

The pillars of creation.

The aftermath of a supernova.

The nebulosity surrounded a star.

Allison Templeton-Miller

Born – January 25th, 1956.

DEDICATION

I dedicate this book to my late father. He inspired me to work hard and always do my best. Thanks, Dad.

ACKNOWLEDGEMENTS

I want to express my special thanks to my son Sam who lives in New Zealand, for his creative graphic designs. A huge hug for my daughter Georgina.

Thank you to my mum and husband, who have given me so much support and love over the last year whilst writing this book.

And as always, keeping my feet warm under the desk, my dog Willow.

ABOUT THE AUTHOR

AK Cooper-Elliot was born in Germany and raised in Yorkshire. After graduating from university in the early nineties, Cooper-Elliot pursued a high-flying career in Accountancy & Procurement. Retiring early from her executive role, she now creates exciting romantic and crime novels in her home office.

PROLOGUE

The Idiomatic Restaurant - New York

2nd December 1971

Paul Freidman sat at a corner table overlooking Orchid Park, cigarette in one hand and a glass of whiskey in the other. Sparkling chandeliers, high ceiling windows, and Doric columns were impressive, but not impressive enough for Paul Freidman.

Eager to get down to business, Paul waited for his visitor to arrive. The sound of plates clattering, glasses clinking and people chatting, increased his perception.

"Mr Freidman, your guest is signing in," the waiter said. "Refill?"

"Please," responded Paul, ogling the arrival of his guest.

The show-stopping platinum blonde walked towards the table in a red figure-hugging dress.

"Paul, darling, how good of you to invite me," the blonde smiled. "Gareth, I'll have the usual, my dear."

"Certainly," the waiter nodded to them both and marched over to the bar.

"Please, sit." Paul gestured.

The blonde held out her hand, and Paul placed a soft kiss upon her pale skin. "I heard you have a business proposition. I must say, I find it quite hard to refuse you." Her alluring green eyes investigated Paul's Eldredge knot.

iv

Gareth placed the whiskey and martini on top of lace coasters before departing with a bow.

Paul offered a cigarette to his new business partner. She accepted it, unthinking.

Placing the cigarette into her black holder she removed a silver lighter from her clutch bag. Leaning over the table Eva Moulin lit Paul's cigarette.

He looked around the occupied restaurant and met the blonde with his piercing blue eyes, inhaling his first smoke.

"You look well, Paul." she said, blowing smoke from her red lips.

Dressed in a grey pinstriped tailored suit, the thirty-five-year-old male of worth took another drag and blew a toxic cloud towards her. "It's an honour to be in the company of such a beautiful woman."

"Thank you," the blonde replied.

"You have something I require." Paul coughed.

"Enlighten me," the blonde smiled, ashing her cigarette.

"A student I'm interested in. You know."

"Miller's daughter?"

"Correct. The daughter in question is a gold mine." Paul smirked, gripping his whiskey glass.

"What are you proposing, Mr Freidman?"

"Five hundred thousand. Bonus for the school."

"Mr Freidman?" Eva licked her lips. "Can you guarantee the girl safety and success?"

"Of course… I am a man of my word."

"Paul, darling." The blonde leaned forward revealing her cleavage. "There's one problem."

"Problem?"

"Allison Templeton-Miller has formed a band called Templeton. Josh Williams, keyboard, and Allison, lead vocalist, are the songwriters. Both are only fifteen."

"Who are the other band members?" Paul asked irritably, annoyed at this news.

"Ricky Brown, lead guitarist, Donny Davis backup, Jack Evens on bass, and Marc Garcia as percussionist. All are ex-students of mine," she blushed.

"These kids got jobs?" Paul said, fuming at the fact that his million-dollar ticket could have been cashed.

"They graduated at eighteen and carried on with their education until twenty. Word in LA: Ricky Brown and Donny Davis are being booked for commercials. Jack plays in a jazz club. Garcia is a studio drummer for Honk Sound."

"Honk Sound? Send my guys a demo, and I'll notify Green Records." Whistling at Gareth, Paul shouted, "Two more," pointing at his empty glass.

"Paul, darling, I will accommodate you in whatever way you desire." Eva Moulin gulped while the waiter placed more drinks on the table.

"Keep the change." Paul stuffed a hundred-dollar bill in Gareth's pocket. "My proposal is that we sign the band with Green Records. Allison will also sign with Sphere Pictures. Green will own the royalties. I get a cut from both contracts. Twenty percent."

"What happens to the band when Allison is filming?"

"Continue recording…My goons will edit them together in post. My focus is Allison. I couldn't care less for the rest of them." Paul scoffed. "Donny Davis…"

"Ruthless."

"Madam Moulin, nobody becomes a multi-millionaire music executive by being polite. Do not forget who funds your school."

"Not my tax money, that's for sure." Eva Moulin looked down at her martini, wondering how many years she had sent innocent lambs to the slaughter. "I will help you with Allison."

"Please accept my gratitude towards the students at Kellie's." Paul raised his glass and smiled a wrathful grimace. "I am not happy with this situation, Eva."

The malevolent executive disguised himself greatly with his handsome looks. Hundreds of young lives had been ruined - promises of fame and fortune, wealth, and success. Initiating eating disorders, bankruptcy, drugs, and even suicide, Paul Freidman produced millions of dollars at their expense.

Allison Templeton-Miller, nearly sixteen years old, was at the mercy of The Kellie School of Performing Arts. She had no idea of the tactics that were being prepared for her.

On a crisp December afternoon, Paul Freidman and Eva Moulin planned their next venture. Encountering failure did not exist in Freidman's world. The future was an open book. Both Paul and Eva were ploughing all their energy into Allison. Mediocrity 1974 would be the turning point to produce one of the world's greatest pop stars that ever lived.

An immense welcome to Allison Templeton-Miller.

CHAPTER 1

Zurich - Switzerland - 25th January 1956.

Snow covered the elegant 1930s mansion, set in dense vegetation, and lined with doubled centennial trees.

American film director Theo-James Miller and his English actress wife Eleanor Templeton-Jones welcomed their fourth child, a healthy baby girl weighing six pounds and two ounces. Strong emotions of joy reverberated around the luxurious Art Deco bedroom, filled with expensive fabrics, sharp mixed metallics, and glamorous Bauhaus furniture.

"We shall name her Allison Marie." With pride, Theo-James Miller handed his daughter to Mrs Whitehouse, the family nanny.

"My darling Theo, I may say it is an excellent name," Eleanor replied, smiling at her pediatrician.

"My love, I shall leave you to rest." Theo-James kissed Eleanor on the forehead. "When you are ready to see the children, let me know."

"How are the children?" Eleanor replied

"Very well. You can see them later, please rest."

Theo-James and Doctor Keller walked out of the room. Eleanor was exhausted. Her hazel eyes blinked beneath black, curling hair. Even at thirty-five, every man in the film industry wanted her. She sat against her pillows and closed her eyes. "This is my fourth child. I cannot handle any more pregnancies," she mumbled.

The household maids replaced the bedding, bathed Eleanor, and dressed her into satin pajamas.

Eleanor's dresser Heidi collected the soiled nightgown from the carpeted floor and asked. "Would you like Earl Grey tea, Ms Templeton-Jones?"

"No, thank you. Gin and tonic, please. Childbirth is quite stressful."

"Better to drink after pregnancy than during. You deserve it Ms Templeton-Jones." Heidi curtsied and vacated the bedroom.

****

Theo-James caught the eye of every female who was lucky enough to star in his films. His tantalizing New York accent matched his designer 1950s suit.

"Congratulations," Keller said.

"Congratulate me? Eleanor did all the work."

"Unpaid labor."

"With overtime. For a moment, I was worried that she…"

"Don't worry, Theo." Doctor Keller shook Theo-James's hand. "That's my job."

Still gripping the wrought iron rail, Theo-James turned around and encountered his firstborn son, Henry.

2

"You're still my little angel," Theo-James said, caressing Henry's dark wavy hair.

"Can we see the baby, Papa?"

"Not yet, Henry. Your new sister is sleeping. You will all meet Allison later." Theo-James patted Henry's back as they strode down the grand staircase into the family room.

Inside the period-featured family room with parquet flooring and luxury fabrics, seven-year-old Henry joined his brother Richard and his sister Annie. The children sat listening to the radio that au pair Sofia had permitted.

Theo-James ordered that under any circumstances were his children allowed to attend school today. Henry, Richard, and Annie were all excited: not because of the baby, but because they were missing school.

"Shall we lunch in the conservatory, children?"

"I'm not a child," said Henry. "I'm almost eight!"

"Almost eight," Theo-James muttered, ambling towards the conservatory. "First one eats the chocolate cake!"

****

Baby Allison laid fast asleep in a white crib. Dark hair and pale rosy skin absorbed her pastel baby suit. Mrs Whitehouse shuffled quietly around the dark wooden floor of the nursery, trying not to disturb the newborn. Beside the crib an old rocking chair stood abandoned ready to commence its work at feeding time.

3

The children visited the nursery after lunch, shattering the tranquil atmosphere. Mrs Whitehouse and Sofia struggled to control the children's excitement. Luckily Allison slept through the commotion.

After seeing their new sister, Henry, Richard and Annie ran into their mama's room and tormented a enervated Eleanor.

The next day a new routine began in Templeton House. Eleanor bonded with Allison and the children played in their playroom.

Theo-James returned to his office and finalised his African filming project. His new movie would keep him away from his beloved family for the next sixteen weeks. Organizing the christening before February 21st took priority.

****

St Paul's Chapel - Zurich - Switzerland
15th February 1956

The paparazzi overlooked the prestigious architecture of the chapel and a growing number of spectators stood outside the gates. Two Silver Ghost Rolls-Royces approached the main entrance, chauffeurs blinded by flashes from the paparazzi's cameras.

Theo-James and Eleanor waved to the press and the surrounding crowds while their staff opened the Rolls-Royce passenger doors. Henry, Richard, and Annie waved and held hands. Eleanor's beauty blossomed in her red Charles Montgomery swing coat, crowned with a faux mink fur hat.

Theo-James, sporting a full-cut designer flannel grey suit, accompanied his wife and children into the chapel. Mrs Whitehouse cradled Allison in her silk lace baptismal gown.

Father Eric Schmid gathered the family around the font. Godparents Sylvester Kay and his wife Judy Grayson waited for their cue.

Allison remained quiet throughout the baptism. Outside the chapel paparazzi yelled questions and waved unsigned notebooks. Theo-James approached the waiting press with a statement.

"Gentlemen, thank you all for attending the christening of my daughter, Allison Marie Templeton-Miller. The service was supposed to be private, but the crowd showed up anyway. My wife and I wanted to invite more guests, but the church would have run out of water. Thank you."

Theo-James walked over to his car and then drove the family to Templeton House. The party was filled with enough film producers, directors, and actors to shoot an award-winning movie. Eleanor entertained the guests with champagne and caviar.

Theo-James escaped into his office with his assistant director. Howard and Theo talked about flying to Africa on their sixteen-week filming project.

Hanging above Theo's desk was a framed portrait of his wife. Theo-James stared into Eleanor's oil painted eyes and blinked. "Life without her is not worth living, Howard. In a couple of days, I shall be gone."

"All will be well, Theo." Howard glared and polished off his whiskey. "The team appreciate their contracts."

"I barely have time for Africa: I have no time for moaning actors."

The office door crashed open. Henry, Richard, and Annie ran into the room, laughing and screaming.

"What the hell?"

"Sorry, papa," Henry blushed.

"You are not allowed in here," Theo-James said, irritated. "Exeunt!"

The children disappeared, and Theo-James sat down in the nearest armchair with his whiskey.

"I detest parties as much as I love Eleanor. The children become disobedient. My staff disappears. Sometimes I wish I could, too."

"This is not like you, Theo. Is it the birth?"

"Forty is old to have a newborn, but I do love children. I am just worried when Allison is twenty, I will be sixty. Grandpapa."

"Rubbish, Theo. Your looks are young; your outlook is young. To get in your bed, most women would die."

"The little death. When you say it like that, I should be proud that I can still father a child in my forties."

"Never too late for fun!"

Howard and Theo-James laughed together beneath Eleanor's painted portrait.

****

Mrs Whitehouse fed, bathed, and dressed baby Allison. She was ready for her sleep. The guests had already made their acquaintances earlier in the day, and the nursery was at last peaceful. Henry, Richard, and Annie constantly ran inside until au pair Sofia was instructed to attend to the children.

Mrs Whitehouse held Allison in her arms, walking around the room with a smile of excellence. "You one day will be famous and beautiful, like your mama, my little one." She gazed down at the baby girl. "You are blessed."

The next morning brought chaos. During breakfast, Eleanor had the most excruciating headache. A concerned Theo-James walked around the table, kissed his wife passionately, and took his seat at the head of the table. Demanding his children be quiet because of Eleanor's condition, Theo disregarded his newspaper and watched his wife struggling with the noise.

A Silver Ghost Rolls-Royce parked directly outside the main doors. At the same time, school satchels laid abandoned across the entrance hall floor.

After breakfast, Eleanor and Theo-James aided their children with their coats and hats. Henry and Richard wore navy peaked caps, blazer, and tie, with long grey trousers, and polished black shoes.

Annie peeped under her boater, wearing a black pinafore dress, tie, and Sarah Jane shoes. All three children were finished to perfection wearing their white shirts.

Eleanor struggled to dress Annie into her school emblem winter coat, and Theo-James also had the same problem with the boys.

Henry, Richard, and Annie attended boarding school. Annie, an all-girls school called St Mary Schule. Henry and Richard, an all-boys school called St Augustine Schule. The children maintained decent grades in music, mathematics, and English.

Theo-James moaned, "Henry, your socks don't match!"

"Sorry, papa, I will change them."

"Too late now, there's no time. The car is waiting."

Richard was trying not to laugh, but Annie was giggling.

"Children, please, your papa is stressed." Eleanor clutched Annie's and Richard's hand and sauntered towards the entrance door. The staff stood in a line and waved goodbye.

Theo-James and Eleanor settled the children into the car and kissed them on the cheek.

"Be good," said Eleanor with tears in her eyes.

"You too," Annie said.

"Goodbye, children, and be good," whispered Theo-James.

The Rolls-Royce slowly moved forward, and the children waved through the windows. Theo-James cuddled Eleanor and waved back to his children. Within moments the vehicle had disappeared through the main gates.

They were gone…

****

Templeton House - Zurich - Switzerland
20th February 1956

Theo-James cuddled Eleanor in his arms, while baby Allison dribbled in her basket next to the bed.

"This is bliss, Theo," Eleanor said.

"My love, I wish I could stay here for the rest of my days."

"Do you need to take part in this African movie?"

"It is my job, Eleanor. My life's work."

"Africa?"

"Movies."

"That's the problem with our lives. No direction." Eleanor stared into his eyes. "I'm sick of acting. The only role I want is to be a mother."

"You are the greatest actress of all time."

"That's the problem, Theo. Strangers have put me on a pedestal. Like a circus act."

"Or a Michelangelo. I have a new script on the coffee table. Are you going to read it?"

"I already did. Max Stedman desires my talents."

"What's the movie called?"

"*The Fluctuation of Two Lovers.*"

"How cliche."

"It's supposed to be a comedy."

"That's what they always say when people laugh." Theo-James kissed Eleanor and climbed out of bed. His naked, tanned body radiated against the morning light. While dark chest hair shielded his sternum.

Eleanor sighed in contentment. In love with her husband, Eleanor fondled the pillow he had just risen from.

Theo-James made his way to the bathroom and turned the faucets on. The luminosity cast a shadow on his handsome face. Eleanor observed him while nursing Allison.

A knock at the door startled Eleanor.

"Yes, what is it?" she said.

"Would Madam care for breakfast in the dining room?"

"Yes, Gabriel?"

"Certainly, Madam."

"Theo!" Eleanor called. "Breakfast will be ready soon."

"Okay." Theo-James smiled in the mirror. "I will not be long."

Eleanor got out of bed and placed Allison back into her basket. She put her silk robe over her pajamas and joined her husband in the bathroom.

Three hours later, Eleanor established her place at the entrance of Templeton House. She waved goodbye to the most attractive man she had ever loved.

Theo-James's Silver Ghost drove through the wrought-iron gateway towards the airport. Theo's film crew were already on flights from LA to Cape Town. Assistant director Howard Levy had telephoned that morning to finalise the arrangements.

Another G.F Award would complete Theo's war chest of four awards, three Onyx, two F&P, and one Picture Makers Award.

Theo-James casually sat in the back in his Rolls, checking his schedule for the next sixteen weeks. Time was precious, almost as precious as his newborn.

****

Eleanor cuddled Allison as she strolled across the hallway. The former propped herself against the iron banister and groaned, feeling empty and lost.

Gabriel approached. "Madam, telephone call."

"Who is it?" Eleanor replied.

"Madam, Mr Stedman."

"Please alert Mrs Whitehouse to collect Allison. This might take a while."

The butler bowed and departed towards the nursery. Mrs Whitehouse arrived quickly and removed Allison from Eleanor's grip.

Eleanor kissed Allison on the cheek and blew a kiss towards her little bundle of joy, while Mrs Whitehouse disappeared up the staircase.

Eleanor paced into Theo's office and sat at his antique desk. Reaching for the French Bakelite telephone, she prepared herself before speaking into the handset.

"Eleanor, darling, how are you?" Max Stedman said on the other end of the line.

"Very well, Max." Eleanor rolled her eyes.

"Have you read the script yet? We are in the process of making you an offer."

"Yes," she said. "But I refuse to participate in any sexual scenes."

"You did nine months ago," Max laughed.

"Gerry Ramsbottom, my agent, will discuss your offer. I presume that filming will be in LA."

"Where else? Thomson & Burrows are waiting to issue the contract."

"I assume that screen tests will be issued, Max?"

"Not for you, my darling. The studio knows your pedigree. We shall be in touch once I get the go-ahead from Gerry."

"Indeed." Eleanor stayed seated with her hands resting on her chin. "What about Alli—"

The line was dead.

"Gabriel!" Eleanor cried.

"Madam?"

"Please get me my agent on the telephone this instant."

"Yes, Madam."

"This will be a long three months." Eleanor sighed.

CHAPTER 2

St Marys Schule - Zurich - Switzerland

3rd March 1966

Allison Templeton-Miller walked through the school grounds looking reserved and angelic. Plaited dark hair and hazel brown eyes, skin as white as snow, wearing her boater and pinafore dress, her looks were simply to die for, even at ten.

Allison was everyone's favourite. She skipped into the music room where Mrs Karson was waiting.

"Alice, we are playing *Symphony No.9* today."

"Yes, Miss Karson." Allison placed herself upon the pianist's seat.

The polished grand piano exploded into a melodic rhythm. Allison was a natural; she played the most exquisite music ever heard.

Mrs Karson applauded. Her A-grade student was excellent, brilliant, and she couldn't contain her excitement. "Bravo!"

"Thank you, Miss Karson."

"Do you practise at home?"

"I practise at the piano."

"Clever girl. Just remember not to be late for your next class. Ballet with Miss Fleur?"

"I won't be late, Miss Karson. Promise."

****

Loitering in the girl's dormitory, twelve-year-old redhead Belinda Ross-Belling stuffed an unopened textbook into her leather satchel. The daughter of US actress Melinda Ross-Belling, disliked school and resented her mother.

Belinda hurried to class, as Mrs Muller held the strictest detention in the school. She ran down the corridor at full speed, taking every step twice as big. Belinda cleared the doorframe just as the bell rang.

"Everyone, sit down. Today we will learn what the Pythagorean Theorem is. Does anyone know who Pythagoras was? Ross-Belling?"

"I didn't read the…" Belinda trailed off. "Geometry section."

"Right, a section within geometry. Now, we calculate the three sides of a triangle to detect if the hypotenuse is equal to the sum of the area on the other two sides."

"Belinda?" Mrs Muller said.

"Miss…?" Belinda coughed.

"Miss what? Do you even know my name?"

"Yes, Miss."

"Then what is it?"

Belinda just stared, clueless, and fell apart at her desk. Mrs Muller stormed over and grabbed Belinda's arm. "With me. Now!"

"Where?"

"The headmistress."

Belinda smiled because she knew this was exactly what she wanted: to be kicked out. She marched along the corridor with Mrs Muller and waited outside the heavy oak door to the headmistress's office.

Belinda knew her executioner would come out momentarily to discuss her case. She was thrilled. At least she would get the day off.

Lucinda La-Mount, the blonde twelve-year-old goddess, excelled in art. She kept busy splattering blue and yellow acrylic paint all over her canvas. Even though she was busy exuding excellence, she still smudged paint on her rosy cheeks.

"Excellent, Lucinda," art teacher Mrs Billon applauded from behind. "Another astonishing piece. I am so proud of you."

"Thank you, Miss. Billon." She continued hurling paint everywhere.

Lucinda stepped back and nodded, raising a thumb to her eye, she examined the perspective of her splashes. Delighted with her masterpiece, Lucinda displayed a huge grin.

As for eleven-year-old Fay-Abigail Lyons, the mousey-haired brunette was covered head to toe in mud. She ran down the field with a hockey stick in hand and wacked a small ball into the opponent's net. Fay disappeared into the nucleus of cheering girls. The crowd lifted her into the air; a whistle alerted the girls to drop the top scorer.

Fay thudded onto the hard ground with a moan and rolled over. Once she was back in focus, she retook her position, placing the curvature of the stick on the ground, and began to move forward, eyeing the ball in sight. Another strike, a smooth goal, piercing the net. With that, the final whistle blew. St Marys had won the match, all thanks to their filthy champion.

It was now lunchtime at St Marys. Allison found Belinda, Fay, and Lucinda, sitting in the school cafeteria.

"Hi," said Allison, looking pleased.

"You, okay, Alice?" Belinda said, glum.

"How did your morning go?"

"Hated every minute and now Mrs Muller has given me detention," Belinda said. "Why can't they just kick me out?"

Allison laughed. "You do some of the silliest things, Belinda."

"I'd be happier if they just kill me. Anyway, you seem happy. Music lesson?"

"Every day, same time."

"Fancy some Danny Bud later, after detention?"

"If they ever let you out."

"Can I get a witness?" Belinda grinned.

"I'll come to your dorm around six."

"That will be the best thing that happened to me in my whole life," Belinda said.

"Are we invited?" Fay pointed at Lucinda and herself.

"Yup, always." Belinda winked. "The four beauties!"

****

Synopsis

Allison Templeton-Miller, Belinda Ross-Belling, Lucinda La-Mount, and Fay-Abigail Lyons remained best friends. All four girls graduated at the age of fifteen, and Allison went her own way from St Marys on July 28th, 1971. Whereas Belinda and Lucinda graduated two years before, Fay graduated in 1970.

Returning to Templeton Hall, East Hampton, New York, Allison continued to play the piano and write music.

Belinda Ross-Belling resided at her family's penthouse suite, Upper West Side, New York. Lucinda La-Mount attended The College of Hospitality in the same state and resided with her father at the La-Mount Building, Manhattan.

At the age of sixteen, Fay-Abigail Lyons made it into law school in New York, following in her father's footsteps. For her birthday, Fay's parents acquired an apartment and chaperone close to Washington Square.

The four friends telephoned each other daily, talking about music, celebrities, and their love lives.

September 4th was the date when Allison and Belinda would reunite once again. Whilst Lucinda and Fay endeavoured another year at college before the four beauties reconciled, in the same place, at the same time, somewhere in September 1972.

CHAPTER 3

Kellie School of Performing Arts - Brooklyn
New York - 4th September 1971.

"Wow, Papa," said Allison, hypnotised by the grand pavilions.

"Only the best for my daughter," said Theo-James, grinning. "Where is your mama?"

"Here, darling." Eleanor smiled with a loving glow.

She wore a 1950s design: a beautiful Charles Montgomery sweeper dress in navy, accompanied by a wide brim hat and a navy ribbon. To that, she added sunglasses, a stylish navy purse, and earthy sandals.

Theo-James sported a Montgomery like his wife. A wide lapel suit in grey plaid with a matching necktie.

Madam Eva Moulin greeted Theo-James, Eleanor, and Allison with a huge bright smile. "Welcome to heaven. Please follow me to the lounge."

"Oh," gasped Allison. Everything emerged into a fairy-tale ballroom; the marbled floors shined as the Miller's walked to the lounge.

"Darling, there is the music area, look!" Eleanor beamed. "A grand piano."

"Mama, I'll love it here." Allison searched around the opulent room with her ball-shaped hazel eyes. She wore a yellow pinafore accompanied by a white polyester blouse, white tights, and branded white Sarah Jane shoes.

All three of them sat down whilst Madam Moulin spoke about the history of the building. Allison accepted a term schedule consisting of Maths, English, English Literature, Music, Drama, Ballet, and Contemporary Dance.

Theo-James and Eleanor had arranged a private car to collect Allison at 8:00 and 17:00 - Monday to Friday. Mr and Mrs Brown-Doyle were Allison's designated guardians at school, and their penthouse was located on 5th Avenue. This would be the residence for Allison for the next four years.

Henry, Richard, and Annie were also the Brown-Doyle's responsibility while attending The Kellie School of Performing Arts. Henry and Richard now worked in theatre, and Annie recorded classical music in Europe.

The following Monday, Allison started her first day with a fresh mind towards her new life. She was hoping to see Belinda, even though their schedules didn't match.

The Cadillac Fleetwood arrived outside the school at 8:30. The Brown-Doyle's chauffeur opened the back door, and Allison stepped out onto the pavement in all her glory, wearing striped, blue trousers and a turquoise blouse. She climbed the entrance steps, flourishing her Charles Montgomery work bag.

Opening the double glass doors, she glanced around the reception area and discovered Belinda Ross-Belling.

"Hi!" Allison waved at her with excitement.

"Come over here!" Belinda squealed.

"So glad to see you." Allison hugged her. "How's your schedule?"

"Maths first thing." Belinda looked at the ceiling in despair. "Double drama and music all afternoon."

"Music all morning and ballet this afternoon." Allison grinned with satisfaction.

"Your timetable seems much better than mine." Belinda sighed.

"I'll see you at breaktime." Allison bade goodbye to Belinda and sauntered towards her music class.

Inside the music room were eight polished grand pianos.

Dan Summers, the music lecturer, introduced himself to the students. "Call me Dan." The teacher announced, taking his seat at one of the pianos. "I'll be your music instructor."

The students followed suit, and each chose a vacant piano. Dan finished his overture from memory and placed a sheet of music on top of the polished lid.

Allison reached for the music sheet and stared at her blonde lecturer.

"Today, you are going to practise *Fur Elise* until you know it better than Beethoven."

All eight students agreed. While playing, Allison noticed a small fifteen-year-old male sitting at the next piano. His melodies were exquisite. After the first lesson, Allison introduced herself.

"Josh Williams," he said, continuing to play. Allison sat down at his piano and accompanied him. Josh, the son of actor Jack Williams, became good friends with her.

Eventually, they were so close that they started writing music together and produced a No.1 hit with their band 'Templeton' three years later, which helped them achieve platinum status.

****

The Kellie School of Performing Arts
4th February 1974

While students stood around chatting and rehearsing, someone yelled, "Talent scouts!" The entire hall fell silent. Belinda, now dating Donny Davis, met Allison in the reception area.

"Alice, what's going on?"

"Scouts."

"Scouting for what?"

"Talent," Alice deadpanned.

"Then they've come to the wrong school," Belinda huffed. "Don says there's a good chance the band could play."

"He hasn't mentioned it to me yet, and I'm the lead singer-songwriter. Anyway, I 've gotta run. Music class!"

Dashing towards the music hall, Dan Summers grabbed Allison's arm. "Allison, did you know we have specialised recruiters in the lesson today? They are particularly interested in Josh and you."

Allison pulled away. "Can we play our own songs?"

"I don't know. Can you?"

"Have you seen Josh?"

"Yes, and he's agreed to play *Heavenly Body* if you're happy with that."

"Sure, that's great."

"Go and do your best. I believe in you, Alice."

"Yes, sir."

Allison departed immediately to the music room, where Josh was waiting for her.

"Did Dan see you?" Josh asked.

"Yes, we are playing *Heavenly Body*, right?"

"Correct."

"Let's blow the socks off them," Allison beamed.

"You go, girl!"

Dan entered the room, followed by two guys wearing black suits and carrying portfolios. Dan introduced Peter McDonald and Greg Marsh from Green Records to the students. Both sat down with notebooks and requested to see the performance of Josh Williams and Allison Templeton-Miller.

24

Dan walked over to Josh and Allison and whispered, "Take your time, guys. I know you can do this."

Josh nodded. "Ready, Alice? One, two, three."

The moving ballad played between two pianos as Allison sang the song lyrics. The audience fell into a silence watching the pair's intense concentration. The soft melody merged with Allison's majestic voice, lighting up the room.

After the encore, Josh and Allison glanced at one another and smiled with satisfaction. They bowed towards the guests from Green Records. Applause engulfed the music room.

Mr McDonald requested once again to meet with Eva Moulin. Josh and Allison continued their studies with the rest of their class, while Dan Summers, a very proud lecturer, couldn't stop himself from taking pride in his students: the best class of 1974.

****

Madam Eva Moulin's office was the perfect place to negotiate. Filled with chic French furniture and expensive furnishings, the office emanated a unique and wonderful style.

Walking into the elegant surroundings, Mr McDonald and Mr Marsh observed Eva's splendour.

"Mr McDonald, Mr Marsh, sit." Eva pulled up a chair. "Tea will be served."

"Green Records are interested in charismatic, attractive, and entertaining artists that fans can connect with. Madam Moulin, think of the artists you look up to."

"If I had to think, it wouldn't be art."

"It's not just their music you admire. It's their personalities, right?" Peter McDonald said, crossing his legs and relaxing in his chair.

"Right, Mr McDonald. But can I inquire, how did you hear about Josh Williams and Allison Templeton-Miller?"

"An anonymous tip from the school."

"Did you now? Well, for your information Mr McDonald, Allison and Josh already have a band. They comprise of my graduated seniors. Donald Davis, Richard Brown, Jack Evens, and Marc Garcia."

"When do the seniors graduate, Ms Moulin?"

"Eighteen. If luck is on their side, they can achieve prosperous careers. Once they do, they graduate. Should their luck fail, they stay on until twenty. If they survive."

"So, we can say that those seniors we have mentioned are unlucky? Ms Moulin, Green Records would like to see this band. Live."

"Certainly. I shall notify my PA to gather my students together. After tea."

One hour later, in the Great Hall, Templeton prepared their equipment. Donny Davis (Guitarist), Ricky Brown

(Lead Guitarist), Jack Evens (Bass Guitarist), Marc Garcia (Drummer), Josh Williams (Pianist/Keyboard), and Allison Templeton-Miller (Singer/Vocals).

While they were setting up, Green Records assembled next to Eva Moulin and waited.

The dense sound echoed through the hall as they were now tuning in. Allison took the stage and began to sing the first track, *Breakdown Summer*. Ricky Brown and Donny Davis accompanied her, backing her up on vocals.

Eva noticed her guests tapping their feet to the beat. The hall resounded with loud cheers. Both men watched intensely, figuring out the accurate photo shots of the band on stage, constantly writing notes and nodding at one another. As the song ended, everyone could sense that this audition was about to be one to remember.

"Bravo. Bravo." Eva saluted her guests with pride. "Gentlemen, shall we proceed to my office for further discussions?"

Listening to Eva, Allison, and the guys high-fived each other. This was just the beginning of their careers, and they couldn't wait to keep shining further.

CHAPTER 4

Green Records Recording Studio - Los Angeles
8th July 1974

Heated banter could be heard from outside the studio's glassed walls. Paul Freidman crushed an offer agreement in his hands. Benedict Shaw couldn't control himself, and Templeton's legal team were not willing to back down.

Benedict Shaw broke the silence. "This agreement allows my artists to record and release material with alternate recording companies. As Green Records CEO & Chairman, I have a commercial interest in protecting our assets," Shaw said. "My assets."

"Mr Chairman, the original constitutional agreement is collective. Templeton justifiably will be contracted to Green Records and licensed to another label. The situation regarding Allison Templeton-Miller's contract, Sphere Pictures, will also be incorporated. Burrows & Burrows will reject the deal unless immunity is guaranteed."

"New York attorneys approach my company and question my authority? I don't even listen to my father, never mind a lawyer!"

"Extenuating circumstances. The contracts will not be signed. Fifty million and two albums are surplus to Green Records' requirements."

Paul Freidman broke in. "I am prepared to manage this group to the top. Our capital turnover is estimated at over two hundred million within the first year. Benedict, we can capitalise on this. Think about it. Allison can perform between Green Records and Sphere Pictures, Green acquiring the major percentage."

Benedict observed with a pragmatic look. "Deal. Let's get the band's signatures before anyone tries to flee the country."

****

Synopsis

Templeton signed a five-year Green Records contract, and because it was a huge deal, the media and influencers attended the event.

Freidman published the band's recording schedule. Photographers surrounded the area, snapping shots of the band while Green Records legal executives made themselves scarce.

Josh Williams and Allison Templeton-Miller nevertheless had to attend The Kellie School of Performing Arts until they had graduated. Both Allison and Josh were constantly in LA and New York until May 26th, 1975.

****

Green Recording Studios Apartments - Los Angeles

31st August 1975

"Alice, where are you?" Josh shouted from his balcony.

"Here," Allison said, walking onto her balcony through the opened patio doors. "Why?"

"Front page! Can you believe it? Our single is going to be released next month, and we are bigger news than Kingston. Wow!"

"Wow."

"What's wrong, Alice?"

"I'm just tired...I have been given a film script to look at. I don't know how the heck I'm going to fit all this into my schedule."

"I'm writing the next two tracks for the album. So don't worry about it."

"Easier said than done."

"When's filming start?"

"October. Sixteen weeks, start to finish. Then I have all the promotions and events."

"The burden of talent," Josh laughed.

"Hmm."

"Paul mentioned you'll be out of the picture. I heard he's setting your recording dates in between filming. You'll be on demo and merged with our recordings."

"Great. My life gets lonelier day by day."

"You are worth millions, Alice. More than us guys put together."

"Shame I haven't seen a penny."

"You're regretting it?"

"No!"

Josh didn't believe her and smirked at his friend.

"My parents, brothers, and sister are in the same game. It's this or the street."

"Alice, you'll own the street. Stop worrying so much and live in the moment!" shouted Josh, walking into his apartment.

"Yeah, yeah, yeah." Allison drooped over the balcony railing, noticing people and cars dashing around the boulevard from the fifteen-story tower block. "I wish I were normal, like everyone else."

Sheer white curtains blew their way out onto the balcony from the open patio doors. Allison ignored the swaying fabric and faded into herself anticipating the major changes that would change her life forever.

****

Green Records Studio Head Quarters - Los Angeles
7th September 1975.

Templeton sat patiently in Paul Freidman's office on a charcoal sofa. Record producers Peter Clarke and Eric Sanders strolled into the available space next to Paul's desk

Paul was listening to the 'Billboard Hit 100' live on air. Templeton's debut album *Not at All Going Back* peaked at number one and their hit single *Heavenly Body* sold 15.8 million.

Everyone except Allison leapt off the couch and cheered.

"This is cause for celebration!" Paul popped a champagne cork. "Alice, you okay with champagne?"

"Yeah...Paul, just pour the champs!"

"Templeton, the band of the future. Cheers!" Paul smirked, with huge dollar signs in his eyes.

"Cheers," shouted everyone.

Allison celebrated with the team until the early hours. She was exhausted, and Templeton had a busy week ahead of them. They had interviews lined up, and they also had to perform on TV.

Templeton travelled across the states to attend photoshoots for magazines, merchandise, and billboards. Allison's time with the band was cut short. Director/producer Stewart Gloss demanded the singer's presence at the Sphere Pictures film studios.

Attending screenings, photoshoots, and voice, script rehearsals, Allison was determined to please the director. She made new friends with the cast, Colin St-Birch, and Stephen-Paul Golding.

Twenty years her senior, Colin St-Birch became her father figure and constantly supported Allison. The connection between them did not go unnoticed. Allison and Colin became a sensational on-screen duo together.

Flying In began shooting on the 3rd of October. The location was at Sphere Pictures, near to her recording studio. This pleased Allison greatly. It offered her the opportunity to continue recording at Green Records late in the evenings.

Stephen-Paul Golding waved at Allison, "Come over here!"

Allison shouted from her dressing room, "I'll be there in a bit!"

"No, no, I'll come to you." Stephen winked at the female script writer.

Stephen-Paul Golding approached the make-up room with his blue eyes and the smile of a demigod. Allison remained sitting in a tall leather salon chair.

"Hey, honey," Stephen smiled at the make-up artist. "Allison, I need you to go over your lines."

"Why?" Allison asked, puzzled.

"Because I like you...No, I adore you!"

"I'm not looking for a date."

"You're almost twenty."

"So what? You'll be twenty-six. I'm not looking for a big brother."

"That hurt," Stephen winked at her. "I won't give up."

Groups of girls constantly hung around the studio gates, hoping to catch glimpse of the film's heartthrob. Allison loved the atmosphere with Stephen and Colin. The film was going to be a hit.

****

The Hexagon Theatre - Los Angeles - 15th March 1976

Allison wore an elegant black Charles Montgomery couture evening dress and sequenced ankle-strapped heels. The stylists tied her hair with diamond hair clips, supporting the dark uplift above her head. She looked amazing.

Camera flashes ignited the red carpet. Security held fans back, and the limos anticipated the next parking slot. TV personnel were busy speaking into their headphones, whereas interviewers were praying for their next victim.

Stephen-Paul Golding and Colin St-Birch, dressed in tuxedos, positioned themselves next to Allison and Gloss. Waving at the crowd both men posed with pride.

Stephen-Paul continually kept touching Allison around her slender waist. Allison tolerated it until she stepped on his foot. "Oops, sorry," she grinned.

"That hurt!"

"You'll get over it," she said. "Now wave to the crowd." Allison walked over to an interviewer and snatched his microphone.

The evening continued to flow after the premier. Stephen-Paul refused to intrude upon Allison's space at the afterparty, all due to the benefit of being surrounded by three curvaceous young women.

Allison endured engagement after engagement with new directors, producers, scriptwriters, and actors. She was bored and tried to scurry away when she bumped into a dark-haired man. The sight of him took her breath away.

Observing the situation at hand, his expressive brown eyes cast over Allison.

"Si McKay."

"You're Si McKay?" she said.

"And you must be Allison Templeton-Miller."

"Yes, I am Allison Templeton-Miller."

"A beautiful woman like yourself, now a movie star as well. Everyone will want a piece of you." Si smiled. "I know I do."

Allison blushed. Her feet refused to move, and the sound of her heart beating made a commotion in her ears.

Si and Allison chatted most of the evening, danced, and exchanged numbers. Allison's security kept close watch.

Paul Freidman stood in the background, observing the couple.

"Paul, how are you?" Stewart Gloss asked, striding over from the bar.

"Very well, Stewart. Great film!"

"We are just in the process of negotiating part two of *Flying In.* I will require the same cast."

"So, you will need Allison?"

"Unless she has a twin."

"My office next week to arrange the schedule. Templeton have a European tour in October."

"No, filming won't start until next year. February."

"The cruellest month."

"That's April, Paul."

"Any month without Allison is the cruellest month."

Paul clinked his glass of bourbon on Stewart's. Both grinned and imagined the dollar signs. Si and Allison made light conversation, while their futures were decided in a dark and smoky room.

****

The following morning, Allison opened her eyes and sat up in bed beside a tanned male. His arm cuddled her middle torso. Lengthy dark brown hair trailed along his shoulders and his long lashes covered his deep brown eyes.

The moment he opened his eyes, he could see Allison staring right at him. Si grabbed her by the waist and pushed her down to the bed on her back. He smiled at her, looked gently into her eyes, and kissed her.

She could feel the intimacy, the connection between them, growing. Si positioned himself around her whispering in her ear. In the heat of the moment, they felt vulnerable.

Posing in Si's arms, Allison knew she had lost her virginity the night before. A woman in the making. She felt wonderful, happy, grown up. Stroking his face, she gave him a sweet peck on his cheek and made her way towards the bathroom. She removed the bedsheet and covered her nakedness with it. Turning around with a smirk, she said, "Do you want to join me in the shower?"

Si jumped out of bed and rushed over. Kissing her intensely, Si pushed Allison into the bathroom and closed the door with his foot.

Two hours later, the door opened, and the couple, sexually refreshed, re-joined the world.

CHAPTER 5

Hans Hotel - Berlin - Germany - 6th October 1976

The European tour gave Templeton three brilliant hits. All the crew and management were ecstatic. Paul Freidman organised a press conference at the hotel before the show.

"Right, guys, just answer questions regarding the tour. No personal answers."

Donny Davis shouted, "Okay, boss!"

"Allison, the press will bother you regarding your love life with Si. Ignore those questions and move on."

"Moving on," Allison answered, worried.

Since learning of their romance, the press published rumours about Si and Allison, including damaging reports of Si's bachelor days. His reputation as a bad boy made the headlines.

The conference room was full of cameras flashing around them and TV screens. Reporters aimed their cameras at the long desk located on a built stage where Templeton were sitting behind their name plates.

"Allison, Allison! Tell us how long you have been seeing Si McKay. Are you in love?"

Allison looked at Josh and said, "I love a lot of things."

"Next question!" Ricky Brown yelled from her opposite side.

The press received the message loud and clear from Ricky and continued to inquire about the tour and the next album. After twenty minutes, Templeton stood up from their seats and walked off the stage.

Paul patted each member on the back. "Good answers, guys. The bus is waiting at the back of the hotel. Five minutes to board."

"I detest press conferences," Allison sighed.

"Just smile and nod. Always remember that."

"Thanks, Paul."

Templeton boarded the bus for Grub Stadium.

****

Dressed in pink shorts and a Templeton white t-shirt, Allison stood on stage and shouted, "Is this a good position?"

"You are always in a good position, Allison," Slick Dylan shouted back.

"We all love you." The technical manager said, offering Allison a mic. "Especially in those shorts."

"Slick!" Allison blushed, looking at his enormous pecs. Straining to climb over the cable, Allison stumbled. Slick rushed over and pulled up the singer. Allison blushed some more grabbing the mic.

"Starting with Alice, guys, let's take it from *Heavenly Body* on three," Slick shouted to the rest of the band, nodding his head with his thumb held high.

"Got it!" Ricky shouted. "Three, two, one."

In a moment, a soul-pleasing melody spread across the stadium, reflecting every word she sang. Allison's amplitude left all dumbfounded, in awe of the moment, they couldn't stop themselves from swaying to the sound of her voice.

Slick and a sound technician checked the speakers to perfection. A designated dimmer tech operated the stage light and backdrop controls, reassuring that the lighting effects coordinated accurately against the sound's intensity.

Rehearsals, sound, voice, and mic checks continued all afternoon. Templeton finally got the time to relax on the grey leather sofas situated in the Blaugrun Room.

While the guys took a breather, Allison sat in Paul Freidman's temporary office, speaking with Si in Japan on the office telephone.

"Alice. How is Germany?" Si asked.

"Good," she paused. "Do you realise that you call me in every city that I am touring?"

"I would kidnap you, but I can't get through security," Si joked.

"How's Japan?"

"Tiring."

"Oh, that's not good. France is our next stop, then London and then home," Allison sounded excited. "Yippee."

"Another month for me." Si moaned.

"What a shame,"

"Alice, I must go, that's my agent."

"Take c…" Allison's farewell was cut short by the dial tone. She returned to the Blaugrun Room. Feeling perturbed Allison avoided any questions regarding Si.

Sitting on a vacant sofa Allison looked around the room. Huge canvases of sunflowers hung on the walls and potted plants were scattered everywhere. The aromatic smell of coffee percolators engulfed the room - silver trays of sandwiches abandoned on wooden tables.

The guys spawled across the sofas, either reading, watching TV, or sleeping. Unfortunately, the moment of peace wasn't going to last long; the VIP audience had arrived. They wanted to see their favourite pop group in person.

Freidman escorted Allison, Donny, and Ricky into the VIP lounge to meet their awaiting fans. The rest of the band continued to lounge in front of the TV.

The three popular members of Templeton signed autographs and chatted with their fans. Within an hour the VIP lounge was empty, and the trio were in make-up.

Josh now dating hairstylist Miranda King sat in his chair drinking orange juice. Miranda, a tall redhead with blonde highlights, and seductive green eyes, enticed Josh into falling in love with her.

Robert Kingly worked on Allison's make-up. With black hair, olive skin, dark eyes, and an effortless promenade enhanced his Latin look. It was fun when Miranda and Robert were together, and Allison loved their gossip.

Ricky Brown engaged to Annie Templeton-Miller was soon to marry. Donny Davis and Belinda Ross-Belling were planning to get engaged. Jack Evens secretly married his childhood sweetheart and had to live a double life, while Marc Garcia a free agent was open to all offers.

Allison loved the band's private life because Miranda and Robert continuously kept their gossip simple. Whatever Allison learned, she never really revealed much of it to the band and believed that it gave her the upper hand, but she understood not everyone needs to know everything.

Later that evening, the concert proceeded without any problems. Templeton signed more autographs that evening than they ever did, and the fans went crazy for them.

****

Back at the hotel, an afterparty was held in the Hannover Suite. In a dark corner, Gregory Sharp was speaking to a stunning Latin male, and Allison was intrigued to meet him.

"Allison, darling," gestured Gregory, grabbing Allison's arm. "Meet Romano Mancini."

"Hi," Allison mumbled, immobilised.

Gregory looked at her worriedly, wondering if she was okay. The Italian/American actor got captivated by her aura. Stepping closer, Allison found herself losing sight of the ground, stumbling. He couldn't stop himself from staring into her eyes, as if he was telling her exactly what he was planning that night.

Gregory did the right thing by inviting him here. Noticing the glow in their eyes, he knew they would hit it off. "Allison, Romano has been nominated for a G.F Award."

"Really? That's cool!"

"Impressed, Miss Templeton-Miller?" said Romano.

Allison nodded. She couldn't stop thinking that she was standing in front of a living, breathing God of the film industry. She didn't realise that her world just made a 180.

The twenty-six-year-old pinup lived in LA and owned property in Tuscany. He was around five-feet-ten inches tall. The A-lister's olive skin glowed against his long raven hair.

Even though Allison was twenty, Romano could feel himself falling for her. He had to have her for his own.

Allison had no words for how she felt. Only just meeting him for the first time had totally confused her. His handsome looks palpitated her heart.

Gregory could feel the tension growing around him, and to make it not look awkward, he had to cut in. "Allison's schedule is hectic next year. Templeton are recording another album. February, she starts filming *Flying In 2*. We are negotiating with her father, Theo."

"Theo?" Romano interrupted.

"He insists that Allison play the leading lady in his latest picture."

"Do you want to work with your father?" Romano gazed at her with his alluring brown eyes. "Allison?"

"No."

"This is the reason we're still under discussion. Not with Theo-James, but with Miss Templeton-Miller," mumbled Gregory.

"Then I will have to persuade you, Allison," Romano said. "I think you will like my methods!"

Allison excused herself and headed off towards Donny and Josh. Trying to avoid Romano, she eventually withdrew to her room.

Romano followed and knocked at the door. Allison peered through the keyhole at Romano standing in the hallway. She opened the door halfway so nobody could see her and invited him in.

The room had a dim lighting effect, more like a faded orange, and was designed to look like an escape into the 18th century. The interior had a touch of how France used to be back in the day.

Romano interjected, "Forgive me for intruding, Allison."

"It's okay," responded Allison, gulping down nervously as her voice broke and her mouth went dry. She urgently needed a drink. "We're just talking."

"I understand that you are dating Si McKay."

"You've heard of him?"

"Sex?"

"Romano, please," blushed Allison, offering him a bottle of water.

"Only the hard stuff!"

"Whiskey?"

"That'll do." Romano made himself comfortable in a regal French chair.

"I have seen him a few times, but with the touring, it has been difficult keeping in touch… I always receive a phone call in every city I tour," Allison responded quietly.

"Only one call per city?" Romano laughed, shaking his head.

"What? If it were you, you would call me all the time?"

"A girl as gorgeous as you should not be relying on one phone call per tour," Romano took the glass of whiskey and sipped a mouthful of the succulent amber liquid. "I thought you would have understood that by now."

Allison stood there, admiring the beauty before her.

"Let me take care of you," Romano said.

"Romano, please." Snapping out of her fantasy, she took a moment to realise what he had just said. "You know I'm dating Si."

In a flash, Romano got up from his seat and whisked her into his athletic arms. He gazed at her out of love and lust, sliding his mouth upon her silken, soft lips. His fingers caressed her thick, entwining dark curls as he kissed her to oblivion.

With a soft moan, she realised she had lost all control. Her legs felt weak within his embrace as she delicately responded with a kiss on his honey-sweet lips. The feeling of his strength against her clear skin and petite body thrilled her.

Romano gazed into her hazel brown eyes. "I am in love with you already," he whispered.

Hearing Romano's sensual words, Allison was shocked, but excitement bubbled inside while she remained silent.

"I will not surrender, Allison." Romano slowly released her. Combing his fingers through his hair, "I have to go."

He walked towards the door without a word. Allison wanted to stop him but knew that it was not right. Before leaving, he gave her a faint smile, as if he were addicted to the silence. He wanted them to address their love, trapped within the room, but Allison couldn't cheat that wasn't who she was. Aware of how she felt about Romano, she had to deal with Si first.

The relationship with Si was not working and she always felt like the other woman for some reason. It was vital that Allison had to end this joke.

Feeling herself opening her heart towards Romano, she had fallen in love with him.

The following day Allison ended her relationship with Si. Sending him a fax was easy. Never looking back Allison joined her band members and flew to France.

Templeton survived another successful concert in Paris. Finally, they ended the tour in London on October 12th, 1976.

Eight weeks later, their third album, *Red Signs*, was finally complete and scheduled to be released on January 6th, 1977.

CHAPTER 6

Templeton House - Zurich - Switzerland
25th December 1976

A snowy landscape surrounded Templeton House. Its long, slender shadows sculptured the 1930's structure. Winter trees shivered in the bitter wind, and the warm radiant antique lanterns illuminated the icy driveway.

Occupying the hallway stood a five meter tall Norwegian Christmas tree, full of festive charm.

Assembled midpoint in the dining room convened a sophisticated handmade bronze table surrounded by sixteen seats of golden flame birch and flanked by armless chairs. A veneered end chair completed the arrangement.

The table design dazzled in its splendour. A sequin banquet tablecloth in gold coordinated against black napkins, and placemats. Holly corsages settled among the crystal wine glasses. Demitasse plates complemented the gold cutlery placed in front of nine seats.

Theo-James and Eleanor seated themselves in authentic brown and gold leather chairs next to the crackling fire. Traditional holly and red berry garlands hung merrily around the fireplace. Assorted candles crystalized the beauty of soft lighting engulfing the dining room.

Henry and his pregnant partner, actress Rene Wilcox, cuddled one another as they sipped champagne mixed with orange juice.

On the opposite sofa, Annie sat with her fiancé Ricky Brown. Soon to be Mr Ricky Brown–Templeton–Miller.

Richard Templeton-Miller sat drinking whiskey with his present girlfriend, model Susan Milroy. Susan chatted with Allison and completely ignored Richard.

This was typical of Richard, to attach himself to a stunning woman and become bored of her. He was never interested in the single life drama in the company of his family: she was just another trophy notch on his bedpost.

Theo-James presented Eleanor with a gold box. Eleanor smiled, dressed in an elegant black Charles Montgomery evening gown.

Eleanor opened the box and gasped. "It is beautiful, darling," she said, pulling out a pearl bracelet.

"Just like you," Theo-James bent down and placed the bracelet around her slim wrist.

Eleanor beamed holding her wrist into the light and examined the expensive pearls. Delighted by her gift she handed over a silver box to Theo.

Theo-James knelt next to his wife and opened his box. Everyone watched in anticipation. Grinning, he said, "A pocket watch! It is not a standard model, but a rare antique…Eleanor this is perfect. I will treasure this forever, thankyou my love." Gripping onto his box, Theo stood up and whispered into Eleanor's ear.

Removing himself from his blushing wife, Theo-James announced to his family, "Because of Alice's busy schedule next year, Eleanor and I have decided to present our baby girl with an early 21st birthday present." Theo handed Allison an envelope. "Wow, I feel old, Alice."

Allison sprung onto her feet and walked over to her parents, while her siblings clapped and cheered. She accepted the envelope from her papa and opened it. Turning pale she muttered. "I don't believe this."

Eleanor and Theo-James nodded at one another in approval. "Problem, my darling?"

"Mama, it's perfect," Allison erupted in delight. "The penthouse suite, Palmer Building, on 72nd Street. Manhattan!"

"Darling, we have requested an interior designer to help with decorations and the furniture," Eleanor beamed. "All expenses paid."

"By giving it to you early, you'll have more time to organise the apartment." Theo-James hugged her in delight. "There is also another delivery, from me. It will arrive on the 7th of January. The Palmer Building staff are aware of the delivery."

"Another present?" Allison squealed at her papa.

"You're the only present I need." Theo-James kissed Allison's forehead.

Allison was overwhelmed: returning to New York would be so different, especially owning her own home.

More presents circulated, and Theo-James and Eleanor acquired cars for their sons. Annie received a spa treatment in Paris along with Allison. Rene, Susan, and Ricky all received jewellery. Celebratory tributes continued until the dining room was occupied in abundance.

Champagne poured; glasses clinked. Different conversations were happening all around. A combination of smoked salmon and caviar appetizers commenced the festivities. Culinary masterpieces of *Wagyu beef* and seasonal vegetables soon followed. Lastly, haute macaroons and cake confections alongside the *crema Mexicana* completed the feast.

The family enjoyed their Christmas celebrations until the late evening.

****

A luxury king-sized bed absorbed Allison. A loud knock emanated from the bedroom door while she browsed through a magazine.

"Yes?" Allison sat up, startled.

"Hey, kid." Richard poked his head around the door. "Can I come in?"

"What's up?"

Richard strolled over to the bed and sat down, resting his head against the pillows. He looked at Allison, saying in a sympathised tone. "You, okay?"

"Okay? I'm a homeowner!"

"No." Richard smirked. "I meant with Si."

"I ended it." Allison paused. "It wasn't working. He was touring, I was touring…"

Richard looked down and fiddled with the magazine Allison had thrown onto the bed covers.

"You want to know why I broke up with him?"

Richard looked shocked. "You have someone else?" His lips parted. "Alice, you dark horse!"

"I met someone in Berlin. I was..." Allison contemplated what she had just said.

"Oh… Love at first sight." Richard laughed.

"Nothing happened!" Allison tossed a pillow at him. "Just because you dip your thingy into every female out there doesn't mean I do."

Richard laughed some more. "Okay, okay. I was just joking!"

"I met Romano Mancini, and I'm not sure if our paths will ever cross again. I know Si was not for me."

"Romano Mancini? He is more popular in the movie world than 'King Kong'. Wow, you certainly go for the big hitters, Alice." Richard stared into Allison's puzzled face. "What was his reaction?"

"He was attracted to me. He couldn't keep his eyes off me. That's why I felt overwhelmed." Allison began to blush.

"If you two made out, it would make world news." Richard sat back against the headboard and rubbed his chin in thought.

"Do you think I will have trouble with the press?" Allison asked, worried.

"No! You have two big brothers and five band members to look after you," Richard responded, clenching his fists.

"What about your love life?" Allison giggled.

"I have met someone else, and I want to marry her." Richard shrugged his shoulders.

"Who?"

"Ami Johns."

"The underwear supermodel?"

"Who else? I am madly in love with her, Alice."

"Why is Susan here?" laughed Allison.

"I 'm struggling to get rid of her!" Richard sighed. "Ami and I have been in a relationship since July."

"Oh!"

"Ami is attending your party. That's when I intend to propose."

"At the club?" Allison bellowed. It was her birthday party, and she didn't want the limelight to go to her brother.

"It's your birthday, silly." Richard looked up at the ceiling. "I wouldn't dream of taking the attention away from you."

"We both have secrets to keep." Allison took Richard's hand and held it tight. "It's like the old days."

Richard kissed Allison's hand while he shuffled off the bed. Saying good night, Richard disappeared from her room.

Allison had major plans for her return to New York, and they all included Romano Mancini.

****

St Moritz - Switzerland - 27th December 1976

The family continued their festive holiday in the alpine resort of St Moritz. The Templeton-Miller's luxury thirty-bedroom chalet cascaded down the mountain, overlooking forests and streams.

Each evening, chefs offered the family a canapé reception. Stewards presented fine wines and beers. Fresh flowers orchestrated the tables, and crystal imitated soft lighting upon the oak flooring.

By day, the family appeared on the snowpack inclines. Eleanor was inclined to relax on the mountain restaurant terraces, drinking pear brandy.

Theo-James challenged his sons to compete in a downhill race. Henry always won his father, to Theo's annoyance.

Esteemed for her exceptional style, wearing a black Cossack faux fur hat, sunglasses, and a fashionable ponytail, Allison skied effortlessly across the terrain of snow.

On her left side a dark-haired male approached. He turned his head towards her and winked. Allison glanced at the man and made a parallel stop. The man continued for another few metres and did the same. Turning around, he lifted his hand and waved at her.

"Allison, my love!" a voice called out.

"Romano! What are you doing here?" shouted Allison, feeling flustered.

"Vacation." Romano stabbed two poles into the snow.

Allison skied towards him and stopped at his side. "Good to see you."

"I selected St Moritz for my vacation because I knew you would be here."

"I see," Allison smiled. "When did you arrive?"

"Yesterday. Just in time for dinner with you tonight."

"Mr Mancini, you don't beat around the bush!"

"I can't stop thinking about you, and I know you hate me." Romano sighed. "That makes me want you more."

"I don't hate you." Allison blushed.

"So? Will you have dinner with me?"

"Alright, I will have dinner with you."

Romano and Allison spoke for another hour on the crispy slopes. That evening, he arranged their dinner date at the Kavalier Hutt Das Hotel. Romano left the scene a very happy man.

****

Kavalier Hutt Das Hotel hosted the world's richest guests. The hotel contained 167 lavish rooms and suites, two restaurants, luxury spa, gym, and an exotic crystal indoor pool.

Allison arrived on time in a beaded ivory godet gown. Gracefully entering the glass door entrance, Hotelier Mr Wagner greeted her with a bow. "Miss Alice, your guest is waiting for you at your table. Please, follow me."

Wagner paced towards the table. Romano stood by the picturesque furnishings dressed in a black dinner suit and tie. He cleared his throat as Allison took her seat. "You look beautiful, Alice."

Waiters poured wine into utopia wine goblets; bread rolls overflowed from prestigious side plates. Allison and

Romano ordered oyster appetizers, followed by the main course of smoked beef.

Romano fidgeted gazing at his companion. "Alice, I want to spend the rest of my life with you."

Allison dropped her fork onto her plate. People around her glared.

"Sorry if I have shocked you," Romano said. "My feelings for you are eternal."

"Sorry...I just don't know what to say!"

"Don't say anything...You are answering me with your eyes." Romano grinned. "Do you believe in love at first sight?"

"I don't believe in anything."

"Alice?"

"In Berlin, I knew…" Allison stopped in mid-sentence, looking down at her plate. "You walked out of my room…"

"I would never walk out on you." Romano grabbed Allison's hand.

Allison gripped Romano's hand and lifted her head. "My heart told me everything when you walked away from my room." She wondered if she would be able to stand back up, her legs quivered like jelly underneath the table.

"Stay the night with me?" Romano whispered.

"Every night." She nodded.

Calming piano music absorbed the romantic atmosphere. People chatted and clinked glasses around them. Everything froze in motion for the couple as Romano gazed into Allison's eyes, and Allison gazed back into Romano's.

Dessert arrived: two Swiss couverture sundaes interrupted the moment. Romano released his hand from Allison's and asked the waiters to take away one sundae. The waiters obliged while Romano and Allison shared the single sundae, feeding each other.

Allison sent a message from the hotel informing her parents that she was staying out. After coffee and mints, Romano directed her to his suite.

The glorious room of green and gold drapes consisted of complementary sofas, a polished oak bureau, and a drink cabinet; beyond the stained-glass casement doors a snow-covered balcony hid in the darkness.

The bedroom concealed itself behind double oak doors on the far side of the suite. Romano opened the doors to reveal a four-poster bed. The drapes matched the interior in the lounge area.

Allison smiled at Romano while he pulled her close to his chest. Leaning in Romano glided his soft, warm lips against Allison's. Sensually kissing him back, she fused her body with his.

Romano scooped Allison into his arms and carried her over to the bed, placing her on top of the mulberry duvet.

Gazing deep into her hazel brown eyes, he whispered. "Bello."

Enshrouding his robust body above hers, he discarded his and her clothing. Their naked legs entwined within the duvet.

Romano continued to whisper in Italian as Allison moaned with pleasure, gasping, purring. His flat chest, broad shoulders, and V-shaped torso, rubbed against hers. The hours evaporated while the couple embraced their love making.

Snuggling under the blanket, Romano hugged Allison in the hollow of his arm, determined never to let her go. Watching the beautiful creature sleep next to him he knew his love would last forever.

CHAPTER 7

Styliani Studio - New York

4th January 1977 - 11.00 a.m.

Standing in Julia Styliani's studio, dressed in her Charles Montgomery grey trouser suit, and trilby. Allison portrayed a business professional, carrying her leather document wallet.

Julia Styliani, an award-winning interior designer, selected several designs and patterns. Placing them ahead on the desk, she said, "If you are going to choose an English theme, I suggest the Chesterfield. Burgundy and walnut flooring. The walls can be painted in old English whites and sienna architrave. Brass chandeliers and wall lights throughout the apartment."

Allison observed the designs. "I think…."

Julia continued interrupting her client. "The master bedroom in white and mahogany." She placed another swatch into Allison's hand. "The guest rooms can include half tester canopy beds in oak. Bedding in cream, drapes to match."

Completely lost Allison drifted off, thinking about Romano.

Julia stopped and tapped her foot. "Are you listening to me, Alice?"

Allison jumped when she heard Julia's voice ring out. "Sorry, I am a little jet lagged."

Julia sat down at her desk. "I understand. My son lives in England, and I too encounter tiredness when I travel."

Observing the aging designer, Allison nodded. "I thought your son lived in New York?"

"Sam does. I have two sons."

"Oh, I didn't realise." Allison stared at Julia feeling a connection to the designer.

Julia smiled hiding her deepest secret away from her niece. Allison had no idea that Julia Styliani was her aunt.

In 1938 Julia had married Allison's uncle, Nathaniel Templeton-Jones. Keeping her single name Styliani prevented the Miller children from knowing any different.

Theo-James insisted on the confidentiality because he did not want Eleanor's career ruined.

Julia gave birth to two boys, Jack, and Sam. In 1966 tragedy struck the family. Natt and his brother Rupert Templeton-Jones died in a car crash, not far from Templeton Manor in England.

Rupert (Viscount Templeton) had never married and Julia's son, Jack, would become the next Viscount after his death.

John Nathaniel Templeton-Jones, known as Jack Jones, now lived in England at Templeton Manor.

Samuel Templeton-Jones remained in New York and worked alongside his mother at Styliani's. Changing his name from Jones to Styliani, he became better known as Sam Styliani.

Allison always felt that Julia was much more than a designer to the family, but she could never work it out.

Browsing the final drawings, Julia completed the dining room and kitchen areas. There was one problem that Julia refused to mention. Theo-James's birthday present: a purple mini grand piano. How on earth would that fit into the theme?

Sam Styliani made the decision to change the open dining room's colour from green to mauve. Allison and Julia agreed on the royal shade.

"Go ahead." Allison coughed. "How long will it take?"

"Three weeks...I promised your father the apartment will be ready for your birthday. Don't forget that I run a team of fifty, working 24/7."

"And I thought my schedule was tough." Allison shook Julia's hand. "I'll leave you to it."

****

The Marianna Hotel - New York

4th January 1977 - 2.00 p.m.

Paul Freidman organised his security outside the conference room door, as the hotelier served tea and refreshments.

"Paul?" Allison scurried past security, addressing each guard by name.

"Alice, we're in here! "Paul shouted.

Following him into the alluring room, Allison noticed an oak table and two cream chairs placed in the centre with no other furniture present.

Sitting down, Paul opened a leather portfolio and spoke. "I am holding this conference without your colleagues...They can learn about this meeting on the news. Allison Templeton-Miller, you are the new face of The House of Sylvester."

"What? Seriously?"

"No, Alice...All your products, clothing, make-up, luggage, even your dental floss, will be designed by Phillippe-Astor-Sylvester. A five-million-dollar deal."

"My appearance will change," she mumbled, crestfallen.

"Correct! Tweed will be your style and dignified ball dresses. Phillippe will also redesign Templeton." Paul smiled, sliding the contract towards Allison. "Sign here."

"Can I read it first?" Allison replied.

"Don't worry, I read it for you," said Paul, handing a pen over to Allison. "Your photo session starts tomorrow morning."

"Okay." Allison signed the contract and slid it across the polished table to Paul. He grinned and placed the contract into the file. The second plan was interrupted by the clattering of tea and coffee cups. Paul cleared his throat. "We want you to go solo."

"Like, alone?" Allison interjected.

"Alice, you got to toughen up. It'll be good for your career."

"Shouldn't I be the one deciding what's good for my career?"

"You did until you signed that contract. Listen, I have three songwriters."

"I write my music with Josh."

"Josh?" Paul seemed confused. A man in black whispered in his ear. "Oh, Mister Williams. Let me finish, please."

"Was letting you finish in the contract, too?" Alice said.

"Templeton will remain as Templeton. Alice, you must go your own way. I am sorry, but Green Records have only released four Number One hit singles and two albums charted at Number One. How many awards do you think Green won, Alice? Guess."

"I don't want to be presumptuous, I would never—"

"Take a stab at it."

"I don't know."

"GUESS."

"T…three?"

"Zero."

"So, what, you want me to make up for it? Bring you home a trophy like its softball practice? I'm under a lot of pressure. My film career, recording with Templeton, tours, red carpet, fashion magazines, and now you want me to go solo?"

"Exactly. I will assign you a PA, Sebastian Dupont. Sebastian answers to me, just like you. His organisational skills are superb. Sebastian will make data entry for your schedule and arrange your deadlines."

"When does Sebastian start?" Allison thought her world was about to crash.

"Next week. He will meet you in London on the 11th of January, at the Sylvester photoshoot…Details are in this envelope." Paul flicked the folder into her lap. "Included in the contract is a private jet and security. Earnings: $150,000 per week."

Allison, dumbfounded, stared at Paul, still holding onto the envelope, speaking in a dazed tone. "D…dollars?"

"$1,000,000 increase to $7,800,000 per year for the solo arrangement. Plus $5,000,000; The House of Sylvester. Plus $15,000,000 for *Flying In 2*. $3,000.000 for royalties. So, for the year 1977..." He scribbled the figure on a napkin and slid it to her.

"$30,000,000?" Allison was stricken with shock and muttered, "Are the guys in Templeton still..."

"Still on the old contract. Josh maintains his share of the royalties," interrupted Paul, checking his watch.

"They will despise me." Allison began to worry. "The band will despise me!"

"No more than they already do, Alice. Come on, toughen up! Business is ruthless." Paul smashed his hand on the table, spilling his coffee. "You are the girl to break these guys."

Allison jumped. The coffee stained her shirt. Immediately three security guards murmured into their earpieces and handed her a replacement. "How did you know my size?"

"I know everything," Paul Freidman smiled.

****

Oak Tree House - Westfield - New Jersey
4th January 1977 - 6.00 p.m.

Overwhelmed and elevated, Allison concluded her meeting at the Marianna Hotel. Obliging to attend dinner at Lucinda La-Mount's house, Allison arranged transportation with her driver. It was a thirty-minute drive to Westfield.

Lucinda La-Mount and Allison's friendship had survived more than fifteen years. They first met at St Marys Schule, Switzerland. Lucinda, two years older than Allison had graduated in 1969, leaving Allison behind.

Lucinda received a call from Allison two years later. Thanks to her parents, she got the chance to attend and gain a scholarship in Hospitality. Lucinda's father Chuck La-Mount yearned for his daughter to take over the La-Mount Hotel's family empire.

Artist Max Martinez married Lucinda in July 1976. Lucinda's parents gave the couple a property in Westfield called Oak Tree House. The twelve-bedroom mansion: a grand residence for Max's studio became a happy family home. Lucinda, expecting her first child in March, was busy designing the baby's nursery.

Allison sat in the back of her limo, thinking how much people's lives had changed over the past year, including her own. She couldn't converse too much regarding today's engagement, but she could look at her reflection in the tinted window and stare at the new face of The House of Sylvester.

The limo approached Oak Tree and accelerated through icy puddles. Lights twinkled along the driveway and tree's overhanging limbs hung across the shadowy path.

At last, the main entrance appeared. Solid oak, rustic doors, and semilunar concrete steps sat within the column pillars.

"Miss Alice, we have arrived."

"Are my bags in the trunk, Stan?"

"Yes, Miss... I shall retrieve them."

"Thank you. Is it possible to collect me around lunchtime tomorrow?"

"Certainly."

Lucinda's Butler Mr Anderson approached the car and opened the door. Stan collected the bags from the boot of the car. Allison stepped out and said goodbye to her chauffeur.

Lucinda, now showing, leant by the door, laughing and waving, "Hurry up, we're starved!"

"Sorry, sorry. It's been a busy day, and I have lots to tell you." Allison climbed the steps and threw her arms around her old friend.

Once everyone was inside, Anderson closed the solid oak doors behind him. A petite housemaid waited ahead of the stairs and carried out instructions from the butler.

Allison established her way into the dining room. Remaining seated, Max signalled a wave while Lucinda held a seat ready for Allison. The three of them chattered into the night.

****

Templeton Hall - The Hamptons
4th January 1977 - 7.30 p.m.

Martyn Simpson-Smyth from Burrows & Burrows Law Ltd crossed his legs and anticipated the reply from Theo-James. Opposite Martyn stood Sebastian Dupont.

"My baby's flying solo. She is signing today, the new face of Sylvester! Gentlemen, what's wrong?"

"Your daughter's signing will increase her fortune by 3.33%. Our agents have Freidman under round-the-clock surveillance." Martyn adjusted his silk tie. "We believe his cut is considerably higher."

Sebastian stepped in. "Obtaining the information will be easy."

Theo-James leaned against his office chair, irritated, pounding the headrest. "I want his head on a platter for this! How many young lives have been destroyed by this money-grubbing nuisance? Alice is my baby, my girl, and he's seizing her earnings...Sebastian, take care of her."

Sebastian adjusted his designer spectacles. Martyn checked his notepad, replying, "The suits at B&B will have no problem collecting enough evidence on Freidman. We'll get him."

"Green Records are issuing Alice's security next week. Craig Welling," grinned Sebastian. "My right hand."

"Goodman, another on board." Theo-James was delighted; he gathered the paperwork on his desk. "I must say, I do believe we will catch the bastard."

"Eventually all bastards get caught. Freidman is working with Madam Moulin. The school amasses potential stars, trading the kids for cash. He exploits them, earns millions. Rehab. Psychological damage. Suicide," Sebastian exhaled.

"We are sorry for the exploitation of your daughter's success, Theo. But Allison will generate her own achievement, with or without Freidman," Martyn butted in, sipping green tea from his elegant cup.

"All I will say is that Alice is not only a Templeton: she's a Templeton-Miller...Success is in her blood. Well, my blood. She'll leave Green Records and Freidman behind. I guarantee it. I'm not sure about the band, though." Theo-James sighed, inhaling long and hard on his oriental cigarette. "Sebastian, make sure she is not overworked. Or you'll have me to answer to!"

Sebastian handed over Allison's agenda. Theo-James seized the document, requesting regular updates, explaining that the next three months were vital because his next filming project would completely remove him from the country. The three men clinked glasses and a teacup together and swore an oath on Paul Freidman's downfall.

CHAPTER 8

Atrium Apartments - Camden - London

11th January 1977 – 5.00 a.m.

Deserting a somber airport, Allison's silver limousine exited onto the M4. Her chauffer pushed a privacy button, closing the window between Allison and himself. Staring into the darkness, Allison relaxed on the rear passenger seat listening to her transiter radio.

Entering through the Atrium Apartment's double wooden gates, Allison's limousine stopped outside the glass entrance doors.

Once she awoke, she opened her eyes and sat up. Allison noticed an attractive man standing with his arms folded behind his back. He wore luxury spectacles and a designer navy pinstriped suit over a crisp pearl shirt.

Cutting off the driver, the elegantly styled male opened the passenger door of the limo and greeted her with a manicured hand. "Miss Alice, Sebastian Dupont. It is an honour to meet you."

She smiled, gazing helplessly through his spectacles into his brown eyes. "You're my PA?"

"Correct. I occupy the apartment above." Sebastian held his arm towards the door, and Allison followed his direction. "Shall we proceed?"

Three red velvet sofas, shiny brass lamps, a coffee table, and red shag rugs aroused Allison's sense of wonder. The kitchen was captivating, with white oak cupboards and a breakfast bar, including grey velvet stools. All four bedrooms displayed white king-sized beds, shag rugs and glass ball lamps.

Unmatched to Sebastian's office. There placed a diamond-encrusted desk, black suede high back chairs, and glittering photo frames. Positioned on top of a wine table stood a gemstone Opis 1921 cable telephone.

Wow! Allison thought… "This guy's got style."

"Do you like my panache, Miss Alice?" Sebastian said in his soft English Californian accent.

"I love i—" Before Allison could finish, he shut the office door. A minute later, it re-opened.

"Right, I almost forgot. Alice, we have an agenda to keep. At eleven the car will arrive to collect us…"

"Where?" Allison beamed with excitement.

"The House of Sylvester…The designers studio."

"Oh yeah, these fashion names are called houses!"

Sebastian looked at the ceiling in despair. "The appointment for your measurements is at noon."

"I'll skip lunch."

"Hair and makeup at one, interview with *Conception Magazine* at 15:00, lunch at 16:00 and photoshoot for the *Tweed Collection* at 18:00."

"Oh, the schedule is so tight."

"At 20:00 we shall dine with my husband, Oliver."

"Your husband?"

"Unless you steal him," Sebastian announced, grinning. "Yes, Oliver and I have been married for two years."

They walked into the kitchen, and Sebastian began to prepare tea.

"So how long did you date Si McKay?"

"Six months and twenty days, but it's over now. I met someone else in Germany, not romantically at first. But then in December, I went skiing in Switzerland, and I bumped into him again. We spent time together, and..."

"Romano Mancini!" Sebastian spilled his tea on the floor.

Allison stooped over to dab it up. "How did you know?"

"It's my job. Does Romano stay in touch?"

"Yes." Allison blushed. "He's filming in LA. I will see him again at my birthday party."

"Happy early twenty-first birthday. Where's the party?"

"Discis, Manhattan." Allison giggled. "You want to come?"

"As long as I can bring Oliver."

Sylvester House - Camden
11th January 1977 - 11.30 a.m.

The silver limo pulled to a halt outside a weather-beaten warehouse below dark clouds and pelting rain. Sebastian opened the car door and offered Allison his hand. Stepping out of the car, she struggled to focus as she followed Sebastian inside the building.

Allison found herself in an atelier full of artisans, fashion designers and illustrators conceiving, designing, and developing Sylvester's new product lines. Concept boards were scattered all over the place, displaying sketches of luxury clothing, shoes, hats, and bags.

The employees were studying fabric constructions and evaluating colour choices. Technicians were engaged in sewing, printing, and embroidery. Large offices with administrative personnel reinforced the back walls.

A tall blonde male in red loafers and an untucked shirt promenaded towards Allison and Sebastian.

"Darlings, darlings, darlings. Handsome as ever, Sebi," Phillippe trilled. "I am so jealous of Oliver!"

"Phillippe," beamed Sebastian. "How exquisite."

Sporting tight tweed trousers and a matching waistcoat, Phillippe revealed his bronze chest through his unbuttoned shirt.

"My new baby girl...Allison Templeton-Miller! Sebi, she is beautiful."

Allison stood motionless while Phillippe Aston-Sylvester upped his pace, stroking, fingering, patting, and tapping. "You look like a Macy's mannequin. We can make beautiful music together! Let's advance to my office...Come now, people. There is much to do!"

Following Phillippe into a lift, Allison and Sebastian emerged on the top floor and into Phillippe's rooftop office. Encircled by the windows from floor to ceiling, the room offered a panoramic view of Camden. Reflecting lights beat down upon a glass desk and high back chairs. The white marble non-slip flooring seemed to have been stolen from heaven.

Two hours later, Allison and Sebastian were still sitting at the glass conference table. The latter was scrolling through his files and Allison browsed the profiles of past Sylvester models, anticipating the arrival of her clothing collection. A telephone rang.

"It's for you," Sebastian said.

Phillippe's team had telephoned her to attend the make-up room. Allison hurried down onto the fifth floor and sat in a barber's chair surrounded by hairstylists and makeup artists.

After being tugged, hauled, jerked, and prodded. She looked at herself in the mirror, she couldn't believe how much she resembled her mother. The radiant brownish-black curls, heart-shaped lips, pale skin, and light pink tinted cheeks said it all.

Now prepared for her first fitting. An elegant ivory floral gown revealed an off-the-shoulder low décolletage and long green bouffant skirt. With that, her opera-length ivory gloves and vintage jewellery complimented the regal dress.

The cameraman instructed Allison to stand in front of a reflective white backdrop. She remained elegant and followed the instructions of the photographer. Standing next to him were Sebastian and Phillippe, gushing in astonishment.

"Good God," whispered Sebastian. "It's Eleanor."

"She's bewildering. Beautiful," answered Phillippe. "The most beautiful thing in the world."

The second dress in the collection was a full-bodied corset with a sweetheart neckline and straps: a glittering royal blue ball gown with a tiara and white opera gloves.

That afternoon Allison exhibited ten dresses in all different styles and colours. After she devoured lunch, it was time for hats.

Sebastian accompanied Phillippe into his office. They were both overwhelmed with the afternoon session, success had prevailed. Allison had changed back into her navy suit while conversing and signing autographs in the dressing rooms.

After she had gathered her belongings, she walked into Phillippe's office, giggling. "Finished!"

"No, no, no!" Phillippe bellowed. "You are not wearing a Charles Montgomery. You are going to wear my collection!"

"I can't wear the entire collection at once." Allison looked at Phillippe, worried.

"All of this!" Phillippe turned around and held out his hand.

Allison counted on her fingers: five wardrobes of clothing, from coats to shoes. "I need a larger apartment!" Allison screamed.

"You admire this cap? It's yours, keep it!" Phillippe flung the flat cap at Allison's forehead. "You'll have to change again, my dear. No one leaves my studio in a Charles Mont…Whatever his name is!"

She changed into a Sylvester royal blue tweed jacket with a white balloon blouse, black Capris, and brown leather high-heeled boots. Allison appeared before Phillippe, followed by an explosion of applause.

****

Cor Restaurant - Camden

11th January 1977 - 8.00 p.m.

A delicate mix of modern and old-fashioned furnishings, red garnished tables, exquisite lighting, and romantic keyboard music enchanted the restaurant's ambience.

Sebastian flaunted his black tuxedo and pulled up a seat at the table next to his husband. On the opposite side, Allison wore a classic love-heart dinner dress: her first Sylvester.

Her new mentor leaned over and kissed the handsome male standing in front of him. "Alice, meet my husband, Oliver Dupont." Sebastian gleamed with pride. "Oliver, Allison Templeton-Miller."

"Allison, so pleased to meet you," said Oliver, kissing the back of her hand.

"Please, call me Alice," she pondered, wondering which male was more attractive.

Whilst they busied themselves with conversation, the attendants served Margaritas and presented three leather menus.

"Alice, a little birdie told me that you are not dating Si McKay any longer." Oliver sipped his drink.

"Darling! You are not interviewing for your magazine," Sebastian said, glaring at Oliver.

"It's okay," Allison said without hesitation. "We're friends."

Oliver glared at Sebastian.

"I dated Si for six months, and I ended it by fax! Three reasons...One, we both had no time together because of our tours...Two, I met someone else…Three, he's bi."

Oliver spat his drink into his napkin and choked with shock. Sebastian patted Oliver on the back while Allison blushed.

"He's what?" Sebastian said, loosening his collar.

"I became friends with an ex-lover of his, Mark." Allison fiddled with her cocktail.

"Mark?" Sebastian said.

"Mark Redruth, sound technician. Templeton's. Mark worked for Si a long time before us..."

"How long?" Oliver said.

Sebastian elbowed Oliver in the stomach.

"Mark had a three-year relationship with Si. He was the one who ended it. Si was seeing other people."

"Like all at once?" Oliver butted in.

"That's disgusting," said Allison.

"Did you know this before you were told"?" Sebastian asked.

"I had an idea...I caught him chatting to a waiter in LA, they exchanged phone numbers. The guy just can't keep his fly up!"

"Allison Templeton-Miller!" Sebastian streaked.

Oliver collapsed, laughing.

"I ended the relationship in Germany after I met Romano."

"Romano Mancini, the film star?" Oliver asked.

"That's what they all say."

"You are dating the Romano Mancini?" Oliver repeated.

"Yup."

"Wow." Oliver's ears perked up. "Big news!"

"Oliver, darling, no! You are not going to interview the couple," remarked Sebastian. "Alice, my husband is employed by *Conception Magazine*. You will meet him again tomorrow. Let's end this conversation."

Oliver and Allison responded with a toast. "To us," they laughed, clinking their cocktail glasses together.

The handsome trio chuckled and gossiped all through the evening over fresh lobster.

****

The following morning Sebastian remained busy on the telephone. Talking through the loudspeaker, he doodled in a notebook and glanced at his watch.

Allison had already departed. Today's schedule involved filming a fragrance commercial in Westminster. Oliver hopped in the limo with her and the security team.

A threatening voice thundered through the phone in Sebastian's office. "Where is she today?"

"She? You mean Miss Templeton-Miller. Miss Alice is in Westminster today."

"Why?"

"Shooting a commercial. Part of the new Sylvester campaign. Today is perfume. The five million deal or was it more, Paul?"

"When do you fly back to New York?"

"Tomorrow. I am accompanying Miss Alice myself," Sebastian said, trying to make the conversation restricted as possible. "Phillippe mentioned a fifteen-million-dollar deal."

"Strange." Paul sharpened his tone. "You do realise, Sebastian, that you work for me?"

"Just something that was said in passing." Sebastian cleared his throat.

"Phillippe is so over the top. Alice received five million, and the company earned one million. I have wages to pay, Dupont!"

The conversation became rote. Paul Freidman was as cunning as ever, but not clever enough. Phillippe Aston-Sylvester had shown a copy of the contract to Sebastian: fifteen million over a three-year term. Sebastian's calculations implied that Freidman had embezzled ten million dollars.

Sarah-Jane copied the contract for Sebastian. Phillippe's PA provided a list of all the 1978 clothing lines for Allison, an additional twenty-five million dollars.

Sebastian hung up on Paul Freidman, walked into the kitchen, and uncorked some whiskey. "Damn you, Freidman."

CHAPTER 9

The Palmer Building - New York - 23rd January 1977

Elevator doors opened into a neo-gothic corridor. A luxurious antique wine table accommodated an inspiring bouquet of pink flowers displayed in a crystal vase.

An antiquated walnut door opened onto the corridor revealing Julia Styliani's design: an assortment of woods, heritage colours and furnishings. Allison observed her picture-perfect home as she tottered towards a purple mini-grand piano.

A polished soundboard displayed a music book, with brass pedals and casters. The piano positioned itself in the spacious dining room exhibiting a gold-trimmed card.

To my baby girl
Today you get to feel special.
It's time to get happy.
I hope you enjoy your special gift as I have enjoyed you over the past 21 years.
Happy Birthday darling
Love Papa xxxx

Reading the card, Allison whimpered, wiping tears from her eyes. Suddenly she noticed a garland of red roses. It was from someone else. She tore open the envelope and braced herself before reading the inscription.

My love.

Welcome to your new home.

I long-await to join you.

Soon we will be together

Love you with all my heart

Romano xxxx

While caressing the card she was interrupted by a cough. Romano stood against the entrance door and smiled. Allison dropped everything and ran towards him, embracing him with a long-overdue hug. At the same time, Romano captured her in his arms and kissed her on the forehead.

Fifteen minutes later, Belinda, Lucinda, and Fay disturbed the couple's passionate kiss with bottles of vintage champagne.

They hugged Allison and Romano as they entered the luxurious apartment.

"A toast to the lovebirds!" Belinda squealed.

"You guys," laughed Allison. "I'll get the glasses."

"Do you know where they are?" Lucinda said.

"Sure do, I helped design the place. But orange juice for you...Mummy?"

Donny Davis walked in and gave Romano a fist bump. He curled his arm around Allison and Belinda, kissing both on the cheek. Fay presented Donny and Romano with a sparkling glass of bubbly.

Next arrived Max La-Mount-Martinez and Michael Simmons, Fay's fiancé. Both shook hands with Romano and hugged Allison in the process. As they walked in, Belinda offered Max and Michael a glass of champagne.

Allison showed the girls around the apartment and explained the idea behind the design of each room while the guys lounged on the sofas, chatting.

Suddenly there was a loud knock at the door. Everybody turned around. Romano stood up from the sofa and walked over to the main entrance. A porter held two designer leather holdalls and spoke. "Your luggage, sir."

"Thank you," said Romano, smiling kindly at the porter, and tipped him a fifty-dollar bill.

The porter left the bags and departed towards the elevator. Romano took the holdalls and left them in the passageway.

The girls made their way over to the sofas. When Allison noticed the two holdalls, she asked, "Are they your bags, Romano?"

"They are now. Where would you like me to put them?"

"Master bedroom, on the left. You have your own dressing area."

"Are you two living together?" Belinda screamed.

"Yes, when I'm in the Big Apple and Alice resides at my place in LA." Romano answered, gesturing with his shot glass towards Allison.

"So, you'll not be at the Green Records Apartments anymore?" Donny frowned.

"Doesn't look like it." Allison hugged her friend.

The housewarming celebration continued into the evening. Later that night, when everyone had gone home, Romano made love to Allison: an early twenty-first birthday present.

****

Discis - New York - 25th January 1977

Allison's security climbed out of the front passenger side of the limousine. Striding around the car, speaking into his radio, Craig Welling authorised the doorman to approach.

Romano wore a burgundy suit and an open-neck white shirt. He stepped out onto the pavement holding out his hand to assist Allison.

Allison followed Romano's instructions and stood by his side in Sylvester hot pants, a diamante boob tube, and sparkling high heeled ankle boots. Clutching her glitter purse, she waved at the crowd.

They were crammed in between the heaving crowds, screaming, shouting, and jumping up and down with their autograph books in hand. Photographers were shouting names, and flashes of light hit everywhere.

Overwhelmed, Romano planted his arm around Allison's slender waist and guided her towards the entrance doors. The couple walked down the red carpet and into the dark.

Electronic sounds thundered around the night club. The club's management greeted the party and escorted them to the refreshment area.

The clique, Templeton and their partners chatted amongst themselves waiting for Allison to arrive. Richard and his brother stood at the bar with Rene and Ami fumbling with their champagne glasses. While Annie and Ricky associated themselves with Green Records executives as Freidman lurked in the background.

Sebastian and Oliver Dupont flirted with film actors and directors, surrounded by another three hundred guests.

Allison arrived holding Romano's hand, and Discis exploded into a firecracker of confetti. With a sparkle in her eyes, she hugged her guests, chatting and walking around, trying to be a good host. Belinda ran behind, placing a glass of champagne into her hand.

Paul Freidman grabbed Allison's arm tightly and pulled her towards him. "We need to chat, tomorrow." He then faked a smile and released her. "Your apartment."

How dare he grab her arm like that. She glared at him angrily whilst walking back towards her friends. *"Damn! He is getting on my nerves! Work! Work! Work! Money! Money! Money!"* she cursed to herself.

Across the darkness towards the private rooms, she recognised a long-haired male chatting with another man: Si and his new boyfriend.

"Oh!" Allison gasped before covering her mouth.

Si stopped kissing Jonathan and winced.

"Hi, Si," she said. "Long time no see, never dreamed I would see you here!"

"Alice!" Si said, agitated. "Happy birthday."

"So, are you going to introduce me?"

Si furrowed his brow. "Jonathan, this is Alice...Alice, Jonathan."

"Hi Jonathan...I hope you are enjoying my party."

Jonathan smiled and nodded.

"I believe Belinda overlooked crossing you off the guest list...I'm so sorry. Just an oopsie."

"Oopsie." Jonathan rolled his eyes.

"Alice, I'm sorry," said Si, swallowing. "I don't know how to tell you this, but I'm b—"

"Goodness, isn't that Jonathan, your tour manager?"

"No. Yes. I mean, I couldn't bear to hear your voice again...I was hurting!"

"I met someone else, Si. I moved on. It prepared me for my new love...I'm happy that you have someone else too." Glancing over at Jonathan. Allison sighed. "He seems like a nice guy."

"I'll always be your friend, Alice." Si leaned down and kissed her cheek.

Lucinda interrupted with a cough. "Come over here, you got to see this..." She tugged Allison down the carpeted steps towards the dance floor. The throbbing crowd sang, *To My Birthday Girl,* a Templeton song.

Romano stood next to a seven-tier birthday cake bedecked with red roses. "My darling, come over and cut the cake."

Stepping out into the centre of the dance floor, Romano placed a silver knife into Allison's hand. They gripped the knife together, slicing into the icing, lifting a small piece of cake towards their mouths. The couple bit into the delicious white chocolate sponge and posed for the cameras as the crowd cheered.

****

Si McKay continued to cavort with Jonathan. Oliver Dupont made his acquaintance. He introduced himself, explaining to Si how lucky he was to have had a brief relationship with Allison. *Conception Magazine* wanted to be the first to print the story.

Oliver arranged an appointment with Si at his New York office to negotiate a million-dollar pay-out to unveil his story. He suggested there would be a clause that Allison Templeton-Miller would not be involved under any circumstances.

Oliver and Si shook hands. Jonathan accepted that it would be a good move on Si's part to increase publicity for his new upcoming album.

Oliver also promised photo shoots and a centrepiece spread for his fans. A successful business plan brightened Oliver's mood, thinking that it would be safe to make this deal while Sebastian would be elsewhere.

****

"Leave Alice alone, Paul! She's booked for the next six months."

"Who the hell do you think you are?" Freidman coughed up from his cigarette. "You work for me."

"For now!" Sebastian glared.

"What, are you thinking of moving elsewhere?"

"Not yet," Sebastian said, smirking at Freidman's displeasure.

"Another million is on the table, and I want it."

"What don't you want? A million here, a million there. It's never enough for you, is it? She's a queen, not your pawn!"

Looking at how things were only elevating to a worst-case scenario, Craig Welling stumbled into the heated conversation. The disagreement echoed through the club's entrance hall. "Hey, break it up!" Craig shouted.

Both men turned their heads towards Craig. Sebastian threw up his hands. "We're done!"

"Craig, you, okay?" Paul said, taking a drag from his cigarette.

"Great, Paul. Could you do me a favour and back off, Sebastian? He's exhausted."

"And I'm not?"

Craig and Sebastian had been good friends for many years, and they hated Paul Freidman for even longer.

"Back off!" he hissed, pointing his finger at Paul.

"Okay, Okay!" Paul wasn't going to argue with a security man who towered over him by a foot. Paul doused his cigarette in Craig's drink and stormed out the back door.

Craig re-joined the party after the cake cutting. Shoving through the crowd to reach the bar, he nodded at the males and smiled at the beautiful women.

He stood against the counter and choked down a chilled glass of water. Richard Templeton-Miller walked over.

"Trouble in the foyer?" Richard scoffed. "Don't tell me it was that idiot Freidman."

"Someone will bring that bastard down. I've had it with him," said Craig, spitting out an ice cube.

"The family is concerned for Alice. Freidman's cheating her."

"People protect her." Craig propped up his elbows on the counter, staring at a stunning redhead across the room. "People like me."

Richard gestured at the redhead. "Does she?"

****

The clique nestled together in the VIP area, surrounded by crushed wine, velvet seating, and bevelled mirrors. The conversation between Paul and Sebastian enthralled Romano.

"Did everyone know?" Allison demanded.

Belinda, Fay, and Lucinda glimpsed at their partners. Max, Donny, and Michael gave a fleeting look back.

"Alice, it was so obvious," Donny Davis declared. "You are so naive!"

"Did the band know?"

"Sure did. On tour, you were hardly on the phone with him. Ricky said it was guilt!"

"Why didn't you tell me?"

"Because we didn't want to upset you," Donny said. "The last thing we needed was our lead singer having a meltdown!"

Belinda stepped in. "That's a bit harsh."

"Excuse me, but what are you guys talking about?" Romano asked while he cuddled Allison.

"Si is here tonight." Michael treaded carefully. "With his boyfriend."

Hearing that, Sebastian and Oliver joined the conversation. "Boyfriend?" They laughed. "You mean Si McKay?"

"Si is extremely attractive," said Oliver, sipping Sebastian's martini.

Romano laughed, trying to restrain himself.

"Oh!" Allison muttered, refilling her drink. "It's an open book."

"Everyone knows, darling. Even the press. Consequently, the number of women he uses to hide his secret." Sebastian butted in.

Romano turned towards Allison. "I love your innocence, baby. You didn't get upset when you realised the truth?"

"I'm shocked that his lover is Jonathan, but I got over him a long time ago. It was only sex."

Belinda and Lucinda cheered. The guys breathed a sigh of relief, and Romano sniggered alongside Sebastian and Oliver.

After the guests had departed, the couple burrowed into one another on the vacant dance floor. Romano whispered, holding Allison tight against his chest. "Someday, I will marry you."

Allison looked up at him and sighed, realising Romano was her future. Beaming with happiness, she knew that one day she would marry him. What a perfect birthday present she had been given.

CHAPTER 10

The Green Record Studios - LA - 28th March 1977

"Theo, this accusation is very serious." Benedict Shaw said, resting against his high back leather chair.

"Mr Freidman isn't just defrauding your company. He's defrauding all of us." Theo slid the binder across the desk, spilling transcripts and photographic evidence. "Burrows & Burrows are preparing an arraignment."

"How long have we known one another, Theo? Forty years?"

Theo-James hoisted himself out of his chair. He placed both hands onto Benedict's desk, leaned over, and whispered, "Long enough for you to trust me. I sold you this place, remember."

"I need additional verification." Benedict flipped through the folder and cast it aside.

Theo-James pulled out his pager and transmitted a message. Within minutes Benedict's office telephone rang.

"Yes, yes," he said. "Send him in."

The door to Benedict's office opened, and Martyn Simpson-Smyth walked into the office with a black leather briefcase.

"Martyn, join us." Theo-James greeted Martyn with a handshake and introduced him to Benedict.

Martyn took a seat next to Theo. Theo-James unfurled a typewritten page from the file and handed it to Benedict. Benedict put his glasses on.

"Good God," he uttered in disbelief.

"If God were good, Paul Freidman would be in hell." Theo-James did not mince his words. "You are employing a criminal and a murderer."

Benedict noticed the Sylvester contract submitted in triplicate. In one, Allison Templeton-Miller had signed a counterfeit copy for five million dollars. The second copy was the original contract for fifteen million dollars. The third was blank.

Over the past five years, a total of sixty million dollars were fabricated from forged contracts. Young potential stars were paid pittance and had failed. Their lives ended either in death or mental illness.

Benedict calculated the figures and held his head in his hands. "He screwed us for fifty-five million."

"Pauls probably pilfered more, but our records only go back five years," explained Martyn.

"Is anyone else involved?"

"We cannot issue names," Martyn said. "Legal reasons."

"What do you mean, legal reasons? You're a lawyer!" Benedict stood up from his chair and faced the window.

"Burrows & Burrows are bringing the case to trial. Green Records can also perform a private prosecution. Benedict, please inform your legal team." Martyn shuffled through his wallet and produced a Burrows & Burrows legal business card before being escorted out of the building.

Benedict tore the business card in half.

****

Sphere Pictures Filming Studio - Los Angeles
28th March 1977 - 6.00 p.m.

Tony ambushed Primrose, police cars in hot pursuit. Primrose screamed.

"Cut!" Stewart Gloss slammed shut his clapper board. "See you at the Cantus Awards!"

A poodle-haircut blonde sauntered from the car wreck, wearing a torn floral cocktail dress. Make-up artists surrounded Allison, placing blankets around her shoulders, and sitting her in a director's chair.

Colin St-Birch and Stephen-Paul Golding rubbernecked off-screen.

"That was amazing, kid." Colin winked at Allison.

"Be more amazing without this awful wig!" Allison moaned.

"It suits you, honey," Stephen-Paul said. His pearly teeth glinted at the costume designer.

Allison glared as strangers jabbed and poked and prodded at her figure.

Stewart Gloss crooked his idiomatic expression towards Allison. His stunning features captured additional female attention. The hunk strode towards the mass of people standing with his sound engineer.

Stewart approached Allison. "Excellent work today, Alice. We have another two roles for you."

As the make-up artist powdered her nose, she tried to reply stopping in mid-track with a sneeze. A costume designer grabbed Allison's blanket and assisted her from the chair.

Wiping her nose Allison took her place on set and handed the soiled tissue to a cameraman.

"Right, then. Jeff striking Primrose. Positions, everyone." Stewart produced his clapper board. "Action!"

The team scattered, leaving the pair in prime position to start the next part of the filming. Two hours later, Allison was sitting in the studio's trailer attempting to remove her impervious cosmetics. Dressed in a white robe, she tore off her wig and allowed the natural curls to cascade over her slender shoulders. In the mirror, she examined her exhausted eyes. "Two more weeks."

She had to move fast. Her recording session had been scheduled for 21:30 and there was no time to eat or drink.

A knock at the trailer door startled her. Alice's driver stepped into the trailer, followed by Craig Welling.

"You ready, Miss Alice?" Stan asked.

"Give me two minutes." She tried on a Sylvester tweed cap.

"You look very English, Alice!" Craig smirked.

"That's the point, my dear Craig." The matching jacket hung over her jeans and t-shirt. Allison grabbed her bag, locked the trailer door, and exited with the two men.

Hopping into the rear of the limousine, she slumped in her leather seat. Both men sat in the front and lowered the privacy window.

"You look tired, Alice." Craig passed her an espresso.

"Thanks, Craig. I wish it was an Earl Grey," she said, taking a sip.

"You're welcome," Craig said, facing the windscreen. "I keep forgetting you half-breeds like tea!"

****

Green Records Recording Studio - Los Angeles
28th March 1977 - 10.30 p.m.

Digital Audio Workstations separated Eric Sands and Allison.

"Alice, *My Heart is on Fire* is being remixed. We need to create a poignant, sexy sound," said Eric.

"So, you want me to sing it naked?" Allison replied.

"Funny girl...I will slow the rhythm and speed up the tempo."

Nodding her head in agreement, Allison relocated to the live room, fully equipped with microphones and mic stands. The square pine studio displayed several assorted instruments, from keyboards to drums and guitars placed in stands. Allison placed her headphones over her ears, ready for the signal.

Listening to the introduction, she sang the first line of the song—the constant volume, tone, pitching, and style propagated through the studio. Energy transmitted the beat through the stale air.

Eric Sands tapped on the glass panel and held both thumbs up. The squawk back sent his message into the live speakers.

"It's a smash!"

Allison laughed. "Can I come up and listen?"

In the control room, Eric played back *My Heart is on Fire*.

"Oh," Allison exclaimed, nodding to the beat while sitting in a brown leather chair. "Disco!"

"This will be played in all the clubs, Alice."

"I would dance to this."

"Could go platinum!" Eric screeched in excitement, high fiving Allison.

My Heart is on Fire was the first of many solo singles for Templeton-Miller. The release date had yet to be discussed, and Green Records would not delay on the matter.

****

Porta Del Castello - Bel-Air - Los Angeles
29th March 1977 - 2.00 a.m.

Concealed in the foothills of the Santa Monica Mountains, luxurious mansions lined the meandering streets. A limousine propelled the clique past sumptuous shrubbery and towards Westside, Los Angeles.

Approaching Porta Del Castello's security gate, the silver limo decelerated until Stan pushed his foot onto the brakes. Instantly the security authorised clearance, and the limo began to accelerate sluggishly through the open gates.

Allison observed shadows dancing below warm illuminations escaping from the architectural mansion. A fluctuating mosaic pathway escorted her towards a pair of gothic iron doors, and exotic landscape gardens defined its domain surrounding her view.

Lounging in the back of the limousine half asleep, she felt the car stop. Stan opened the rear passenger door while Allison struggled to remove herself from her seat.

Holding his hand out Stan helped her out of the car and assisted her towards the main entrance doors.

Saying goodbye to her driver, Allison entered the grand hallway presenting a white marble floor and a dual staircase. Greek pillars obstructed her balance as she veered upwards towards the master bedroom, exhausted.

Opening the master bedroom oak doors, she noticed Romano lying face down on top of the sheets, naked. His sweeping dark hair suspended against his olive skin. Allison collapsed onto the bed next to him.

"You home, baby?" he murmured, half asleep.

"Hmm?" she responded, closing her eyes.

He pulled her closer. They slept peacefully for the next three hours, until the alarm sounded.

"Alice, you are never getting up." Romano moaned.

"I must. The car is collecting me in an hour, and I'm desperate for a shower!"

"I'm not letting you go!" Romano held her tight.

"I wish I could stay. Filming starts at eight, and I have make-up. Oh no!" Allison screeched.

Swinging both legs together, she escaped Romano and headed to the bathroom. Romano followed her, grinning. "You are still wearing your clothes from yesterday."

"I know...I needed my bed last night."

"You mean this morning. Can I join you in the shower?" Romano asked, seductively positioning his body close.

"Okay," she giggled, "But don't make me late!"

Allison climbed into the rear of the car while Craig Welling spoke to Romano. Soon the silver limo would disappear out of the gates leaving the Italian film star behind.

Thirty minutes later, Allison arrived at Sphere Pictures Filming Studios. Sebastian Dupont waited, delivering hot bacon bagels and Earl Grey tea from Martha's.

"Sebastian!" Allison hugged him as she stepped into the trailer.

"My dear Alice…I brought bagels."

"Do I have time for breakfast?" Allison asked, smelling the delicious smoked aroma of bacon.

"Yes, I have made time for you. Please sit and enjoy." Sebastian appropriated his seat at the table. "Alice, I am worried about your weight."

"Great thing to tell a woman!" she said, biting into the bagel.

"You haven't been eating. Look at you! You're half starved." Sebastian glared. "It is my job to prevent you from overworking, and nothing can stop me from completing a mission."

"So, you're going to babysit me?"

"Yes!" Sebastian retorted, walking into the kitchen, and pouring himself a glass of water.

"Romano is worried about me," she mumbled.

"We are all worried about you." Sebastian turned around. "Believe me, Alice, everyone loves you."

"You should write that on a greeting card."

Sebastian cleared his throat trying to ignore Allison's last comment. "Filming stops at six. No recording studio. Home by seven."

"Stewart will not like it!"

"My little chat with our friend Stewart went well, and Gloss has agreed to it. Your screenings are going to take priority from now on."

"You're my fairy godmother!" Allison screeched, throwing her arms around him.

"Darling, I have been called worse!"

CHAPTER 11

The Kellie School of Performing Arts - Brooklyn

New York - 5th April 1977 - 7.00 p.m.

Elle Sidorov lit a cigarette and closed her legs. A cloud of smoke escaped from her luscious lips. Positioning his strong arms behind his head atop the chaise lounge sofa, Paul Freidman exhaled in satisfaction.

Opposite Paul, the curvaceous Eva offered him a cigarette while sprawled naked on a Louis XIV chair.

"Paul, darling!" she pulled on her panties as Elle caressed her left nipple. "You said earlier that we needed to chat."

"Look, Eva, I can't even listen to women when they are wearing clothes!"

Eva laughed. "Like any girl would waste time talking to you."

Standing up from the French-style chair and strutting over to the closet, Eva opened the door and produced two silk kimonos. With the cigarette between her lips, she flung a black kimono at Paul, concealing herself in the process.

Eva's assistant Elle, departing from the office nude, pecked Paul on the cheek and disappeared from the scene.

Positioning herself back down into the same chair she had left seconds ago, Eva smiled. "Well, what's the urgent news?"

"I'm being investigated," Paul said, crossing his legs and lighting up a cigarette. "We're being investigated."

"Who's doing the investigating?" Eva replied, unbothered.

"Green Records!" Paul slammed an ashtray down on the Regina Baroque coffee table, scattering his ashes.

"They can't make us testify against each other. What's it called? Spousal…"

"Spousal privilege? That only applies to married couples."

"Don't you want to…"

"Marry you?" Paul said. "I don't even like you."

"You bastard."

"I'm a bastard? What does that make Benedict Shaw? He's not accepting my appointments."

"Maybe he's away on business."

"His secretary away too?"

Eva lit another cigarette and occupied herself next to Paul. "Where should we go?"

"Prison," Paul laughed.

"On what charges?" chortled Eva.

"Charges? How about fraud, embezzlement, third-degree m—"

Eva put her hand over Paul's mouth.

"You'll go down with me," he mumbled. "I'll make sure of it."

"That's the most romantic thing you ever said to me."

Eva untied her white kimono. Silk fabric flowed over the chaise lounge cushions as she invited him in. Paul slithered towards her, bending down on both knees, supplicating, demanding, and kissing her lower leg. Slowly meandering his way up, sensing her delicate pale, supple skin with his tongue, he had reached his destination – Eva's core.

An accumulation of silk including a pair of panties crumpled onto the prismatic rug. Muffled giggles and groans dispersed from the sofa. Eva devoured the moment and impaled Paul alongside her.

"We're still not getting married," Paul said relaxing into his thrusts.

****

Elle, quickly dressed and grabbed her bag, sprinting out the door. A red Chevrolet Impala lingered outside the performing arts school. Darting down the stone steps towards the car, Elle noticed the rear passenger door was open. Checking the area for clearance she jumped inside. As soon as the door closed, the Chevy accelerated eastward into the night.

An hour later, motionless outside a secluded diner, the car's paintwork reflected blue and red flashing lights that irradiated the night sky. Beer billboards and broken windows surrounded the parking lot.

"Ask for booth four," said the driver, facing forward.

"Booth four?" Elle replied.

The driver remained silent as he unlocked the door. Slamming it shut, Elle advanced towards an 'OPEN' sign on the diner's glass window. She walked into the warm atmosphere and took a deep breath.

Elle lingered at the reservation desk, observing hurrying waitresses and cooks placing meals on elongated counters.

"Can I help?" smiled the well-groomed male at the reception.

"Booth four?" Elle murmured.

"Certainly, follow me."

Elle shadowed the receptionist until she reached booth four. He handed her a menu while she removed her coat and took a seat. "Thank you," she said, throwing her bag into the booth.

"Good evening, Elle." The voice seemed to come from the walls themselves.

"Evening," she responded, producing a brown file from her bag. The striking gentleman snatched the portfolio and rifled through the contents.

"The agreed amount," he said, sliding a brown envelope across the table towards Elle. "One thousand."

"Thank you," she responded, putting the envelope into her bag. Looking across at the gentleman, she whispered, "He knows something is wrong. He's panicking!"

"He should be...The madam?"

"Doesn't flinch."

"She will." The gentleman grinned. "In time. Keep me apprised: you know the procedure."

Elle gulped. Standing up, putting her coat on, she shifted away from the booth and walked out of the diner, never looking back.

****

Conception Magazine - New York
5th April 1977 - 10.00 p.m.

Light refracted from the Manhattan skyline, illuminating a tall, dark-haired man clutching a telephone receiver in one hand and a cigarette in the other.

"I have it right here on my desk. Yep. Yep," he said, stretching over the black granite and grabbed a coordinating ashtray.

"You'll have it in ten. Fax. Yep. Yep."

Walking around the desk and opening the file, he gripped a sheet of paper. "Another victim. Emily-Jane Collins, sixteen. Yep. No, One Film Studios are contracting. How much? Sixty mil? Yep, five years. One million to Emily-Jane. I said one, not two. What do I look like, a chump?

Twenty-nine million to Eva. Thirty million to Freidman. Yep."

The monotone voice on the other end of the receiver muffled, "Freidman pilfered Elle's lover!"

"No, he's going down. I refuse a female scorned…My husband. You are not a bitch!" Oliver laughed. "Sebastian, I do love you, and I miss you terribly." Oliver sat down at his desk, browsed at the file, and asked, "How's the babysitting job?"

Laughing again and playing with the telephone cord, he said, "I told you it would be hard work," pausing, shifting his tone. "I can't wait. Love you too. Bye."

Placing the receiver onto the receiver cap, Oliver grabbed the file and walked across the office floor. Standing in front of the fax machine, he began to scan the pages from the file.

Dialling the correct facsimile number, the machine emitted a screeching sound and vomited out the copies, crowning them with a cover sheet.

"Success!" Oliver said, alone.

Locking the brown file into his desk drawer, Oliver swung his suede high back chair towards the windows. He gazed out into the night: peace, quiet, and solitude surrounded him.

"No emotional conflicts. No guilt," he added, calm and contended. Oliver had guaranteed the scoop of the century. He felt like a hunter, ready and patiently waiting, anticipating the kill. Thanks to Oliver Dupont, *Conception Magazine* would remain the world's foremost publication for many more years to come.

****

Templeton Hall - The Hamptons
6th April 1977 - 10.00 a.m.

Theo-James entered his home office and advances towards the fax machine. Wrenching out the paper, Theo paces towards his chair at great speed.

Sitting at his Chippendale antique desk, reaching for a GPO classic telephone, Theo-James turned the dial and hollered for Edwards, attendance.

Edwards knocked three times at the door and entered.

"Sir." Edwards bowed.

"I would like to request tea, please," Theo-James said, placing the receiver to his left ear.

"English breakfast, sir?"

"Yes, please and a plate of Mrs Wagner's shortbread biscuits."

Edwards bowed and departed quicky.

"Martyn!" Theo-James gushed. "Did you receive the fax?"

Martyn Simpson-Smyth reclined in his office chair. Paperwork scattered upon paperwork. The modern X-line metal desk submerged into chaos.

"Theo! I received your fax late last night."

"We have to stop this contract!" Theo-James demanded.

"I disagree, we require Emily to sign."

"Why?" Theo-James mused.

"Elle Sidorov is available to record the signing. The evidence will be admissible in court."

"Excellent." Theo-James waved Edwards forward, carrying a silver tea tray.

Lowering it onto a nest of tables, Edwards lifted the teapot and slowly poured the contents into the teacup, adding a drop of milk and two teaspoons of sugar. Edwards placed the cup and saucer on Theo's desk, complementing a plate of shortbread biscuits and a napkin.

Theo-James grabbed a biscuit and started to nibble.

"So, what happens next?" he crunched, dropping crumbs onto his plate.

"We wait six weeks before the pre-trial processes a decision. If successful, the legal authority can remove Freidman."

"How long will the trial last?" Theo-James continued to munch on his shortbread.

Martyn swivelled in his chair. "Nine months."

"Good, Freidman will remain in custody," Theo-James said with a sip. "My concern is Eva Moulin. She unnerves me."

"Theo, are you on the school's board of governors?" Martyn asked.

"My colleague is."

"Great! After the papers are served and Freidman is arrested, reference your colleague a valid reason to remove Eva Moulin from the board. Be conscientious not to implicate her with Freidman."

"I understand. It could affect the trial."

"Affect the trial?" Martyn said. "It will decide it."

****

NYC International Airport - New York
6th April 1977 - 11.30 a.m.

Arriving at the terminal, Paul Freidman dismounted from his golf cart. Personnel escorted Paul to the VIP lounge. The relaxing atmosphere did not fix his mood.

Thirty minutes later, an executive approached Paul. Freidman smiled at his chaperone and offered a handshake. The executive feigned a cough and directed Paul to a private hangar. Insulted, Paul "VIP" Freidman boarded his plane.

The jet disembarked the runway. Taking off at speed and climbing into the clouds it began to slow its acceleration.

Observing through the porthole, Paul perceived ice crystals made from contrails from the engine fuel.

"Mr Freidman, care for a glass of champagne?" asked the steward, holding a bottle of Dom Perignon.

"Please," replied Paul. "Leave the bottle."

The steward stopped pouring the prestigious pearls into the flute and handed it to Paul. "Is there anything else, sir?"

Paul sipped his drink and shook his head. The steward smiled and retreated towards the rear of the jet.

Emptying his glass, Paul was delighted to leave behind New York for LA. He licked the champagne off his lips as he prepared to accept the counterfeit contracts on behalf of Eva Moulin.

****

Los Angeles - 10th April 1977

Wrapping up filming on *Flying-in 2*, Allison spent Easter relaxing with Romano at their home in Bel-Air. Friends and family celebrated the festivities with the couple.

A week later, Romano travelled to New Mexico and endured a twelve-week filming schedule while Allison resided in their New York apartment, alone.

Sebastian visited The Palmer Building Apartments, bringing bacon bagels and Earl Grey for Allison. He announced that Green Records were releasing *My Heart is on Fire* on the 15th of May. She would have to endure a challenging music video, and worse, a new schedule.

****

Green Records Recording Studio - Los Angeles
24th April 1977

Allison noticed Sebastian's accomplishments within her management administration, supervising and organising everything. Looking puzzled she said. "Where is Paul? I haven't seen him since my party."

"Darling, the man is busy with other projects." Sebastian said gripping his cup of tea.

"I was supposed to see him after my party, he was not pleased with me."

"Yes, that is about right. Anger management is needed in his case."

Allison grinned and quietly sipped her drink. Sitting in Sebastian's office would become customary for the superstar.

Not one person in Green Records said anything about Paul's disappearance! How strange...

CHAPTER 12

Templeton Hall - The Hamptons - 2nd May 1977

Framed in a full-length mirror, Eleanor Templeton-Jones placed a diamond pendant around her daughter's neck. Stepping back from the bride, Eleanor said, "This was my mother's gift to me on my wedding day."

Exhibiting a glamourous balloon-sleeved white fishtail lace dress, Annie's reflection caressed the pendant.

"My gift to you, darling!" Eleanor smiled behind her.

Charles Montgomery stepped forward holding an elegant cathedral veil, situating the one-tier crystal edged lace onto Annie's head. He and his team arranged the three-metre length garment.

Annie Templeton-Miller dazzled when Montgomery's team refined her to perfection. Passing Annie her prestigious bouquet of jasmine white roses and gypsophila, Eleanor ordered the photographers into the room.

Conception Magazine remunerated a two-million-dollar deal for the exclusive. The family commissioned Pyramid Imitari Photo Studios to capture the unforgettable day.

The sound of clinking crystal flutes commenced the celebrations. Charles Montgomery announced that a successful morning had been achieved. Eleanor, supporting his striking salmon pink two-piece, wore matching stilettos, a luxurious antique pearl headpiece, and a coordinating clutch bag.

Five delightful bridesmaids were wearing his floral white and cerise A-line silk off the shoulder dresses, matching satin court shoes, silver tiaras, and bouquets of dark cerise-scented roses. Not forgetting twenty-four charcoal grey morning suits, silk waistcoats, cravats, and pocket handkerchiefs for the groomsmen and Theo.

Only one person who omitted Charles's designs was Allison Templeton-Miller. Contracted to The House of Sylvester it had caused terrible problems over the past months, but both designers had compromised over an agreement.

****

Phillippe dressed Allison to perfection. Standing in front of a full-length mirror, beholding her cerise A-line bridesmaid dress, Allison noticed the capturing waterfall train flowing behind the fabric. Her dark hair held in a sophisticated twisted low bun; diamantes sprinkled the elements with a silver tiara placed towards the front of her forehead.

Turning round and hugging Phillippe, Allison cried out in excitement. "It's beautiful!"

"Perfection, Alice! You make the dress shine."

Phillippe stepped back and opened the door, allowing the photographers from *Conception Magazine* to enter.

Smiling smugly to himself, he said… "My beautiful petite angel will infiltrate this dress design with her beauty."

Already notifying his seamstress in London, Phillippe prepared to collate the orders.

****

Thirty tables decorated in white linen and deep pink cattleya orchids stood elegantly inside the marquee. Stewards delicately situated crystal champagne flutes and exotic wine glasses against fine silver cutlery. Monogrammed place cards, and luxury silver silk napkins completed the tables.

Pink silk sashes dangled from the marquess's interior ceiling. Numerous designers arranged blush-pink roses in silver pedestals and technicians rolled out a red carpet leading to the top table.

Outside in the gardens three hundred gold coloured banqueting chairs sat against a flowered rose path. A solid white wooden gazebo stood at the bottom of the aisle displaying a hanging cascade of scented pink roses and ivy.

Waiters and waitresses dressed in smart uniforms rushed around. Engineering technicians worked in the music marquee doing last minute adjustments. A chequered dance floor, assorted lighting, and stage created the finished look.

Chauffeured limousines, Ferraris, Lamborghinis, and other prestigious vehicles parked along the driveway.

Parking attendants and wedding coordinators assisted individuals towards the ceremony area. Champagne and assorted wines flowed as the sun embraced the gardens of Templeton Hall.

Social hierarchy laughed, chatted, and greeted one another. The Templeton-Miller brothers met their guests while the remaining family were screened from the outside world.

Inside Templeton Hall, garlands of glamorous pink and white flowers surged in every direction. Exquisite guest bedrooms on the second floor disturbed the bustling chaos from downstairs.

Lucinda complained, "I look fat!"

"Lucinda, you just had a baby!" Belinda said.

"Five weeks ago." Lucinda breathed in and stood sideways looking into the mirror. "My fitness instructor is not doing a very good job. I should be skinny by now!"

"How is baby David? He's so cute!" Belinda chuckled.

"He's beautiful like his father." Sighing, Lucinda sat on the bed. "I will never let him go."

"I think David will have other ideas once he's eighteen," Belinda laughed, agreeing with her hairstylist.

Fay entered the room, already dressed in her off the shoulder bridesmaid dress.

"Wow!" Belinda said. "We all look gorgeous."

"Did you hear the arguments between Montgomery and Sylvester earlier?" Lucinda twirled her blonde coils around her finger.

"Yup," Fay replied, adjusting the tiara located between her caramel curls.

Belinda's hairstylist listened to the gossip while pinning the silver tiara onto Belinda's head. Red princess curls hung majestically against Belinda's face as she continued to tittle-tattle.

"Alice is under contract to wear Sylvester, whether Montgomery likes it or not," Belinda blurted.

"I wonder what she will look like." Lucinda grinned.

"Perfect!" Belinda screeched.

****

The photographers finalised their shots. Allison and Eleanor departed downstairs. Waiting patiently in the foyer, five bridesmaids gossiped: two were friends of Annie, and three were the clique: Fay, Lucinda, and Belinda.

"Alice, Alice, you look absolutely stunning!" Belinda shouted.

"Wait until you see Annie. Oh, she is so beautiful! Look at you, guys." Allison hugged her friends standing on the bottom step.

"We have a surprise for you," Fay said, pulling away from her.

"What, for me?" Allison replied, confused.

"Close your eyes. No peeking!" Belinda squealed.

Romano, dressed in his morning suit strolled towards the girls, arm-in-arm with Eleanor. Allison opened her eyes. "Oh! Romano!" she screamed and hurdled towards him.

Romano and Allison passionately kissed one another.

"Romano, darling! Do be careful with her make-up," Eleanor insisted. "Edwards, please send for the Montgomery make-up artist. Immediately!"

"Mama, did you sort all of this?" Allison said, lifting her head.

"Your papa and I, darling. Romano is part of the family, and it is a family celebration."

Edwards conveyed Montgomery's make- up artist, Miss Elizabeth C Knowles.

"Thank you, Edwards. Please, Lizzy, can you powder Allison's face and apply more lip gloss?" Eleanor stressed.

The bridesmaids giggled. Romano blushed once the make-up was in place again. A cough interrupted the ramblings in the foyer. Everyone looked up at the balcony and gasped.

Walking down the staircase, Theo-James—on his left arm, Annie. Charles's team clasped the three-metre veil from behind.

"Positions!" shouted the wedding coordinator.

Romano kissed Allison and withdrew towards the ceremony area while Eleanor rolled her eyes in despair at Allison's smudged make-up.

Annie relished in her beauty. Her chocolate brown hair styled in a classic updo intensified her green oval-shaped eyes, and diamonds bathed against her soft milk-white skin.

The bridesmaids got steered away, and Eleanor kissed Annie and Theo-James before departing. Head bridesmaid Allison remained with her papa and sister.

Stepping down the rose pathway, Allison searched for Romano. She noticed Sebastian and Oliver in matching morning suits.

"You're a sensational couple!" she whispered to herself.

Oliver waved at Allison, while Sebastian tapped his husband's hand with his programme.

All the Templeton band members sat together in their morning suits. But when arriving at the gazebo, Allison noticed the terrified look on Ricky's face and Donny Davis smiling at him. Trusting Donny to be his best man was like being in a cage with a ravenous lion.

Annie followed the chief bridesmaid on the arm of her proud papa. Happy and contented, Theo-James announced his daughter to the priest, placing Annie's right hand over Ricky's alluring bronze palm.

The ceremony commenced beautifully, and Allison desperately searched the congregation for Romano. At last, she had found him sitting with her brothers Henry and Richard. Romano caught Allison's attention, winking, and blowing her kisses. Ami and Rene giggled, looking at the man she loved.

****

Performing *Heavenly Body*, Allison watched her sister and brother-in-law dancing their first dance. People gathered around the edge of the dance floor to spectate, snapping photographs.

Finishing the song, Allison bowed to the audience and blew a kiss towards Annie and Ricky. The crowd of people went ballistic, clapping and whistling.

Discovering where her friends were located, she removed herself from the stage. Grabbing a drink, Allison went over to join them.

Romano chatted nearby to Oliver Dupont. "I'll be ready soon!" he shouted to her, waving his hand.

"Okay," she shouted back.

Belinda, Fay, and Lucinda hugged Allison, nearly spilling her drink. Gripping Belinda around the waist, Donny Davis said, "Great song!"

"Very funny," Allison sarcastically replied.

"I thought all the band would have sung it tonight." Max interrupted.

"Annie requested that her loving sister sang it."

"A sister thing!" Michael Simmons laughed. "Never get in the way of a sister thing!"

Everyone started laughing but the laughter soon stopped when Jake Pullman barged into the clique. Drunk, and chaotic he grabbed Allison's breasts. Craig Welling saw the incident and ran over. Jumping amongst the disoriented group, he seized Jake by the collar, and they fell to the floor. While falling backwards, Jake bashed his head against Allison's.

Romano watched in horror as he witnessed Craig running over to the crowd. Both he and Oliver dropped their drinks and fled towards the scene.

Allison remained unconscious on the floor.

"Alice, Alice, wake up!" Dropping to his knees, Romano cuddled her in his arms. Donny Davis checked her pulse and crumbled into pieces.

Eleanor and Theo-James ran towards their daughter.

"What the hell happened?" Theo-James screamed, as the crowd around his daughter surrounded them tightly.

"Call 911!" Eleanor shouted, stumbling while trying to hold herself between the gathering crowd.

Lowering herself to her daughter's level, she began caressing her forehead, trying to wake her up. "My darling, you will be alright."

"The emergency services are on the premises, madam," Edwards informed, shepherding people away from the area.

Craig Welling and his security started clearing guests out of the marquee. Two medics rushed towards Allison.

Theo-James, Eleanor, Romano, Donny, and Belinda stayed at Allison's side. One medic tried listening for her heartbeat while the other placed a canular into her vein. She was still unconscious: No response. They lifted her onto a stretcher.

****

Allison remained unresponsive, wearing an oxygen mask and an IV. Eleanor sat across the rocking interior from her helpless baby. Theo-James held Eleanor's hand.

"Please don't run the sirens. Her heart can't take it."

"I'm fine," Eleanor said, blowing her nose.

Romano and Craig's limousine followed the ambulance. Stan kept the partition closed between Romano and himself.

"What happened, Craig?" Romano said, looking out of the rear passenger window.

"Jake Pullman. That's what happened."

"Who the hell is Jake Pullman?"

"He's been after Alice for years. His father is Senator WJ Pullman."

"I didn't ask for his family tree. I asked who the hell he is."

"I will explain. Elizabeth Pullman was best friends with Eleanor,"

"Was?"

"She died; in fact, she was murdered in broad daylight with her bodyguard. Her husband WJ sank to an all-time low. Nine-year-old Jake ran off the tracks."

"Wow."

"His father married a gold digger and Jake was forced into boarding school. The Pullman's and Miller's happy family vacations ended after that."

"Why?"

"Jake always made a play for Alice since she was eleven. Sometimes she would return to the lodge and have bruises on her."

"No way," Romano said.

"Templeton security always kept a close eye on him."

"How do you know all this?"

"Sebastian gave me a copy of his file. Alice was rushed to hospital in 1968 with a broken wrist. At the time, Jake Pullman was with her. Nothing got proven, but the guys say he was the one who did it."

"I'll end him."

"If the alcohol doesn't. His father has put him into rehab so many times that I have lost count."

"So, it didn't work?"

"Theo-James is good friends with WJ. Very close like brothers."

"I'll pay for a hitman for the bastard." Romano said under his breath. "I suppose daddy paid hush money for his sons mistakes!"

"Someone did."

"The ambulance!" Romano knocked on the partition and the window started to move down. "What's happening Stan?"

Stan shrugged his shoulders and pulled into the layby.

****

The medic in the back of the ambulance shouted, "Stop!" An ear-piercing alarm went off.

"What's happening?" Theo-James stood up, looking over at Allison.

"Please remain seated, sir," the head medic replied.

Opening the door and climbing into the back, the medic from the driver's seat opened a drawer, pulled out a syringe and held it at eye level. He flicked the side of the syringe with his finger and positioned it into Allison's canular. Both medics started CPR and checked the monitors. After a few

128

minutes, a bleeping sound came from the monitor. The pair sighed.

"Mr Miller, your daughter is in critical condition. We have no choice…"

"Do it," Theo said.

Sirens pelted an ear-splitting echo, and the vehicle accelerated at lightning speed.

****

An emergency team of nurses and doctors rushed Allison into a solitary room. Eleanor, Theo-James, Romano, Craig, and the Templeton security were escorted into a VIP family room. Eleanor, distraught, reached over to grab a tissue from the glass coffee table. Theo-James paced lengthways against the mocha floor tiles. Romano stared through the metal blinds evaluating the crowd of press gathered outside.

"Good evening, Mr Miller. My name is Doctor Andreas Tellerman, St Eliza's Chief Director. My team are working on Allison as we speak. We have found a few complications with a DVT, or blood clot, as the kids call it. The bang to the head has caused a DVT and obstructed the coronary artery. Myocardial infarction. In Allison's case, it was mild."

"A heart attack?" Theo-James said.

"Yes, the clot travelled to the arteries."

Sitting down, Theo-James held Eleanor. "Now what?"

"We are treating her condition with blood thinners; they are improving her circulation as we speak. The good news is that the CT scan showed good brain activity. She will not require surgery."

"Is she awake?" Eleanor sniffled.

"No, we are expecting Allison to wake within the next twenty-four hours. My staff is preparing her room. She will be moved into a private suite."

"What about her heart?" Romano cut in.

"Allison's heart is strong, and the DVT caused a mild attack. No damage."

Romano sighed in relief next to Eleanor. Theo-James smiled and stood up from the sofa.

"Thank you, Doctor Tellerman. Please give our regards to your staff."

"When the team is happy with her healing, you can visit." He shook hands with Theo.

"If," Eleanor added.

****

Plastic tubes appeared from the cannula that submerged into Allison's soft pale skin. As she breathed in, buzzing reverberated from the monitors. Unconscious, Allison appeared to be fast asleep.

Eleanor and Theo-James sat on either side of Allison's hospital bed. She caressed her daughter's cheek, exhausted, still wearing the Montgomery salmon two-piece from earlier. Theo-James held his wife's hand and massaged Allison's leg.

Romano, tolerating his morning suit, stood outside the room with Craig and the Templeton-Miller security. The family issued strict instructions: under no circumstances was anyone allowed to enter the room unless they were family, close friends, or hospital staff. Identification had to be certified.

Theo-James paced outside. "Gareth, I'm taking Eleanor home. She's exhausted. Have you arranged for staff to cover the room?"

"It's all organised, sir. Tony and Zack are on night duty. I will replace them in the morning with Phil."

"Craig, I know you are Allison's personal security. What are your plans?" Theo-James asked.

"I'll accompany Sebastian in the morning. Tonight, I'll get some rest."

"Good man. Romano, the hospital staff are bringing you a divan so you can stay with Alice. I will arrange a change of clothing for you and a wash bag. One of my staff will deliver it. Also, nightwear for my daughter."

Craig and Gareth accompanied Theo-James and Eleanor out of the hospital. Their limousine waited at the rear of the building, as usual, avoiding the press.

131

****

Romano's and Allison's overnight bags got delivered successfully, without any hassle. Having taken a shower and removing the grey soiled morning suit, Romano exhibited a white Templeton t-shirt and grey jog pants. After an hour of speaking to Allison, he climbed into the provisional divan the hospital had installed.

Closing his weary eyes, he heard a murmur. Romano pulled back the sheet, jumped off the bed, and rushed to Allison's side. He pressed the alarm button. Two nurses ran into the room past security and started checking her OBS.

Stirring, Allison uttered a few confused words.

"Yes, its Romano. I'm here, Alice," he said, holding her hand, "I'm here."

"Allison, can you hear me?" one of the nurses asked, paging a doctor.

After a moment, Allison opened her eyes, looked at her lover, and started to cry. Stroking her hair away from her forehead, Romano tried to assure her, "Don't cry, baby. I'm here."

A short red-haired male wearing a white lab coat came into the room and asked Romano to stand back so he could record Allison's condition. Checking her credentials, he shook his head in approval.

"Miss Templeton-Miller, good to have you back. You bumped your head. It caused a blood clot. The IVs are clearing that clot away. You are in good hands. Don't panic."

"Panic?" Allison looked even more confused. "I... need...a."

"The nurse will get you a glass of water." The doctor scribbled on a clipboard. "I will monitor you for the next couple of days."

Allison foreshadowed a smile while her bed was adjusted. She sat up while the nurse handed her glass of water with a straw. Allison managed to take a couple of sips.

"She is very tired now, so take your time with her. Don't panic if she suddenly falls asleep. It is natural with concussion," the doctor explained to Romano.

After all the assessments and satisfactory results, the hospital staff vacated Allison's suite. Romano reclined in a brown leather chair close to Allison. He kissed her hand. "You scared me," he muttered.

"I... sor..."

"Don't apologise. I should have protected you more."

****

St Elizas Hospital - The Hamptons
3rd May 1977 - 9.00 a.m.

Sebastian Dupont dabbed at Allison's warm forehead with his silk handkerchief.

133

"My darling Alice, I'm so sorry for what happened yesterday."

Though imprisoned by IV lines, Allison was feeling heaps better. Earlier that morning, nursing staff had given her a bed bath and dressed her into a pair of satin floral pyjamas.

A nurse called Jenny combed and plaited Allison's long dark hair. "Miss Alice, that was a terrible bump you received yesterday. You had us all worried."

Allison stared forward while Jenny pulled tight her hair. "I can't remember a thing. I thought I had too many drinks."

"Yeah, your sister married Ricky Brown, he's so hot."

Allison laughed. "I take it he's your favourite band member?"

Sitting on the bed with Allison, Jenny said. "No ...Marc Garcia is my favourite."

Allison and Jenny giggled. "All finished." Jenny said positioning the final hair grip.

"Thank you, hand me over your notebook." Allison asked. Jenny scrambled to collect her notebook from the side table and passed it to the superstar.

"To Jenny thank you for styling my hair, Alice," she said, writing on a blank page.

"Miss Alice, I shall treasure this forever." Jenny gazed at the page. "I shall now leave you in peace." Jenny smiled, collecting her notebook.

Another nurse walked into the room carrying breakfast. Allison made herself comfortable and smelt the aroma of eggs.

Sebastian stood in the lounge area of the suite. "Your fan club is overwhelming. I am surprised you have the energy to sign notebooks. Recovery is vital."

"I'm okay," said Allison, eating a boiled egg and soldiers.

"Did the hospital explain what happened?" Sebastian selected his seat on the luxurious red sofa.

"The hospital didn't say anything. The doctor did."

"Where's Romano?"

"Shower," said Allison, crunching on brown toast.

Sebastian searched the room with his keen eyes. "Your schedule has changed, Alice. You cannot attend the TV tour. The boys are happy to stay at plan B."

Templeton's plan B always established itself when Allison wasn't available. Ricky and Donny took the lead.

"Green Records have delayed your music video until you are well again. But the release date of your single will remain the same."

"I figured."

"Who is Jake Pullman?" Sebastian asked, knowing very well the full history of the guy.

"Friend of the family. We have known each other since we were two. I admit he can be a problem."

"A problem? I'm increasing your security, Alice." Sebastian crossed his legs. "Pullman is obsessed with you."

"Jake?" Allison nearly choked on a piece of bread.

"Annie has expressed concern regarding Mr Pullman. He's aggressive, abusive. The broken wrist!"

Allison fell silent.

"Somehow I doubt that you'd slipped in the snow."

"I was twelve years old; Jake was thirteen. We were skiing in an isolated area, and I fell over. I thought Jake was coming to help me get up. Instead, Jake jumped on top of me, tried to kiss me...I screamed. He grabbed my wrist, twisting it back towards him, telling me to shut up."

"Then what?"

Allison looked down at the remaining breakfast that existed on her plate. "He skied away," she replied.

"You never told anyone, did you?"

"Annie had an idea. Papa thought I fell over."

"Your sister identifies more with Jake than you know." Sebastian hoisted himself from the sofa and approached Allison. "He's dangerous. Theo told me he wants this incident yesterday to be the final one."

"I agree, he's out of hand." Allison muttered.

Turning his back to her, he asked, "Are you frightened of him?"

"No. I'm frightened of what he could do."

"You will be protected, Alice." Sebastian looked out the window at the ambulances massed in the hospital parking lot. "I swear on my life."

****

Templeton Hall - The Hamptons
3rd May 1977 - 11.00 a.m.

Theo-James and Eleanor accompanied Annie and her new husband Ricky, for a spectacular morning brunch. The newlyweds were travelling to the Maldives for their honeymoon, courtesy of Annie's brothers. Eleanor and Theo-James had purchased a twenty-million-dollar mansion for the couple. The new mansion was only ten minutes away from Templeton Hall.

"Please pass a message on to Alice that we are thinking about her." Annie smiled, buttering a roll. "If we were not flying today, I would have called to see her."

"Annie, darling, your sister will understand."

"Romano rang us this morning. Alice is feeling much better."

"She is a fighter, Papa!"

"Romano is a good man. Your papa is trying to discuss an extended stay from his filming." Eleanor smiled at Theo-James.

"Where?" Ricky stepped in.

"New Mexico," Theo-James scoffed. "A western!"

****

Templeton Hall - The Hamptons
3rd May 1977 - 7.00 p.m.

Theo-James rearranged the tabloids on top of his desk and checked his pocket watch: 7:00 p.m.

"Damn it, Dupont. Where are you?" He sank deeply into his Chesterfield high back, reading the dreadful stories about his little girl. Theo slammed his fist on the desk, scattering the newspapers. "When I'm finished with Freidman, Pullman is next."

CHAPTER 13

Green Records Recording Studios - Los Angeles

4th May 1977

Viewing the mountain range skyline from his office window, Benedict Shaw prepared himself for the final showdown.

Observing the unscrupulous male in the reflection of his window. Shaw gripped his fists tight.

Paul Freidman sat self-assured, exhibiting a dark blue designer suit and polished brogues.

"Benedict, at last! I suppose your secretary lost my number. Maybe I should carve it into the walls."

Benedict glared and turned around to face Freidman. Walking over to his desk, Shaw pressed a button on his telephone. "Please send in Mark and Todd."

A tempered glass door opened. Two suited executives walked into the office. Offering them both a seat, Benedict remained standing. He handed Paul a white envelope. "Paul, the board of directors have confirmed their decision to dismiss you."

"Dismiss me?" Paul slammed his feet on the floor, rose from his chair, and leaned over Benedict's desk. "What do you think I am, Shaw? A cheap hooker?"

Benedict opened a packet of cigarettes. "No, a fraud. You have cheated, lied, manipulated. You've stolen things that don't even exist. Shall I continue?"

"Go on," Paul said, leaning more deeply into Shaw's desk.

Green Records Legal Representative Mark Jammer walked over and confiscated a letter opener that Freidman was edging towards. "Mr Freidman, you will be receiving a summons from the Supreme Court."

Paul pounded Mark Jammer right in the face with his fist. Mark hit the floor with tremendous force. Benedict sounded the alarm, and security burst into his office.

Three uniformed security guards apprehended Paul, forcing him down onto his knees and tying his hands behind his back.

"You all right, sir?" the guard asked Shaw, gripping Freidman by the shoulder.

"I'm fine," Benedict said, helping Mark to his feet.

"Police are on their way," shouted Mary from reception.

"Get him out of here," Benedict ordered, crashing both palms onto his desk. "Now!"

Mark stumbled back towards the sofa and held a tissue over his nose. Blood dripped everywhere. Mary ran into the office and handed Todd a first aid box.

Benedict propelled himself through the door and into the reception area, waiting for law enforcement to arrive. Minutes later, the elevator door opened, and three cops paced towards Benedict.

"He's in there," he said, pointing to a small office.

"Please remain calm and tell us what happened," the police sergeant said, pulling out his gun.

"I will provide you with a statement shortly," Benedict mumbled, walking into the small office, and observing the disorder caused by Freidman.

Sitting with Benedict's security, hands behind his back, a fanatical Paul Freidman spat at Benedict.

Three cops followed.

"You have the right to remain silent…" the officer said, cuffing Freidman and escorting him into the elevator.

Directing the police sergeant into Benedict's office, Mary inquired if anyone would like tea or coffee.

Everyone declined. Noticing Mark, the sergeant walked towards him and said, "You'll need to go to the hospital with that."

"Mary, arrange my car to transport Mark to the hospital," Benedict demanded.

Benedict described the situation of the incident to the police sergeant. Todd remained in the office with Shaw and provided his summary of events. The showdown was over, and Benedict Shaw had won hands down.

****

Paul Freidman sat handcuffed in the back of the squad car as they approached the police precinct. Two cops pulled Paul out of the vehicle and walked him into the custody area.

A detention officer asked for his details and booked him. Paul had all his personal belongings removed and then a custody officer escorted him into a small secure cell.

Loud cries and yells echoed in the background. Humiliated, Paul sunk, trapped in a cage with nowhere to run, waiting for the next slaughter. Waking up from a dreaded nightmare, he was startled by the sound of keys.

A tall Caribbean male frowned at him. "What happened, Paul? I always knew you were a wild animal, but that don't mean you should be locked up."

Lieutenant Bob John "JJ Handsome" Jones placed himself next to Paul and said, "I couldn't believe the guys when they told me who the force just dragged in."

Paul shrugged. "I'm having a bad day."

"In jail, every day is a bad day."

"Lost my job, freaked out," Paul said, looking down at his feet.

"So that's why you beat a man."

"He deserved it."

"Everybody does, that don't mean you should be the one to beat them. Look at you, Paul. Templeton's Manager."

"I was."

"What got you fired this time?"

"Some bitch in New York."

"You gotta be more specific."

"The bitch is forging contracts. She discovers the talent and forwards them onto me. I am unaware what they have signed. Suddenly the talent fails and boom, they are no more. Green blames me for destroying the kid's future."

"Who is the bitch?"

"Eva Moulin. You forgot my cut: zero, because she's the one forging the contracts." Paul said.

"Green thinks it's you."

"Enough to summon me for court."

JJ asked, "Do you have a lawyer? We can get recognisance bail."

Paul passed on his lawyer's details to JJ. Twelve hours later, bail was set at two million dollars. Freidman remunerated his bail and approved the conditions set by the judge.

Paul walked free from the police precinct, flagging down a cab.

****

Alexander House Apartments - New York

5th May 1977.

Oliver Dupont rolled over and felt the missing space next to him. Silk sheets tossed to one side and the warm indentation began to fade. Opening one eye, he glanced into the mirror and could see Sebastian accommodating his favourite crushed pink and gold Baroque armchair, clutching the antique house phone whilst dressed in his red silk dressing gown.

Unhurried, Sebastian plopped down onto the mattress. Oliver grunted. "Been talking business?"

"My darling Oliver, you are looking at Allison Templeton-Miller's new appointed manager!"

Oliver jolted upright against the pillows and rubbed his eyes. "Sebi, that's wonderful news." Oliver smirked, "What about Freidman?"

"All hell broke loose yesterday at the studio. Freidman got fired and punched a legal executive. The cops arrested him."

"I thought Burrows & Burrows were waiting to issue the summons."

"Benedict actioned his dismissal and invited Freidman into the office. The studio sent in their legal department guys, but it turned into a boxing match."

"Was it bad?"

"Legal guy had to go to the hospital. The cops arrested Freidman for assault."

"You're kidding!" Oliver gasped, unbelievably shaking his head in disgust. "Where is he now?"

"Paid his own bail. I'm attending a press conference tomorrow at the Marianna," Sebastian said.

"How are you going to manage Templeton and Alice?"

"I'm not. Marshall Rusk is."

"Didn't Rusk manage Kingston in the early seventies?"

"Manage? He made them! We both will be at the Marianna at 10:00."

Oliver produced a huge grin. "Does the band know?"

"They will. Alice and the gang need new contracts, this time prepared by Green Records Legal, not Paul Freidman."

Sebastian pulled Oliver into his arms. Placing his warm luscious lips against Oliver's, Sebastian acquainted himself above him, "I love you, Oliver Dupont," he whispered.

Both slid beneath the silky sheets, embracing the lovemaking that would transpire for hours.

****

Mare Casa - The Hamptons - 5th May 1977.

Belinda sighed. "You have to fly today?"

"I do, Honey Bun." Donny Davis responded, blowing a kiss towards Belinda. "Huge meeting at the studio, attendance mandatory."

Turquoise waves splashed the nearby rocks, and sunlight absorbed the placid sea. A soothing breeze escaped into the cheval glass veranda.

Spitting out her breakfast, Belinda replied, "No, you're wrong. What about Alice?"

"I'm not sure what's happening there. All I know is that we must attend this meeting tonight. The jet takes off at noon!"

"I could stay for a few days at the apartment."

"Alice needs you, and you're filming in Toronto next week," Donny laughed. "This is why I love you, Belinda. We have been together. How long?"

"Long enough to know you're an idiot."

"Right." Donny took a knee. "Belinda Ross-Belling, will you be my wife?"

Feeling on top of the world, she squealed, "Yes!"

Donny stood up and walked into the house. Minutes later, he emerged with a platinum emerald-cut diamond ring and a bouquet of red roses. "I love you more than music."

Belinda winked, "I'm louder, too."

A polished limousine parked on the driveway at Mare Casa. The clock struck ten and Donny Davis kissed Belinda whilst the chauffeur packed the car's trunk with designer luggage.

"I will call when I land. Love you, future Mrs Davis."

"Love you too, from the future Mrs Belling-Davis."

"I'm marrying you before September, but you can keep Belling!"

"I can't wait to show Alice my ring!"

"Send her my love. Don't tire her out with your fuzziness."

"You know me!" Belinda laughed.

****

St Elizas Hospital - The Hamptons
5th May 1977 - 6.00 p.m.

Allison reminisced about the day she and Belinda had endured. Several wedding magazines were scattered everywhere. Belinda reclined on a hospital bed for the entire day, discussing honeymoons, food, and venues. She exhibited her sparkling diamond as nurses attended to Allison.

After Belinda left, Allison felt exhausted. She smiled, feeling happy for her two best friends, and eventually drifted off to sleep.

"Hello, my darling!" Sebastian yelled as he pounced through the security outside.

"Hey, Sebastian," came a groggy reply.

"Did I wake you, my dear girl?" Sebastian asked, placing a basket of exotic fruits on the glass coffee table. Dressed in his splendour, Sebastian assumed his place on the sofa.

"I am officially your new manager, Alice." A huge smile stretched from ear to ear on Sebastian's face.

"Sebastian! Congratulations." Allison rubbed her eyes and glanced at him. "What about Paul?"

"Fired! Tomorrow, I attend a press conference, and I didn't want you to see it before I told you."

"I see. Fired?"

"Templeton have achieved four number one hits all over the world, but no awards. When did you ever see him, Alice? Let's see; you only met him when there were contracts to be signed and money to be made." Sebastian said, crossing his arms in front of his chest.

"You're right. The last time I met him on business was for the Sylvester contract. And briefly at my party."

"Briefly, indeed!" Sebastian looked at her in bed and asked, "How much did you receive from that contract, Alice?"

"Five million."

"The contract was worth fifteen. The man scammed you out of ten million dollars!"

"I did have an idea, but the circumstances were never right," Allison replied.

"Now that I am your friendly, handsome, debonair manager, Green Records are going to compensate you for your losses." Turning around to view the window behind him, he continued, "We need you to sign a new contract for Sphere Pictures and a separate contract for Green Records. I plan to spring you into space with your solo career."

"Do the guys have to sign new contracts as well?"

"Tonight."

"When do I sign?"

"Next week, after you're discharged."

"Do I have to keep the security?" Allison looked towards the locked door. "It feels like prison here."

"Afraid so. This is your life now, Alice. Templeton also have a new manager, Marshall Rusk."

"Marshall Rusk, Kingston's manager?"

"Rusk will not manage you, only the guys. Because of your solo career, Templeton will be performing excessive amounts of plan Bs." Sebastian laughed out loud. "Alice, you are my world, and we are going to make it big!"

****

The Marianna Hotel - New York
6th May 1977 – 10.00 a.m.

The hotel featured elegant antique fireplaces and luxury decorations of an 18th century mansion located in the prime of New York City. American television stations and networks assigned their prime positions; the tabloid press seated patiently.

The Parlour Room displayed gold and red fabrics. Glimmering warm chandeliers sparkled vivaciously upon two antique solid oak tables.

Sebastian Dupont and Marshall Rusk greeted one another with a pat on the back; for Sebastian, that was far too manly.

Both guys strode through a glass side entrance. Press officials and their cameras brimmed through the entirety of the room. Sebastian waved and nodded before the audience.

Dressed in a Sylvester grey checked suit and accompanying a pink cravat, Sebastian played the part very well. Wearing his designer spectacles, he settled at one of the tables, pouring himself a glass of water.

Rusk followed, not as glamourous but very attractive. He wore an off-the-rail black jacket, white shirt, and black denim jeans. He, too, positioned himself at the available table and poured himself water.

Camera flashes, papers rustling, and hushed gossip filled the room. Sebastian tapped on a wine glass to get the crowd's attention. "Good morning. My name is Sebastian Dupont, Allison Templeton-Miller's manager. My job is to oversee that my client is satisfying her fans, her producers, and herself. I intend to implement new business strategies and delegate new film roles. Any questions?"

Sebastian glanced over at a young male holding his hand up. "Yes..."

"Mr Dupont, why have you replaced Paul Freidman?"

Sebastian took a sip of water. "Mr Freidman achieved great success with Templeton and has moved onto new projects. Next!"

"Is it true that Freidman was arrested in LA?" shouted a man in the front row.

"Ask the LAPD," smiled Sebastian.

"Is Miss Templeton–Miller well enough to start performing again after her accident?" another voice rang out.

"She will be discharged tomorrow from St Elizas. Alice has recovered, ready to continue her solo career."

A deep and exotic voice shouted, "Is Allison not performing with Templeton anymore?"

"She will continue to sing with the group. Mr Rusk…" Sebastian turned towards Marshall.

Marshall bent his head low into the microphone. "My name is Marshall Rusk. As you well know, I managed Kingston before Templeton were discovered. I will not be working with Allison Templeton-Miller, but I will be supporting her. Mr Dupont and I are a team. Any questions?"

"How long are you planning to work with Templeton?" shouted an attractive blonde.

"That depends on the group. If they are successful, we carry on. If not…"

"Is that why Green Records fired Freidman?" a voice sounded from the back.

"Freidman was not fired; he is pursuing other opportunities. Next."

"Can you all work together or will your schedules clash?" sounded a female voice from the middle.

"I have not seen the Schedules." Both men laughed and shook hands. "We will be a good team."

CHAPTER 14

Green Records Recording Studios - Los Angeles
13th May 1977 - 11.00 a.m.

Only a week after being released from the hospital, Allison accommodated her position with Green Records legal representatives, Shaw, and Dupont. Gripping a bulky silver biro, she signed two contracts: Green Records, Templeton, and Green Records, solo. Later her schedule would take her to Sphere Pictures to sign another two-year contract.

Clapping and smiling, Benedict said, "My dear girl, it's a pleasure to be honoured by your presence, and this time, success will be yours. Green Records are obliged to fulfil your contract."

Pouring champagne into flutes, Mary winked at Allison, passing a glass to each member in the office. They raised a toast to Allison Templeton-Miller.

After the pleasantries, Sebastian and Allison progressed into his office. Entering a chalky white conceptual room, Sebastian placed himself behind his new state-of-the-art desk. Offering Allison, a comfortable black retro chair, he said, "Alice, this is today's schedule. The car will be collecting us in sixty minutes. I believe it should take a couple of hours to complete our business at Sphere Pictures. We also have a table booked at Fernando's at 3:00. The car should collect us around 5:00 and take us to Connors. Your filming is scheduled for around three hours. You with me, Alice?"

"Sitting in a hospital bed for days and then being fussed by your mama for a week, it's luxury," smiled Allison.

"Craig and Tony will be joining us as well."

"I'm getting used to them. I wasn't sure about Ted this morning."

"He's a pussy cat, although he's the size of Godzilla!" Sebastian laughed.

Allison examined Sebastian's office. *Through the Looking-Glass* came to mind. Giant flamingos and teacups, floated around her imagination.

"It's Bauhaus, darling!" Sebastian's voice awakened her.

"Oh. It's simple but effective," replied Allison, "Black and white is professional."

"We are nothing if not professional."

Sebastian went over his paperwork, and Allison just sat around until Mary came into the office. "Car is here, Mr Dupont," she said, popping her head around the doorframe.

"Ready, Alice?"

"I am, Mr Dupont!"

"Allison Templeton-Miller!" Sebastian grinned, grabbing his jacket and briefcase. "You're not too old!"

"Romano is always telling me I need a spanking."

Connors - Los Angeles - 13th May 1977 - 5:30 p.m.

Cassandra Joy strolled around the prime wooden dance floor, wearing a black leotard and ballet skirt. "Lovely to see you, Sebastian. My people are taking care of Alice. Your strapping bodyguards are keeping a watchful eye on her as well."

"Good to see you, Cassy. Filming is tomorrow, right?" Sebastian observed the forty-five-year-old choreographer.

"If we are struggling, then it could be a couple of days."

"The song is released after tomorrow, Cassy."

"Certainly, I will hurry the filming Mr Dupont. How is Oliver?"

"Very well! *Conception Magazine* promoted Oliver to Senior Correspondent Executive."

"Impressive! You both looked happy when I saw you."

"We are." Sebastian smiled with Cassandra. "He's everything."

Five gorgeous six-foot-tall male dancers stepped into the room. Sebastian did a double-take and adjusted his tie while he breathed.

"My boys! Justin, Marlow, Stanley, Mars, and Jack, meet Sebastian Dupont."

Each male bowed to Sebastian in turn. Sitting hot and flustered, he returned a smile. Allison walked into the room, dressed in a white leotard, skirt, ballet shoes, and tights. With her dark hair tied back; she looked the part.

"Alice, my dear, these are your backing dancers."

Cassandra introduced each one to her. All were African Americans with beautiful brown deep-set eyes and soft, supple dark skin. Their bodies were toned with muscle definition and shape.

Allison observed their prominent physiques wearing black dance belts and leggings.

"Oh!" she said. "You're perfect."

Each one smiled with their attractive full-bodied pink lips. "We are honoured to work with you, Miss Alice."

"We will all be good friends. But don't drop me, okay?"

Laughing and shouting, they chanted, "Promise!"

Cassandra played *My Heart is on Fire* as the boys rehearsed. Allison, Sebastian, and security watched from the back of the room. Cassandra demonstrated the dance moves with her boys.

It was time for Allison to take centre stage. She stepped into the centre of the dance floor and Mars lifted her onto his shoulder. Straightening her arms out and folding her legs into him, Allison began to perform her routine.

Stanley swung behind the couple, reaching out, reaching in, turning against them. Jack and Justin repeated the same movement at the side of the couple. Marlow lay on the floor in front of the couple, stretching, rolling, and touching Mars. Swinging Allison around, she leaned backward, facing Stanley. The process repeated while Allison was passed to each one.

"She's a natural." Cassandra winked at Sebastian.

"How long did it take you to arrange this piece?"

"A couple days. Cassy is just a genius!"

"Okay, Miss Joy." Sebastian moved his head towards the group of dancers.

"Mr Dupont, filming will commence tomorrow. Make-up at 9:00, costume fitting at 10:00. Leo will take charge after that. Happy?"

"I am," Sebastian said. "We've got this one, Cassy!"

****

Porta Del Castello - Bel-Air - Los Angeles
13th May 1977 – 8.00 p.m.

Lounging on top of the mammoth king-sized bed, submerged beneath satin scatter cushions, Allison sighed when Romano had to hang up.

Romano's call to Allison had consumed all his twenty-minute break. Still filming in Mexico, he managed to telephone Allison daily. Missing her like crazy, obsessed, and very much in love, Romano couldn't wait for them to reunite.

157

After Allison's accident, Theo-James had spoken with the director of the movie to extend his stay at the Hamptons. It was declined, and after a few days with her in hospital, Romano had to fly back to Mexico.

Allison understood, both were in an industry that was not a nine-to-five job. Glamour and fame required sacrifices. If love prevailed, their relationship would last.

An emitting resonant sound appeared from a baby pink retro telephone that was situated upon an abandoned cushion.

"Hi, Alice speaking."

"Babe, it's me!" Belinda screeched, down the line.

"Hey, you! How's Canada?" Allison sank back down into the cushions and laid on her back. Facing the ceiling, she held the pink phone to her right ear.

"You'll never believe this." Belinda was trying to calm herself but was failing fast. "Dougie Jimi was caught in his trailer with Estelle Grade. It'll be in all the tabloids tomorrow morning!" Taking a breath, Belinda continued. "Mike cut filming early."

"Who caught them?" Allison turned over onto her stomach and kicked both legs behind her.

"Me!"

"What? No."

"Mike asked me to drop off his latest draft of the script. I could hear moans through the trailer door. So, I thought he might be sick, and..."

Allison collapsed, laughing.

"I walked in, and he was giving it to Estelle from behind."

"What did you do?" Allison rubbed her eyes, crying with laughter.

"I dropped the script and ran back to Mike."

"How will the press know?"

"They could have heard the moaning from New York! I think that someone from the team must have overheard my conversation with Mike. Mike was on the phone later, trying to cover the story up, swearing."

"Really? This is good publicity."

"The best thing, Alice? Dougie told me to join in!"

Allison screamed with laughter. "You kill me, Belinda. You really do."

"That's not all. I have a scene with Dougie tomorrow - a sex scene!"

Belinda heard a thud.

"Ouch!"

"Are you okay, Alice?" Belinda yelled down the phone.

"Yep, just fallen off the bed. It's you. I have the stitch."
Red in the face with laughter, Allison had to lean against the
bed.

After an hour on the telephone with Belinda, Allison
hung up and made her way to the bathroom. Turning on the
faucets and pouring lavender bath salts into the hot water,
she heard Craig doing his security checks.

Allison replied with an okay when Craig shouted through
the doorway. Checking the water, she climbed in and
emersed under the soothing heat. Allison sighed; her life was
perfect with Romano, Sebastian, and Belinda. You had to
love them, didn't you!

****

Connors - Los Angeles - 14th May 1977 – 11.30 a.m.

Dressed in gold from head to toe, Allison appeared
spectacular, supporting herself in Ali Baba trousers, bandeau
top and arm bangles. Mars, Stanley, Jack, Justin, and
Marlow donned tight silver jumpsuits and matching costume
jewellery. Sebastian's temperature was at an all-time high.
With five silver gods strutting their thing, he was going to
burst.

Leo Kandinsky, filmmaker extraordinaire, rubbed his
chin with delight. An immense screen enclosed the back area
of the studio: assistants, production staff, and technicians
took their positions behind the camera.

Sitting in the director's chair, Sebastian chatted with Cassandra Joy. Both were deep in conversation, concealed by the darkness.

"Action!" A voiced bellowed from the shadows.

Multicoloured swirls of light animated the studio, and loud, thunderous music encompassed the whole scene. Leo scrutinised the whole story. After four minutes, the song came to an end. Everyone clapped, and Leo nodded in satisfaction.

"Done in two takes. Great job!" Rushing out of the studio, Leo Kandinsky was no more.

Allison, damp with perspiration, mumbled to Marlow, "Is that it?"

One of the other dancers replied, "Leo does his thing and goes."

"Goes where?" Allison asked.

Sebastian and Cassandra walked over and congratulated the team.

"Alice, you must change. Lunch, then studio. Okay?" Sebastian said. "Go!"

Allison thanked her dancers and made a break for the dressing room. Inside a shower stood vacant and waiting. She plummeted into the cubicle and propped herself under the showerhead. Forcing her eyes closed, she softy sang *Heavenly Body* to herself. Grabbing a soft towel and stepping out of the shower cubicle, she dried herself in a rush.

Laying down a pair of cropped jeans, a shirt, and Sylvester lace underwear, the hairstylist and make-up artist caught her off-guard in the dressing room.

"How long have you been standing there?" Allison quizzed both males.

"Not long enough to see you naked, Miss Alice."

"Thanks, I think." Holding her towel tight, she added, "You are make-up, right?"

"He's make-up, I'm hair. Your security is outside the door if there's a problem."

"No, no, no. Can I get dressed first, please?"

"We'll be here." Smiling, both men disappeared outside the dressing room.

Allison changed into her clothing and ushered both men back into the room. Sitting in a leather barber chair, the artists transformed Allison back into a superstar.

****

Green Records Recording Studios - Los Angeles

14th May 1977 – 4.00 p.m.

Stepping out onto the pavement waving to fans that were secured by security gates, Allison walked into the thirty-storey high-rise building, followed by Sebastian and her security.

The staff at the reception desk smiled as Allison made her way to the elevators. Pressing the up button, she waited while Sebastian, Tony, and Craig sheltered her from behind.

A few minutes later, all four of them stepped out onto floor twenty-five. The opened doors revealed a milky-coloured corridor, with sapphire blue carpets and poster-size prints of famous musicians scattered along the milky wall. Greenery placed in dark blue pots dispersed the tedious colour of white.

A solid oak fire door exhibited a sign: Studio Seven. A baton suspended above the door was unilluminated, but along the corridor, some batons were lit bright red like a firecracker.

Inside the studio, the live room displayed antique oak flooring, sombre lighting, drum kit, synthesisers, assorted guitars, and microphones.

Accompanying Sebastian into the control room, Allison laughed and removed her famous Sylvester flat cap. "Hi, guys!"

Eric Sands and Peter Clarke rose from their chairs and hugged her senseless.

"Do I get a hug?" Sebastian said.

"Okay, a small one." Eric laughed.

Both Allison and Sebastian took their place on the control room sofa. Eric wheeled over his deluxe leather chair. "We are on the second track today. If it runs well, GR is hoping for a release in late July."

"What is the song called?" Allison piped up.

"*Feeling Me Again*. The B side *You*."

"Disco?"

"All your tracks, Alice, are disco," smiled Eric. "Third track *Live* and B side *Good Again,* all written by Josh!"

"What's Green's target release date for the third?" asked Sebastian, taking notes.

"November."

"You okay with this, Alice?" Sebastian said.

Allison nodded and headed for the live room.

"Ready for the first track?" Peter shouted from the control desk.

Everyone answered with their thumbs up.

After four successful hours of recording, Allison made her way from the live room to the control room. "Happy with it, guys?" She anticipated the rejection.

"Tracks two and three are good to go." Eric said, spinning around in his chair.

"Thank heavens." Allison breathed, looking at Sebastian.

"I'm scheduling another music film." Looking up at her tired, pale face, Sebastian frowned.

"Can I keep the same backing dancers?" Allison asked.

"I don't know the storyboard yet. I will have to discuss that with Cassandra."

Allison bent down and kissed Sebastian on the cheek. "Thank you," she said.

Sebastian stared and muttered, "What for?"

"Being you." She sat down next to him, resting her head on his left shoulder. "Being here with me."

"Alice, you are a loony at times, but I love you." Sebastian took her hand and kissed it with tears in his eyes. "Ready to go home?"

Allison stood up and put on her tweed jacket. "After you, Mr Dupont."

****

Synopsis

August was the next time Allison entered the recording studio. Templeton recorded their fourth album, and all six members spent eight weeks together singing, writing music, partying, performing on TV, taking magazine interviews, and starring in photoshoots.

Green Records announced *Heavenly Body* had gone platinum on its second release.

My Heart is on Fire, Allison's first solo record, also reached platinum and hit the chart top slots worldwide.

Feeling Me Again proceeded its release date 7th July 1977. Number one all over the world, every nightclub in existence played the song.

Both music films were finished: *Feeling Me Again* and *Good Again.* Allison received her wish, appearing in both films with the same backing dancers from May. Romano completed filming in Mexico and resided at his Bel-Aire home with Allison.

Busy lives transpired over the summer months, but vigorously - love prevailed.

CHAPTER 15

The Hexagon Theatre - Los Angeles

20th September 1977

Rows of limousines queued against the pavement of the Hexagon Theatre. Depositing its guests, one limo drove away, and the next pulled into the vacant space. Romano Mancini secured three tickets to the premiere of *Sal De La Vida.* One for the love of his life, Allison Templeton-Miller, and two for Donny Davis and Belinda Ross-Belling.

Cream leather interior surrounded the two couples in their limo. They screeched every five minutes when an actor passed.

"That's him. You know, the guy in *Marry Me Dotty*," Belinda said.

"Oh, Belinda. Stop, my mascara will run!" Allison cried with laughter.

"Romano, whose idea was it to have these two in the car with us?" Donny said.

"I hope they stop soon, or we'll need a make-up artist in the car," replied Romano.

The car jerked forward, and an attendant opened the rear passenger door. "Here we are, children." Romano winked at Allison and Belinda.

Craig Welling stood behind the attendant observing the atmosphere, or in Craig's case, looking for suspicious people.

Romano stepped out of the car, wearing a designer black tuxedo, and waving to his fans. Donny Davis followed wearing a light-coloured tuxedo. Belinda's Charles Montgomery diamond evening dress sent crowds wild.

The paparazzi cheered. Cameras flashed. Romano positioned his hand into Allison's as she shuffled sidewards towards the car door. Making an entrance to the world, she stepped over the car rim onto the pavement. The crowds screamed even louder.

Phillippe Aston-Sylvester designed a magnificent bottle green princess dress, enhanced with black lace, long opera gloves and a choker, redolent of an 19th century Italian dinner party. Allison's dark hair flaunted diamantes, each embedded into the curl.

On the red carpet, photographers demanded more shots of the two couples. Romano got beckoned over by the film director to join the cast for more photographs. Allison, Belinda, and Donny were interviewed by inviting TV and newspaper reporters.

Inside the theatre, Belinda noticed a leggy actress drooling all over Romano.

"Who the hell is that?" Belinda cursed.

Allison shuffled around to view the blonde.

"Stella Jane Bing, Romano's leading lady."

"I thought you were Romano's leading lady," Belinda frowned.

"She's nothing to worry about," Allison said.

Craig Welling bent down into her ear. "I'll keep an eye on that one. Don't worry," he said, pointing his head towards Stella.

Walking into the auditorium, Romano assumed his position at the front, looking around for Allison. Swamped by B-listers and trying to escape their small talk, Alice noticed Romano waving.

"What the hell are you doing, Stella?" Romano snapped as the woman took her place at his side.

"The leading lady is commissioned to sit next to the leading man. It's tradition."

"Leading lady? You couldn't lead a circus parade."

"I have a right to be here." Stella sat in her seat.

The film director leaned towards Romano. "Is there a problem?"

"Sure is. There's no seat for Alice."

"Behind you. My wife is there," he said, pointing to a brunette in deep conversation with another woman.

"Not happening. Alice will sit next to me, or I'm gone!" Romano raged.

"Okay, okay. Second row. I'll trade with you."

"Thank you, sir." Romano wiped his forehead.

The film director's wife moved onto the front row while Romano climbed over the seat onto the second row and waited for Allison to appear.

Romano kissed Allison when she finally arrived and sat in her seat. Altogether, there were five empty seats: Romano, Allison Belinda, Donny, and Craig filled the remaining gap.

Stella glared at Allison sitting in front of Belinda.

"I will beat the birth control out of her," Belinda whispered.

Allison took Romano's hand. "No need. I think Craig will."

The two-hour film achieved great success, and everyone applauded. Removing themselves from their seats, the group of five proceeded to the afterparty.

The Hexagon Theatre held a conference room and bar that accommodated two hundred people. Twenty round tables exhibited Mexican nibbles and dips. Bottles of champagne were placed alongside buckets of ice containing bottles of lager. Each table displayed a name place card with an embossed Mexican flag.

"Where are our names?" Belinda said, walking around each table and picking up the place cards.

Donny shouted, "We're here! Table five."

Belinda grabbed Allison's hand and shouted over to Donny while Romano followed with Craig.

Looking down at the place settings, Allison got her bearings next to Craig and Donny. Romano was located next to the film director and Stella. "No way!" Romano yelled.

The film director looked over at Romano. "Same problem?"

"Same problem."

"I'll handle it." The film director exchanged Stella's place with his wife, and Romano took Craig's.

The leggy blonde marched across to table five. "Who moved the name cards around?" she demanded.

"I did…" The director said.

"Why?"

"Because the person who has arranged the seating is deranged! My wife and I were separated, and Romano…"

"I sorted the seating arrangements!" Stella shouted.

"Some arrangements," Belinda said.

Stella, on the verge of lashing out, instantly crashed down onto her chair. Craig had grabbed her by the arm and yanked her down. "If I were you, I'd shut the…" Craig whispered in her ear.

The table remained calm, and everyone enjoyed each other's company, except Stella. In the corner of the room, a band had assembled their instruments and began to play. The lights dimmed over the dance floor.

"May I take this waltz, Miss Templeton-Miller?" Romano grinned.

"You may, Mr Mancini."

Allison and Romano walked hand in hand onto the dance floor and smooched as Belinda and Donny followed. Craig sat at table five, watching Stella flirting with guys from other tables. Noticing her flaunting her cleavage, Craig wanted to vomit at the sight.

When the song had ended, Romano and Donny walked back to the table while Allison and Belinda excused themselves to the powder room. Craig followed, lingering outside the facilities.

Exhibiting floral fabrics and perfumed roses, the powder room displayed full femininity. It had pink vanity tables and matching cubicles, lengthy, delicate lit mirrors, and hampers of assorted soaps and sprays.

Belinda ran into the first cubicle and bolted the door. Allison opened her purse, retrieved a red lipstick, and leaned into the mirror. A cubicle door behind her opened. In the mirror, Allison could see the reflection of a blonde coming straight for her.

"Romano and I made love for hours in Mexico. He couldn't keep his hands off me," she snapped, while tapping callously one foot on the carpeted floor.

"Really?" Allison turned around.

"He only wants you for your money. He loves me," she screamed. "Me!"

Allison ignored her.

"You are a bitch. You always get what you want," Stella said. "Little rich kid! Get the best films, best guys, best executives…"

Stella grabbed Allison's hair and smashed her to the ground. She continually slammed Allison's head on the carpet. The cubicle door flung open, and Belinda ran into the chaos. Craig Welling crashed through the door and jumped on top of Stella. She screamed and scratched Craig's face with her painted nails.

"Alice, Alice! You, okay?" Belinda tried to help her up.

Security ran into the powder room and detained Stella. Standing the blonde upright, one of the security men cuffed her and marched her out of the room as she sobbed.

Romano ran past Stella towards his lover. Stopping at the entrance, looking into the room, he could see Allison laid out on the floor. "My God," he whispered.

Belinda's red eyes looked at Romano. "She's in shock."

"Alice!" Romano shrieked. "It's me!"

Allison grabbed his hand and held it close to her chest.

Romano shot a dirty look at Craig. "What happened? Where were you?"

"The blonde charged her," said Craig. "I didn't want to follow Alice into the powder room. Should never have let her out of my sight."

"I heard it all!" Belinda yelled, cradling Allison in her arms.

Officials interrupted the conversion between Belinda and Craig. Romano demanded a medic, but Allison refused. Police arrested Stella in the manager's office for being drunk and disorderly, while a press official lingered outside taking notes. The tabloids will have a field day with this story.

The limo parked behind the Hexagon Theatre and waited while Craig smuggled Allison out. Romano escaped prying eyes by slipping out the back.

"I will have to notify Sebastian of the incident," Craig said through the partition.

"We need to cover this up. That's why there were no charges pressed. Belinda wasn't too pleased. The last thing we need is the police," Romano finished.

Allison was out cold, and Romano laid her flat on the opposite seat. He sighed and pointed his head at the ceiling. "I'm going to kill Stella," he whispered.

"What did happen in Mexico, Romano?" Craig said.

"Stella made a play for me. I refused. She came on to me all throughout filming."

"A woman scorned!" Craig smiled.

"A nut job," snorted Romano.

The limo approached Porta Del Castello. Passing the security checkpoint, it accelerated to the front doors. Carrying Allison out of the back of the car, Tony opened the double doors and helped Romano carry her into the house.

Romano undressed Allison, making sure she was comfortable. He tucked her in and headed downstairs to join Tony and Craig.

Picking up the receiver on the telephone, Romano dialled Sebastian.

Explaining the details of the incident, it didn't take long for Sebastian to arrive at Porta Del Castello.

"So, what's the situation?" Sebastian took his jacket off and walked into the lounge, looking at Craig and Tony settled on the sofas.

"Stella was arrested for being drunk and disorderly." Romano said, pouring whiskey from a decanter into four crystal tumblers. "We did not press charges."

"Did law enforcement see Alice on the floor?"

"Hexagon Security did. We told them Alice couldn't be involved in such matters; it would cause a scandal."

"Good man," Sebastian smiled, accepting his whiskey glass with gratification. "I know the owner. I will arrange a meeting with him tomorrow."

"I'll join you." Romano took a swig from his glass.

"You screw her, Romano? Is that why she plotted revenge?"

"I would never cheat on Alice. The bitch made a pass at me, and I rejected her."

"I'm sorry I had to ask the question. We all know you are mad for Alice. But when incidents happen like this, who knows?"

"I can't keep living like this. I need her so bad, Sebastian. It's driving me mad." Romano took another drink.

"You can't marry her yet. She's not free until January 79," Sebastian jumped in.

"Her schedule?" Romano laughed. "My life is on hold because of a schedule."

"Take a weekend off. Propose, get engaged. Press and the world will go bananas if they find out. That upsets my apple cart, as well."

Romano stared at Sebastian. "Help me."

"Look," Sebastian said, "Get engaged quietly, no press, no party, just you two and, of course, me. Then in 1979, tell the world."

"Good idea, but I want to do it properly."

"You can take her home to Italy at Christmas or do it in Switzerland with her parents," Sebastian said. "But it's a secret."

Romano started thinking about setting a date in June 1979, Tuscany. He had no choice but to come second to the schedule.

****

Romano cuddled Allison between the black silk sheets. Moans and groans escaped from her delicate lips. Rolling her over, Romano gasped. "My poor baby, what did she do to you?"

Allison's eyes were tinted a light shade of purple. Her cheekbones and forehead were marked.

"You are seeing a medic today."

"No," Allison said. "I'm okay."

"Alice, you have already had a head injury, please," Romano demanded.

"If you insist!"

"I'll get Dr Monroe." Jumping out of bed naked, Romano ran into the bathroom and used the facilities. Flushing the toilet and slipping on his jog pants, he rushed downstairs.

Within twenty minutes Romano returned rushing around the bedroom. "Dr Monroe is coming over to examine you."

"What time?" A groggy voice sounded from underneath the duvet.

"9:30 sharp. That gives me just enough time for a shower. You stay there!" Romano went into the bathroom and started running the shower.

"Can you run me a bath?" Allison croaked from the bed.

Romano bobbed his head around the bathroom door. "Are you sure you are fit enough?"

"I can try," Allison moaned as she struggled to sit up. "My head hurts."

Striding across the bedroom floor in all his glory, Romano grabbed Allison, "Baby, you don't look okay."

"Please."

"Okay, I'll go in with you." Romano looked concerned and gently caressed Allison.

Stopping the shower and turning on the faucet, he added a drop of lilac bubble bath into the hot water. He walked into the bedroom and picked up Allison, carrying her into the bathroom.

Romano fussed checking the water temperature, while a naked Allison sat on top of the vanity unit watching him.

Once the bath was half-full, Romano gently lifted Allison and placed her into the tub. He followed behind and opened his legs to cushion her.

Romano noticed more bruising near Allison's ribs as he leaned her against his chest. He carefully sponged her back, making sure not to hurt her. Muffled moans resonated as the water speckled her skin, thousands of pins and needles stabbing, penetrating her tired membrane.

Kissing the top of her head, a tear emerged from his eye and trickled into her hair. "Are you feeling a little better, baby?" Romano said, sniffling.

Allison turned around and stroked his unkempt face. "You need a shave," she smiled.

Laughing back his tears, he said, "You don't like the designer stubble?"

Silence hit the bathroom and the couple relaxed in the soothing water. Eventually Romano climbed out of the tub, tying a towel around his hips. He gently lifted Allison over the rim and snuggled his love into a warm fleecy towel.

Guiding Allison towards her vanity stool, Romano stopped and knelt on the floor. He held both of her hands and kissed her.

"I love you with all my heart, don't ever leave me or I will die," he whispered.

"I will never leave you. "Allison said, wiping away a tear with her thumb.

The couple held each other tight and promised one another, until death do us part.

****

Eagleton House - Bel-Aire - Los Angeles
21st September 1977 - 11.00 a.m.

Standing on the doorstep, Sebastian Dupont engaged in conversation with Markus Lemming. The sturdy oak doors opened, and Sebastian handed the middle-aged butler his business card.

Entering the foyer, he and Markus waited. Sebastian observed the sophistication of colour or the lack of it and Markus gently hummed, tapping his foot against the unique black and white tiled floor.

The sound of running water swirled into the silence while koi swam in tranquillity in a prefabricated pool.

"Good morning, Seb!" Tobias called out. The fifty-year-old salt-and-pepper-haired male walked towards the pair, holding out his hand.

"Tobias! Good to see you," Sebastian greeted him. "This, Tobias, is Markus Lemming."

"Good to meet you, Markus. Both of you, please come join me in my office," Tobias said, guiding the two gents into his office. "My first job is to order tea and coffee." He rang a bell and a butler stepped inside the spacious room.

Tobias ordered tea and coffee and placed himself on a sofa opposite Sebastian and Markus. "To what do I owe the pleasure of this meeting, Seb?"

Sebastian fluffed a cushion and sat in a corner of the emerald, green sofa. "I assume you heard about the incident that occurred last night at the theatre."

Tobias nodded.

"Alice acquired severe injuries from her attack, caused by Markus's client."

"Allison Templeton-Miller and Stella Jane Bing, right?" Tobias said.

"Your staff did an incredible job containing the event. The tabloids didn't catch a whiff of news, and that is the way we're going to keep it."

"I agree," Tobias said, helping his butler place the silver tray of tea and coffee onto the coffee table. "It is crucial that my theatre's reputation is unscathed. I maintain major contracts with the film companies, and I can't afford to lose them over a woman."

"Everything is always lost over a woman. I'm afraid it is my client's fault. Stella is obsessed with Mr Mancini," Markus cut in, grabbing his china cup.

"He's famous; obsession is the cost of doing business. I know Theo-James very well. His family are a prime breed."

"Stella's in custody." Markus looked at Sebastian. "I'm going to bail her out."

"She's dangerous, Markus," Sebastian replied, sipping his tea.

"I'm dropping her, but I'll force her to sign a disclaimer regarding her silence."

"She's not even worth a commercial." Sebastian snorted.

"Anyone is worth a commercial for the right price," Tobias stepped in.

"If Stella speaks or sells her story, Sphere Pictures will sue...I, too, will sue on the grounds of defamation of character against my client. She will not work in the film industry again." Sebastian barked.

Markus stared at both gentlemen, still drinking his tea.

"Hexagon Theatre will also situate a lawsuit against her as well," replied Tobias.

"It's a deal...I have established enough complications to rid her from my company." Markus huffed.

"Mr Lemming, how many people are on your books, if you don't mind me asking?" Tobias pried.

"Fifty in total. Twenty are A-listers, fifteen are commercials, and the remaining are in theatre."

"Theatre died with Shakespeare, so thirty-five," Tobias said. "Good figure. I shall put in a good word around the industry for your company, whose name has tragically slipped my mind..."

"LPA, Lemming Production Agency."

Sebastian grinned at both men rising his cup. "The conversation remains in this room."

"Agreed."

****

90th Street Police Department - Los Angeles
21st September 1977 - 1.00 p.m.

Markus Lemming positioned himself in a confined interview room consisting of dark blue walls, dim strip lighting, a chipped MDF table, and four black plastic chairs. Stella Jane Bing was perp-walked by a stocky police officer.

Standing miserably whilst the female officer unlocked the cuffs and realised both hands. The low-cut designer dress displayed dirt and shreds of fabric. Running over to hug Markus, crying profusely, she stopped when he did not respond.

Leaving the room, the uniformed officer gave the pair some privacy.

"You have gone too far this time!" Markus yelled and banged his hand against the table.

"What are you talking about?" Stella sobbed in her chair.

"Maybe we should ask Allison Templeton-Miller."

"She attacked me!"

"You need help, Stella."

"I'm not insane." She stared at the prison wall. Dried mascara runs had stained her blushed face.

"You're right, I am. For putting up with you!"

Not replying, Stella refused to look at Markus.

183

"I just paid your bail. You're going home and rethinking your life."

"What life?"

"I bribed the LPD for an undercover to drive you home. The press won't get a glimpse." Walking towards the door, he turned around and looked at the tattered actress. "Tomorrow morning at 9:00, my office!"

"Are you not accompanying me?" Stella's voice was weak.

"Accompany you? After I walk out of this room, I don't know you." Markus didn't reply again and walked out of the room.

****

Porta Del Castello - Bel-Air - Los Angeles
21st September 1977 - 1.00 p.m.

Entering the house, Romano greeted Sebastian with relief. "The doc said she's fine, no damage, her heart rate is good and blood pressure too, but I must warn you, Sebastian, that she's not a pretty sight now."

Climbing the stone steps holding onto the banister rail, he turned to Romano and snacked on a grape. "Why?"

"The bruising is purple around her eyes and cheeks."

"I see…" Sebastian choked. Romano struck him on the back until he coughed it up. They opened the bedroom door and froze.

"My God," Sebastian dropped the remaining bushel.

"Hi…Sebastian." Allison tried to smile, hitting the pain barrier.

Sebastian fell to his knees. "My dear Alice, you look terrible."

"I'm okay." Allison's eyes resembled a boxer who had lost his match. "Really!"

"I am so sorry this had to happen to you…"

"You dropped your g-grapes," she said.

Sebastian blinked back tears. "Darling, I was just saving them for later."

"So, you had your get-together?" Romano remarked from the basket weaved chair in the corner.

"We certainly did, and the press will never know." Rising from the bed, Sebastian walked over to Romano and picked the grapes back up off the floor. "Are we having lunch in here?" he queried, looking around the bedroom.

"On the balcony." Romano pointed to the French windows. "Table's ready."

"Alice, you will need a robe to wear over those Sylvester PJs." Sebastian tried to smile. "I'm famished…I do hope I'm treated to an excellent bottle of Premier Cru Montee de Tonnerre."

"Make that two," laughed Romano.

Romano carried Allison onto the balcony and placed her into a natural princess chair. Sebastian took his seat opposite her.

It was a glorious autumn sunny day. A breeze floated amongst the branches of the California Ash. Prolonged rays of sunshine intermingled with the shadows being cast by the greenery.

Sitting in his princess chair, Sebastian played with his Waldorf salad. "Your TV appearances will have to be cancelled, Alice."

"Do you think Stella did this to me to ruin my career?" Allison struggled to chew her lettuce.

"More like ruin your life," Romano piped in.

"She succeeded." Allison whinged in pain. "Soup, please?"

"Leave it to me, baby." Romano excused himself and went downstairs into the kitchen to ask the cook.

"Alice, I'm glad Romano has left us alone," Sebastian said, moving closer. "I received notification yesterday from the Recording Academy. You, my girl, are nominated for five Cantus Awards."

"I hope they don't want a photo." Allison tried to laugh.

"What's going on, you two?" Romano shouted, balancing a tray of hot vegetable soup.

"I have just broken the good news to Alice." Sebastian grinned.

"What, good news?" He placed the bowl in front of her.

"Alice has been nominated for five Cantus Awards. Templeton, Best Group; Alice, Best Female; *Heavenly Body* or *My Heart is on Fire,* Best Song; Templeton or Alice, Best Music Video; Alice or Templeton, Best Album; and Best Composer, Alice, or Josh."

"Josh better not, steal your award!" Romano stood up and hugged her so tight that Allison yelped in agony. Romano jumped back. "I'm sorry, baby. I forgot about the bruising."

"I'll be okay after I win Best Song," Allison frowned.

"Let's celebrate!" Sebastian raised his glass to toast, focusing on the couple before him. "I will schedule the Cantus event for January…Romano, you best be there!"

"Not even Stella can stop me!"

The three of them remained on the balcony chatting for most of the afternoon. Allison then retired to bed, leaving Sebastian and Romano to enjoy the autumn air over a glass of bourbon.

****

LPA Office - LA - 22nd September 1977 - 9.00 a.m.

Telephones ringing, fax machines beeping, paperwork scattered upon desks situated in discrete cubicles, created a vibrant environment in the LPA open plan office.

Making her way through the bustling office, Stella Jane Bing displayed a short black leather skirt exposing her long, tanned legs and a leopard effect shirt, buttoned low, revealing a lace pink bra. High stilettos captured her height that succoured the bounce from her long straight hair. Knocking on the glass panel door, Stella opened it without permission.

Markus Lemming lounged at his office desk, waiting for Stella to arrive. Glancing at his wristwatch, he made no efforts with his introductions when the film star made her presence known.

"My lovely Lemming." Make-up smothered Stella's face like a Picasso. "I'm here...9:00 on the dot."

"Stella, please sit down. Oh, you already have," Markus said, scratching the back of his neck below his flaming red hair. He pulled out a file from his desk drawer and slammed it on the table. "Right, let's get down to business."

"What's my next movie? I'm very reluctant to star with certain particulars," she raised her eyebrows at Markus. "My choices are very limited these days. The minimum I will work for is ten million dollars. I'm not taking the role for anything lower."

"We're all overjoyed to hear that, Stella," Markus said, offering her a gold-plated pen. "Now sign this disclaimer."

"Is this connected to my next film role?"

"If there is one," he smiled.

Taking the pen from his fingers, Stella signed the disclaimer without reading it. "So what date is my screen test?"

"There is no film role. A commercial maybe, but not with LPA."

"What do you mean no film role?" Stella barked.

"Well, there is. But not for you."

Stella flung herself from the chair she was sitting on and barged into Markus's desk. "What the hell are you talking about? I am your number one actress!" Pointing a finger directly into his face, "I make LPA millions. You can't get rid of me!"

Markus calmly rolled his chair away from the desk. "Yeah, you make us millions, and lose us triple in legal fees."

"I will go to the press!"

"I own the press," Markus said. "And you just signed a disclaimer."

"So what? I sign a lot of things."

"If anything leaks about LPA, Hexagon Theatre, or Allison Templeton-Miller, you're headed straight to jail."

"Good, I'll see you there!" Stella replied, straightening herself into a reputable position. "You think I can't bring you down with me, Markus Lemming?"

"You think I care about going to prison? I could use a vacation."

"You bastard!!" Stella yelled, straightening herself into a reputable position. "I have not finished with you, Markus Lemming. You have not heard the last of me."

Stella sauntered into the open-plan office whilst slamming Markus's door behind her. Glamorously smiling and nodding to people as she passed them. Stella soon disappeared out of sight into the elevator.

An exasperated sigh escaped from Markus's mouth has he stamped Stella's file 'CLOSED' in red ink. Later that day it got filed into a metal cabinet with the rest of LPA's failures.

CHAPTER 16

Montague Hills - Echo Park - Los Angeles

22nd October 1977

Paul Freidman's home overlooked well-constructed thick steel security gates, towering twenty feet in height. Cameras concealed themselves within artificial shrubbery and Mexican fan palms. Two security gatehouses secured the top and bottom of the concrete driveway.

The new construction double-height windows encouraged sunlight to engulf the entire house. Minimal furnishings amplified the spacious area with alluring mural ceilings. A typical millionaire's home.

Paul lounged in his burgundy leather chair, arranging assorted paperwork. He crumpled up several contracts and threw them into a metal bin. Sunlight bounced through the vaulted windows behind him.

Vanishing from the public for six months was an organised and calculated move, or so he told himself. Eva Moulin had even failed to contact him regarding new talent and their next scheme. A visit to New York beckoned.

The past few weeks were eventful: business deals in the Far East, remittance investments into offshore bank accounts, pumping and dumping corporate stocks. Also, sponsoring Jake Pullman through college would boost his business deals.

WJ Pullman, perhaps the only senator who wasn't for sale, had asked his friend for the good deed. The arrangement between WJ and Paul included sponsorship at Lex University of Law, until he reached the age of twenty-five. His main target: Constitutional Qualification.

Within their agreement, there was no room for faults. WJ's associates paid thousands to cover up the drug, drink, and rape allegations that haunted Jake. Pullman was a loose cannon, and Paul had heard the news regarding the Allison Templeton-Miller incident at her sister's wedding. The guy had to be reeled in.

Jake's flight landed at noon on May 3rd, the day after the incident with Allison. Already drunk, Jake attempted to divert the chauffeur-driven car into Chinatown.

Freidman's driver was under strict instructions to escort Jake directly from the airport to Montague Hills. Angry that his suggestions were unsuccessful, Pullman pried at the partition window. Approaching the security gate, the driver spoke into the intercom. Freidman's security checked the chauffeur's credentials. The gates creaked open.

Paul Freidman waited at the entrance of his home as the car drove up the driveway. Coming to a sudden stop, the chauffeur stepped out of the car and hurried over to Freidman. "Pullmans in the back, sir! He wanted to go to Chinatown."

"Forget it, James. This is Freidman's Chinatown."

192

Paul walked over to the car and opened the back passenger door. Shouting and swearing, Jake could be heard a mile away. Paul grabbed him by the collar and dragged him out of the car. Still aggressive, bellowing, and punching, Jake was not giving up. In one clean sweep, Jake laid out cold on top of the concrete floor. Paul shook his fist and ordered his staff to clear the piece of garbage off his drive.

Locking Jake into a guest room that did not possess a balcony, the staff continued with their work. Paul remained seated in the lounge, courting a brandy. Tasting the succulent smokiness of the dark liquid relaxed him back into the sofa.

Muttering to himself, "That boy will either survive sixteen weeks or die."

Morning approached Montague Hills. Paul had taken his early morning swim and placed himself on the terrace, ready for breakfast.

"Sir," a mature voice interrupted the peace and quiet.

"Yes, Sid?" he said, shaking his newspaper straight.

"Shall we wake Mr Pullman?"

"I doubt anything could wake Mr Pullman," Paul philosophised.

Ten minutes later, Paul's butler walked up to the table on the terrace. "I'm afraid, sir, that he told me to…"

Paul slammed down his newspaper, grabbed a jug of cold water, and marched up to Jake's bedroom, leaving his butler behind.

Opening the door to Jake's bedroom opened Paul's nostrils to fumes of stale alcohol, vomit, and urine. Lying face down on top of a king-sized bed was the kid. Emptying the water jug over his head, Paul grabbed him by the arm and yanked him off the bed.

Dragging him fully clothed into the shower and turning on fully the cold-water nozzle on top of a startled Jake, the boy screamed and kicked. Paul held the shower door closed.

"You listen to me, boy. This is my house, and you will obey my orders and my rules. Now strip and take a shower, or I'm burying you in the family cemetery!"

Jake nodded.

Paul walked out of the bathroom and glared in astonishment at the mess. He summoned his staff, demanding clean sheets and disinfectant products to rid the stench.

Paul arrived back downstairs and relaxed at his table. His cook had laid out a breakfast of poached eggs, rye bread, orange juice, and coffee. Half an hour later, a befuddled Jake dressed in jeans, a t-shirt, and sneakers stood before Paul on the terrace.

"Sit!" Paul snapped.

Jake took his place across from Freidman.

"Eat."

Jake shook his head no.

"You're having toast, eggs, bacon, and juice." Paul yelled for his cook and repeated the order. "You will attend LUL and emerge a changed man. I have money riding on this, and you don't want to see what happens when I lose money."

Jake struggled, but Freidman would not let him leave the table until he ate everything. "You're joining me in my office. No TV, no music, no whores. I checked your bags for drugs. By the way, that cocaine was 33% flour. 67 is still a D+.

"You trashed it?"

"I'll trash you, if I find anymore!"

Later that morning, Freidman sat at his desk signing papers. In the corner of the office, a dining room chair appeared to be out of place. The red leather high back and metal pencil-thin legs didn't look vigorous enough to hold Jake's weight. Uncomfortable, Jake had to read *US Politics of the 19th Century*.

"This is boring," moaned Jake.

"This is your life. US Politics of the 20th Century is next." Paul growled.

At lunchtime, both men sat in the dining room and split a Reuben sandwich in silence. Back in Freidman's office, Paul sat at his desk smoking a cigarette, shuffling paperwork. Jake read about politics while sitting on a very uncomfortable chair.

Paul challenged Jake once more for refusing to shower before dinner. Forcing him into the shower for a second time, Paul punched Jake across the chin and the kid hit the tiled floor so hard that blood splattered the white vanity unit at the side of him.

"Dinner at seven," Paul mumbled. "Don't be late!"

Every day for the first week, Jake received a punch and was locked into his room. Eventually, realising that the old Jake Pullman could not exist in this torturous house, he decided to play Freidman's game.

> 6:00. Morning workouts, swimming with Freidman, no conversation
>
> 7:00. Breakfast, bacon, eggs, toast, and orange juice
>
> 8:30. Freidman's office, read politics
>
> 10:00. Orange juice
>
> 12:30. Lunch, Reuben sandwich and orange juice
>
> 13:30. Freidman's office
>
> 15:00. Orange juice
>
> 15:30. Freidman's office
>
> 17:30. Shower
>
> 19:00. Dinner, rice, chicken, and salad. Dessert, fruit.
>
> 21:00. Bed, No TV

Fourteen weeks passed expeditiously; Paul Freidman had brainwashed Jake into a functional member of society. Jake's outstanding manners and attitude excelled when in conversation. Even his dress sense had changed: he wore chinos instead of jeans, shirts substituted t-shirts, and loafers replaced sneakers. He was ready for LUL.

Paul assigned security personnel to accompany Jake to Lex and report any misdemeanours. Unknown to Jake, for the next three years he was under the watchful eye of Paul Freidman. That is what Freidman thought.

August 30th, Jake's flight to New York had arrived. He thanked Paul for all his efforts. Jake exited the limousine from the back passenger door and arranged himself on the pavement, accompanied by two muscular security bodyguards. Freidman pressed the window control button-down.

"Jake, you know the score. No drink, no drugs, and high grades. Remember, if I receive a summons from your father, you lose a finger!"

Jake, dressed in a smart navy-blue suit, bowed down to the rear passenger window. "You have my word, sir."

"Good boy!" Paul pulled up the window. The limo drove away.

It was now October 22nd, and his security reports were excellent. Jake was Lex's valedictorian, the perfect student, achieving high grades and brilliant appraisals. True to his word, WJ Pullman offered Freidman a two-million-dollar cheque.

Paul smiled at the cheque, holding it up into the sunlight at his desk - he loved the kid – really, he did, especially when he used him as a punching bag. It was a great stress relief.

****

The Kellie School of Performing Arts - Brooklyn
New York - 5th November 1977 - 8.00 p.m.

Madam Eva Moulin lounged in her exquisite office chair, cigarette in one hand and a pearl rollerball pen in the other. A Charles Montgomery desk lamp glowed warm light around her desk, casting dark shadows in the corners of the office. Eva closed her files, tossing the completed ones into a gold desk organiser.

Eva sighed and reclined against the chair headrest. Craning her neck, she refocused on a passing shadow. It coughed and revealed itself.

"My darling, I thought you had died!" Eva sat upright at the desk, shuffling her files.

Paul Freidman never said a word.

"Cat got your tongue, Paul?" Eva stabbed her cigarette into the ashtray.

Paul approached the desk, gently twisting her chair around and pulling her up towards him, clutching her back and kissing her on the neck. Reaching into his trench coat pocket, he produced a handkerchief and smothered Moulin's nose and mouth.

Eva collapsed. Kicking away the chair, he positioned the limp body face down across the desk. He knelt, unlocked his briefcase, and removed a syringe containing heroin and fentanyl. He then pulled on pair of latex gloves.

Ligaturing the top of Eva's right arm, Paul flicked the syringe with his middle finger, pulled back the plunger, and drew the lethal cocktail out of the vial into her veins.

Pulling a small plastic bag of white powder from his pocket, Paul tapped out a line onto the desk and rubbed the remainder on Eva's lips and teeth.

With a deep breath, Paul flipped through a batch of forged contracts with every client Eva had sent to him. He threw the folder down on her chest, evidence flying everywhere. Collecting his briefcase, he pocketed the gloves and left the crime scene.

Avoiding the security cameras in reception, Paul made his way through the staff side entrance while his security waited patiently in a sedan by the staff exit door. Paul Freidman's work was done, and the sedan drove away from Kellie's for the very last time.

****

Templeton Hall - The Hamptons
6th November 1977 - 11.00 a.m.

"You light up my mornings, Eleanor." Theo-James said, devouring his honey pancakes.

"Thank you, my darling." Eleanor's smile told him that she was still deeply in love with him.

The sunroom's intense mono colouring created a modern theme. With its bold black and white striped ceiling blinds, chic built-in-bench, wishbone-styled dining chairs and grey plush cushions.

Eleanor's sunroom became her haven and every morning she would enjoy brunch with her husband in this romantic setting.

"Excuse me, sir." Edwards bowed. "A visitor."

Theo-James accepted the calling card from Edwards and started reading. "My darling, I must attend this meeting."

Patting his mouth with a silk napkin, Theo-James stood up and walked over to his wife and kiss her hand before leaving with Edwards.

Waiting in the foyer, Martyn Simpson-Smyth said, "Theo!"

"Marty, pleasure to see you." Theo-James held his hand out to greet Martyn. "Please come into my office. Edwards, can you bring the gentleman some tea?"

Edwards bowed and walked towards the kitchens. Theo-James invited Martyn to take a seat in his office. Martyn frowned at Theo-James while he was making himself comfortable on the opposite sofa. "Eva Moulin is dead."

Theo-James suddenly stopped. "What?"

"Elle Sidorov found her this morning."

"Where?"

"At the school, apparent overdose…"

"She had a habit?"

"She had every habit. They found her covered in forged contracts."

"You are kidding me…"

"I know it sounds absurd. But Eva Moulin embezzled millions. Maybe the greater good…"

"A stitch up."

"Did you hear that the forged contracts have Eva's prints all over them but none of Freidman's?"

"What about the central account?"

"Paul Freidman will deny any involvement because the money he withdrew was for the payment to the school and the kids' wages. Madam Moulin has withdrawn millions from the account. Case closed."

"We all know that Freidman is the one who forged the contracts and withdrew the funds." Theo-James shook his head.

"Maybe we all know, but the judge doesn't. Freidman must have forged the withdrawal in Eva's name into his own offshore account."

"Are the police treating the death as suspicious?"

"Every death is suspicious, Theo," Martyn remarked. "But they just think she's a glamourous junkie. All that work, and we were so close to serving him with the summons."

"At least he's not working in the industry anymore. I know for a fact no one will touch him." Theo-James poured himself and Martyn a stiffer drink.

Martyn accepted the whiskey, while Edwards re-entered the room carrying a tray of Earl Grey.

"On second thought," Theo said, "Forget the tea."

Edwards assented, and Martyn began to speak about the school board. "They're closing for two weeks to mourn the loss."

"Two weeks?" Theo-James said, taking a sip from his glass. "Jonathan-Lee Nimbly will take charge."

"Is he good?"

"The best, brilliant singer-songwriter. Classical."

"Why did he not get offered the position before?"

"Didn't open his legs wide enough, I'm afraid. Eva Moulin entered the equation at the last minute. The Performance Art Council closed the date for the chancellor position just before her name was submitted."

"Who did she sleep with?" Martyn enquired.

"Simon Pescis, head of the board of trustees."

"I wonder what he's thinking now. The woman will be tarnished with fraud, murder, you name it."

"I feel terribly for the families who lost their kids to drugs and suicide." Theo-James sighed and lowered his glass.

"Alice was very lucky to have Sebastian."

"I paid Benedict to take him on. He was originally Freidman's assistant."

"You mean Green Record's spy."

Theo laughed. "I kept tabs on Freidman, yes. Sebastian stepped into his role very easily, but it cost me."

"Cash?"

"Lots of it. Did you hear that my daughter has been nominated for five Cantus?"

"Did she stop at five to give the other musicians a turn?"

"Maybe. I think my baby is going to be the top dog," Theo-James said with pride.

"You regret not having more children, Theo?"

"We all have regrets. But Eleanor, with her filming commitments, was struggling. When she was pregnant with Alice, I thought she was going to lose the baby. Eleanor was so fragile and pale; she had to cancel a film premiere and guest dinner. I always worried that..."

"So, she struggled giving birth?"

"No, my daughter popped out into the world within a couple of hours. It was strange, it was like she had to arrive without delay. Like God created the earth for man, Allison had arrived to entertain her fans."

"Everyone believes in Alice," sighed Martyn. "I do love Templeton's music; it's really catchy." Looking up at Theo-

James, he added, "Is it true that the band were arguing over names when Paul Freidman suggested Templeton?"

"You've seen what happens when Paul doesn't get his way."

"Yeah, powerful."

"Correct! He was always after Alice wasn't interested in the guys. That's why he registered the name Templeton."

Earlier Martyn had received the summary of Eva's death from an associate in the state law enforcement, and within hours all the TV stations and tabloids would broadcast the shocking news to the world.

CHAPTER 17

Ash Drive - New Jersey - 21st November 1977

Romano Mancini obligated a detour from his scheduled filming in Turin, Italy. Establishing himself in the foyer of a grand mansion, he surrounded himself with three suited guys holding tape measures, notebooks, and pencils.

"Twenty guest bedrooms, nursery, dance studio, recording studio, office, indoor pool and spa, gym, and an eight-seater dining room," Romano said, walking outside onto the crunching gravel. "Twelve detached five-bedroom houses, six over there in the wooded area and a state-of-the-art gatehouse at the bottom of the drive." Romano clicked his fingers towards the house. "Shall we proceed into the library, gentlemen?"

The architects and surveyors rolled out a blueprint of the house. Romano inclined his head into the drawing and pointed to the area where he wanted modifications. Two hundred hectares of land surrounded the mansion, and Romano knew exactly where the new houses had to be located.

"Good morning, Romano," a voice sounded from the doorway. Julia Styliani clattered across the wooden floor in high-heeled stilettos.

Romano introduced her to the three professionals and continued with his plans. It was priority that all four of them had to work together to complete the project by February 1979.

Purchasing a mansion was easy but completing the construction work was hard. Employing interior designers, architects, surveyors, staff recruiters, and landscapers contributed to a sizable headache for Romano.

Ending the consultation, he bid farewell and stepped into the rear passenger seat of a silver limousine as his chauffeur closed the door behind him. Checking his watch, Romano decided it was time for some shuteye.

Enduring a two-month filming schedule in Turin created more problems. The thought of skipping Christmas in Switzerland nearly killed Romano. At least his parents, Maria and Giuseppe would be delighted that their only son would joining them for the festivities.

The chauffeur drew up the partition window between Romano and himself as he exited the expressway to the airport. In twelve hours, Romano would be residing in Europe without his love.

****

Sphere Pictures Filming Studio - Los Angeles

21st November 1977

Slumped against the carpeted trailer wall, Allison Templeton-Miller comprehended the death of her character. Four weeks of filming in *Flying In 3* and she was dead!

"You still have some fake blood on your lip," Sebastian entered the trailer and handed her a napkin.

"Just thinking about Eva. She was a great ballet tutor," Allison accepted the napkin and wiped her face. "I still believe her death is suspicious!"

Sebastian perched himself on the harmonising chair opposite the superstar. "On the bright side, when they adapt her death into a movie, maybe you can play Eva."

"I would turn down the part."

"That's what everyone says until they see the check. Look alive, Alice. Women like Eva Moulin are ruthless, and a sweet young girl like you. Tea!" Sebastian leaped into the kitchen area as the kettle whistled. "I have some news! Oliver and I are joining the Templeton-Millers in Switzerland for Christmas."

"Really? How?"

"Your papa, of course."

"I can't wait," said Allison. "Are you skiing with us?"

"Oliver pre-arranged ski lessons."

"Bring a helmet," laughed Allison.

"Cheeky!" Sebastian replied, transporting two china cups exhibiting Earl Grey teabag tags. "Oliver and I are travelling with you on the 19th."

"What's it like to be a fairy godmother, Sebastian?"

"Allison Templeton-Miller!" Sebastian laughed.

A knock at the door stopped the pair from giggling. Craig peered through the keyhole. "Visitor, Alice."

"For me?"

Craig opened the door.

"Alice, my baby girl! Sebastian." Eleanor Templeton-Jones ran past Sebastian and hugged Allison. She was wearing a customised Charles Montgomery emerald, green two-piece.

"What a lovely surprise, Mama." Allison hugged her mother.

"We're filming in Studio Six, so I thought I would come see my baby girl."

"Please sit, Mama, would you like some Earl Grey?"

Taking her place next to Sebastian, she smiled. "Yes, please."

Allison walked into the kitchen area and saturated the kettle under the cold-water tap. Opening the cupboard door and searching for the teapot, she asked if there were any news.

Removing her gloves, Eleanor sat with her legs crossed and back straight. "Of course, there is news, darling! Your sister is pregnant."

"Wow! That didn't take Annie and Ricky long! "Allison replied throwing the teabags into the teapot.

Sebastian frowned at Allison and kindly smiled at Eleanor. "Your daughter is in a facetious mood today, Eleanor, I'm afraid."

"I am not! It's wonderful news. Auntie again!" Allison answered, placing the cups upside down upon their sauces, with silver teaspoons beside them.

Allison walked over into the lounge area and placed the afternoon tea set on top of the coffee table, removing the teacups from Sebastian's earlier attempts.

Sebastian, the perfect gentleman, poured Eleanor's tea and handed her a cup.

"Marriage, that is what you need, my dear." Eleanor gripped her saucer and blew the steam off her tea.

"That is a good idea, Mama, but Romano is away until January. My schedule is fully booked."

"Your schedule is flawless for 1979!" Sebastian bit in.

"Does Romano talk of marriage, darling?"

"Not to me," Allison replied.

Sebastian sipped at his tea nervously.

"Children, lots of children to make a family, Alice. Mr Dupont will understand!" Eleanor leaned her head to one side with a wink.

"Yes, Eleanor," Sebastian muttered.

"A loving husband, lots of adorable, beautiful children, and a career to fit in between." Eleanor leaned towards Allison. "You are twenty-two in January!"

Sebastian nearly choked on a mouth full of tea that he refused to swallow.

"Annie and Ricky are very happy, darling, and I'm helping with the new designs of the nursery. Charles Montgomery's team are stripping the old guest bedroom."

"Didn't they have the house decorated before the wedding?" Allison asked.

"With the baby on the way, we require a nursery. The old guest room facing the beach is ideal."

Once Eleanor had damaged Allison's mind with weddings and pregnancies, she departed into studio six.

Sebastian's head was going to explode. Eleanor, beautiful as she was, had given Allison ideas. That's all he needed a brooding superstar.

"Alice, you're not worried about babies and—"

Allison butted in. "No, I listen to Mama because family talk makes her happy. Marriage? Romano and I are too busy to even dream."

Sebastian muttered to himself, "Thank goodness."

A knock at the trailer door interrupted the conversation.

"Miss Alice, your makeup is ready."

"Right, another afternoon of Primrose fighting for her life!" Allison huffed, walking out of the door.

Sebastian remained in the trailer and pondered. Allison's attitude had changed, and he could see the creation of a mega-star.

****

Sphere Pictures Filming Studio - Los Angeles
15th December 1977

"Cut. Cut!" Stewart Gloss yelled. "Alice, you are dying. Act dead!"

"I can't!" Allison said between fits of laughter. "It's Stephen: he's really crying!"

"What an actor," blushed an extra.

"Sorry," Stephen sniffled. "It's my last day with Alice. I'm emotional."

"The studio is paying for your character's emotions, not yours!" Stewart yelled through the megaphone.

Take two: Allison laid in bed for around ten minutes soundless, keeping both eyes closed and thinking of Romano to prevent her brain from transmitting laughing signals to her mouth.

"Cut!" Stewart clapped with the rest of the team.

Allison squinted from the overhead lighting, sitting upright, and rubbing the back of her neck.

"That was so sad," Stephen gulped.

"I'm never starring in another film with you again!" laughed Allison, taking his hand to pull her out of bed.

"Not until next year," Stephen sobbed. *The Crystal Cage!*

A makeup artist handed Stephen some tissues as an assistant wrapped Allison in a robe.

"Come to my trailer for a goodbye drink?" Stephen blew his nose.

"Okay," she accepted, feeling safe and knowing that Craig would be standing outside his trailer.

Walking towards Craig standing behind a camera. Allison explained that she was having a goodbye drink with Stephen. Craig excepted the proposition and escorted the duo to Stephen's trailer.

Inside the lavished, marbled decor trailer, Stephen poured red wine into two wine glasses. Still dressed in her robe, she accepted her wine from Stephen and relaxed in a leather chair.

"I have always admired you, Allison Templeton-Miller. You are funny, glamourous, beautiful." Stephen said, sitting on a barstool and spinning his glass in his hands.

"That's really nice of you, Stephen," said Allison.

He smiled back at her with piercing blue eyes. Faultless pearl white teeth radiated against his snowy blonde hair that curled below his neck. "You are very welcome."

"Why aren't you married?" Allison inquired, draining her glass.

"Because there is only one woman for me, and it can never be."

"Is that why you sleep around?"

Stephen laughed, shaking his head. "I love your innocence, Alice. I'm a movie star. It's my job."

"I hope Romano doesn't have that attitude."

"That is the reason why I cannot have the woman I love."

Going off the subject, Allison replied, "You could have any woman in the world. I thought you might be thinking of settling down. You're nearly thirty."

"I would settle down if she loved me." Sadness appeared in his eyes has he guzzled a mouthful of wine.

"So, who is she?"

"If I tell you, don't walk away, Alice."

"I can't," she said. "I'm dead, remember?"

"Primrose is dead not you!"

"Who is she?"

"You!"

Allison looked shocked. "No, you have always flirted with other women. You even took them to bed. I witnessed it all at the premiers and on film sets. How many have you had in here?" Allison pointed towards the bedroom.

"I wasn't counting. I admit you're right…I have had quite a few in my trailer and outside of my trailer.

"You weren't counting?" Allison blinked at him innocently.

"Would you have had a relationship with me?"

"Maybe, but Romano would have had something to say."

"Alice, do you have any feelings for me?"

"Like a brother."

"I love you! Always have."

"You can't…Romano," she whispered.

"I'd marry you tomorrow if you'd say yes. The annoying thing is that you dated that gay singer who used you to cover up his double life. Then you met Romano, a Mexican movie star."

"He's Italian?" Allison said.

"I regret everything, Alice," he hesitated. "I really do."

"Sometimes, I feel as if I need more experience with men. Romano has had his fair share of women, as well." Looking up at Stephen, she felt something stir in her heart.

"What are you saying, Alice?" Stephen shifted on the barstool, pouring himself and Alice another round. "Are you having doubts?"

"No, but I feel his career between here and Italy is going to be hard for us if we marry."

"How do you feel about me? Would it work for you to leave me in the states if you were touring? Could you trust me?"

"The women you slept with do."

"So, you are admitting you do have feelings for me?" Stephen was breaking her barrier. Removing himself from the stool, he walked over to the leather recliner chair and knelt in front of Allison. "I love you, Alice."

Allison stroked his hair while he closed his eyes. Lifting his head, he placed his own lips upon hers. Allison tenderly kissed him back. Holding her in his arms, Stephen pulled her into him.

"I can't do this," she whispered into his mouth.

"Neither can I." Stephen continued kissing her.

"My bodyguard is outside," she moaned while he kissed her neck.

"Let me make love to you, Alice." Stephen groaned.

"No, I can't...I love Romano." Her weight continued to lean against the six-foot male on the floor, surrendering into his advances.

Stephen stopped and pulled Allison away from him. "This is the reason why I can never have the woman I love. You love Mancini and I will always be second."

Allison looked embarrassed at Stephen.

"I will always love you. I promise I will never flirt or sleep with anyone else again."

"You can't. You must live your life…"

"You will always be my leading lady. How can I live my life if you are not there?"

"Why couldn't you have told me all this earlier?" Allison snapped, sitting back in the chair. "This is a mess!"

"I'm sorry. I'm sorry." Stephen's eyes began to water.

"I should go," she whispered.

Truthfully deep down, she didn't want to leave him heartbroken and alone. Her heart broke at the sight of her friend, colleague, and possible lover.

"See you at the premiere." Stephen sobbed.

"Okay, we'll talk again…I promise." Allison held her palm against his cheek. Kissing him on his forehead, Allison stood up and walked out of the trailer door, leaving Stephen kneeling on the floor.

Craig stamped out his cigarette when he noticed Allison appearing from the door. "You okay, Alice?" Craig smiled.

Alice looked back at the trailer. "Yes…I just hate saying goodbye.

****

Porta Del Castello - Bel-Air - Los Angeles

15th December 1977 - 7.00 p.m.

Allison picked up the pink retro telephone in her bedroom.

"Merry Christmas, chick!" Belinda replied from the Hamptons.

"Belinda! I have something to tell you, but it must remain a secret." Allison hid beneath the scatter cushions on top of her bed.

"Gossip? I'm all ears." Belinda muted the background music.

"Stephen-Paul Golding..."

"Oh, he's so handsome. Whenever he bends over, I have to change my—"

"Belinda!"

"What?"

"He said he loves me!"

"Men say a lot of things," Belinda mused.

"He cried because it was my last day of filming today, even though I start filming the adventure thingy next February with him. We kissed."

"Like, on the mouth?" Belinda hyperventilated.

"Belinda!"

"Does he really have a scar on his—?"

"Belinda!"

"What about Romano?"

"I love him with all my heart and nothing else happened between Stephen…."

"Do you think that Romano will propose?"

"To me?"

"You're supposed to be a superstar, not a comedian. Listen, Donny has overheard Sebastian say your schedule comes before Romano."

"I know the next year is busy because of the awards, but Sebastian promised I'll be free most of 1979."

"I'll quiz Romano, but he's not with you for Christmas."

"I hid his Christmas present in his luggage, a necklace from Charles Montgomery's exclusive design catalogue."

"You mean Santa hid it," Belinda laughed.

"At least you got your ring from Donny," sighed Allison.

"Is he staying in his usual hotel in Turin?" Belinda enquired.

"Yes, until the 24th. Then he leaves for Tuscany to see his parents. Remember, Belinda: they are six hours in front."

"In front of what?"

"It's seven o'clock here, and it is one in the morning there," Allison said.

"I'm on it, leave it with me, chick. You shall marry your prince."

219

BFF to Allison Templeton-Miller became Belinda's ultimate gift in life, and she would find the answers for Allison, even if it killed her.

****

Mare Casa - The Hamptons
16th December 1977 - 2.00 a.m.

Belinda relaxed by the stone fireplace as she spoke on the telephone to an exhausted Romano Mancini. She curled her woollen socked feet between her bottom and the fireside armchair.

"I have big plans for the future, Belinda," Romano said.

"She is worried that you'll never propose. Did you know Annie is pregnant?"

The line went dead.

"Are you still there? Romano!" She smashed the telephone receiver against the chair arm.

"I'm here!" a muffled sound called out.

"I want you to marry her and have babies."

"Can I trust you?" Romano stepped in, speaking more clearly.

"Cross my heart!"

Silence hit the phone line again. Belinda looked down at the receiver, shaking it in her hand.

A voice suddenly sounded through the silence. "Right! I want to marry her now! It's impossible to live without her,

Belinda. I asked Sebastian if he could release Alice from her schedule, but he refused."

"I think it's unfair!" Belinda pointed out, irritated.

"I purchased a New Jersey mansion a while ago. I have people working in it as we speak."

Belinda held her breath.

"My plan is to have the house completed by February 1979. Take Alice on vacation to Tuscany around June of that year and propose to her on a medieval hilltop, surrounded by scenic vineyards. How does that sound?"

"Wow!" Belinda exclaimed. "The wedding?"

"Quick as possible! Either Italy or New York." Romano replied.

"Do you need help with the ring?"

"I know a jewellery designer, and he's taking care of it." Laughing, Romano said, "It's a surprise."

"Damn! You think of everything, Romano." Fiddling with the telephone cord, Belinda exhaled. "Stephen-Paul Golding told Alice that he loved her."

"Of course. Everyone loves Alice."

"You knew!" Belinda replied, surprised.

"I read the tabloids too, Belinda. Golding is besotted by her, and Sphere Pictures demand Alice as his leading lady."

"So, you are okay with the set-up!"

"It would break my heart if she slept with him, but a kiss or hug I can handle. We have all done stupid stuff."

"Stella Jane Bing? Romano, did you…?"

"I kissed her, or she kissed me. I never slept with her."

"What happened?"

"She came into my trailer naked. I was half asleep at the time and she climbed into my bed. I admit Stella did kiss me first, but I made the mistake of kissing her back…I regret that."

"Then what happened?"

"I woke up and pushed her off me."

Belinda felt much better, an eye for an eye. Romano and Allison were even. Her position was to assist Romano and Allison into 1979.

"I have to go, Belinda; I'm due on set in an hour."

"Okay, Romano, I promise I will not say anything." Belinda smiled, crossing her heart.

Placing the phone onto its switch hook, Belinda stood up and stretched. Donny would be home in the next couple of days, and she couldn't wait. Project Templeton-Mancini had commenced.

CHAPTER 18

The Palmer Building - New York - 19th December 1977

Snuggling under her warm, luxurious duvet, trickles of light emerged under the unlatched bathroom door. Sleeping in red satin pyjamas and a corresponding sleep mask, Allison moaned beneath the crushed satin duvet.

"Get up." Oliver Dupont tugged the duvet from Allison's grip. "Wakey, wakey!"

Allison moaned in a destitute manner, "Oh, what time is it?"

"Going to the airport time!" Oliver sang.

"I need a shower," she grunted from her pillow.

"You need a makeover, darling!" Sebastian walked into the bedroom wearing an extended black cashmere double-breasted coat.

"Oliver, my love, grab her feet," Sebastian instructed whilst placing his hands above Allison's shoulders.

"Okay, Okay, Okay!" Allison screamed, stumbling over Sebastian's shoe. "I'm going in the shower. Happy?"

Oliver smiled at Sebastian. "Tea?"

"My favourite letter, my love," Sebastian said. "You have thirty minutes, Allison Templeton-Miller," he shouted towards the bathroom.

Twenty minutes later, Allison emerged from the bedroom, standing at the lounge doorway, detecting

Sebastian and Oliver holding a tea party with her China tea set.

"You two look the part this morning." Allison smirked claiming a vacant sofa. "You do realise it is almost 3:00?"

"My darling Alice, you look superb," Sebastian cut her off. "Are those tweed trousers Sylvester?"

"Sure are. My contract dictates Sylvester clothing morning, noon, and night."

"We have ten minutes before the car collects us," reminded Sebastian. "Tea?"

"I made tea." Oliver beamed.

"Are you saying my tea is bad?" Sebastian frowned, clutching his cup and saucer.

"No, my darling, you just don't use a teapot. Earl Grey infuses much better in a teapot. Ask Alice!" Oliver laughed, pouring Allison a cup, and passing it over.

A knock sounded from the solid walnut entrance door, letting himself in, Roger stood and smiled in his green uniform. "Miss Alice, your car is ready."

"Thank you, Roger," Allison said, pointing at two Sylvester suitcases placed next to the door.

Roger pulled a brass trolly into the foyer and loaded the designer baggage onto his trolly.

Sebastian and Oliver followed in matching cashmere coats. Allison flicked the switch, and the apartment went black. Closing the door behind her, she buttoned her tweed swing coat and walked towards the lift.

Allison always used the rear entrance of the Palmer Building. It prevented fans and the press from invading her privacy. Regularly, Templeton and Allison's fans camped outside the apartment block, hoping a catch a glimpse of her or anyone else who was famous.

Walking towards a black Range Rover, Allison remarked. "No limo?"

"I'm afraid with Oliver's clothing and Christmas presents, it would be an understatement to say size doesn't fit!" Sebastian frowned.

Allison stepped into the rear with Oliver and Sebastian. She considered herself to be a slice of salami sitting in between two slices of oatmeal bread.

"Miss Alice!" Craig Welling was riding shotgun, and probably armed with one too. "Are you well?"

"Craig! I thought you were on Christmas vacation?"

"Security is with you twenty-four seven. Tony took a few days off."

"Don't you have a family?" she said sadly.

"You're my family," Craig grinned, putting his sunglasses on to hide his glassy eyes.

"So, have you been here all the time?"

"With Gareth."

"Who is relieving you in Switzerland?"

Sebastian cut in, "Stop the questions, Alice! Let's go!"

The Range Rover accelerated from the underground car park at the rear of the building. The force of the car flung Sebastian, Allison, and Oliver backwards into their seats.

Noticing a crowd of fans around the entrance, Allison realised she would never lead a normal life. Sighing to herself, she snuggled in between her two slices of bread.

Approaching their destination, the Range Rover was diverted into an under-cover carport. Staff organised a meet-and-greet at the entrance. Craig, Sebastian, Oliver, and Allison hurried into the checking-in area. Allison laughed when she noticed two golf carts with running engines and a mountain of luggage.

"What's funny, Alice?" Oliver said.

"How many bags do you have?" Allison giggled pointing at Oliver.

"Well let's see... Craig has one holdall. Sebastian has two medium Montgomery suitcases and a ski equipment bag. You have two medium-sized Sylvester suitcases. I have three large Montgomery suitcases, a ski equipment bag, and two small hand luggage bags." Oliver beamed.

"My darling husband is a nightmare when it comes to travelling," Sebastian complained.

Allison and Craig climbed into one of the golf carts and Sebastian and Oliver into the other. Allison continued giggling all the way.

"What time is the flight?" she shouted towards the other golf cart?"

Oliver raised six fingers.

"What? Over three hours, wait!" Allison shouted.

Craig stepped in. "We came early to avoid the press!"

"I suppose I can have breakfast," replied Allison.

Arriving at the VIP lounge, the party of four met two stewards dressed in uniform: white shirts, red ties, and black trousers. The stewards accompanied the group to a white and red linen table with four place settings.

When everyone had settled at the table a waiter served drinks: Buck's Fizz, Earl Grey tea, and a latte. Reading their menus: Craig opted for the full English breakfast. Sebastian, poached egg on rye bread, Oliver, scrambled egg no bread and Allison, bacon bagel, two boiled eggs, and soldiers.

"Wow, Alice. You're not watching your weight," joked Oliver.

"You're not pregnant!" Sebastian bellowed.

"I'm just hungry. You two dragged me out of bed early, and I have a three-hour wait!" Allison scoffed.

A steward interrupted the conversation. "Newspaper?"

Sebastian straight away nodded and requested the new issue of *America Today*. The steward handed him the newspaper from his tray.

Skipping through the pages, he buried his face in the newspaper. "Well, I must... Hmm? Excellent!" Sebastian grinned. "My darling, you've gone platinum. *Good Again* is number one in France, the UK, Germany, Italy, and the colonies. Well done!"

"Oh," Allison exclaimed.

"You're back in the studio in January," winked Sebastian. "Album time!"

"I just wrote a whole portfolio of songs for singles." Allison started to butter her bagel, but Sebastian stole the knife to reduce her calorie intake.

"You have? When have you written those?" Sebastian said, putting his crumpled newspaper down.

"At home. That's what I do when Romano isn't there. I fill my emptiness with songs."

Sebastian was speechless. Grabbing Allison's hand, "You are such a special young lady."

Rising a glass of Bucks Fizz, he toasted the beautiful, talented superstar"

****

Boarding their Swiss flight, the captain and cabin crew greeted Allison, Sebastian, and Oliver. She took her seat in first class and waited for Craig to check in with the air marshal, whoever he or she was.

Sebastian and Oliver sat across from her. Oliver put in his earplugs and offered Sebastian a boiled sweet. Allison smiled at the progressive couple. More people joined the flight in first class and did a doubled take when they passed her seat. Whispering and turning around, they wondered if that was Allison from Templeton.

She ignored the attention. Craig placed himself at her side. "All sorted, Miss Alice."

The whispers grew louder: "Allison Templeton-Miller."

Craig flagged down a stewardess. A beautiful African American lady bent before Craig. "How can I help?" she asked in a low silky voice.

"Could you possibly tell the people in first class, in confidence, that it is the real Allison Templeton-Miller? It stops all the whispering," Craig smiled.

"Certainly, sir," she said, looking at Allison. "Can I ask for your autograph later? My little girl is a huge fan."

Leaning over Craig, Allison whispered, "I'll have one better; my manager carries photographs for autograph signing; I will sign one of those for your daughter."

"Oh, she will be over the moon. Thank you so much, Miss Templeton-Miller."

"You're welcome. Please call me Alice," she smiled at the stewardess.

Craig scribbled "Craig Welling" on a cocktail napkin and handed it to the stewardess. "You can have mine." Craig winked.

The flight began to taxi on the runway twenty-five minutes later. Craig had decided to snooze, while Oliver munched furiously on boiled sweets. Sebastian casually browsed out of the window without a care in the world.

In eight hours', time, Allison would be home in Switzerland to enjoy Christmas with her family.

****

Templeton House - Zurich - Switzerland
19th December 1977 - 4.00 p.m.

A twenty-four-foot Norwegian Christmas tree glittered in the late afternoon sunlight as two Silver Ghost Rolls-Royces drove over the snow-channelled driveway and stopped.

Gabriel greeted the guests as they exited their vehicles. Instructing his staff to carry the luggage to the correct rooms, Gabriel directed Allison and her guests into the foyer.

Sebastian stood outside admiring the entrenched icicles dangling from each tree branch, swaying in a nonchalant breeze.

"Sir, Mr Miller is waiting in the sitting room." Gabriel bowed.

Sebastian nodded and walked towards the entrance.

Theo-James and Eleanor embraced the moment when their visitors entered the spectacular hallway. Red and gold garlands draped the main staircase. Beautiful velvet red ribbons and large golden baubles accompanied the sparkling three thousand fairy lights bringing to life the extravagant foyer.

Oliver Dupont gazed in amazement, while holding Sebastian's hand. Craig Welling nodded towards Theo-James and bowed to Eleanor.

"Mama, Papa!" Allison screeched, rushing over and hugged the pair of them.

"My darling, you look exhausted." Eleanor brushed a manicured hand over her little girl's right cheek.

"My baby girl, congratulations on going platinum." Theo-James embraced Allison, holding her tight.

Twenty minutes later, everyone had gathered in the lounge for lunch. Henry, Rene, and baby Ann chatted with Eleanor and Theo-James. Annie relaxed, drinking warm water with Oliver. Richard and Ami were in awe of Sebastian's presence.

Allison accepted a glass of sparkling champagne and accommodated herself by the French windows. No communication from Romano over the past few days had broken her heart.

The next few days provided plenty of different activities for each person staying in the Templeton household. Allison played the grand piano, creating new melodies. Sebastian hid in the room next door, scribbling notes in his leather journal.

Theo-James completed his filming contracts in his office. Eleanor and Oliver arranged menus and entertainment for their Christmas party. Henry and Rene played with baby Ann in the snow. Richard and Ami drove into the village and Annie suffered from morning sickness.

The time ticked away and a secrete surprise remained hidden within Templeton House.

****

Templeton House - Zurich - Switzerland
24th December 1977 - 11.00 a.m.

Leaning against her black piano and daydreaming out of the panelled window. Allison noticed a Silver Ghost Rolls-Royce driving up the embedded white track. She wondered who could be calling at the house on Christmas Eve.

Ricky had arrived two days ago from the UK, and all the guests and family had been accounted for: twelve people, plus baby Ann. Pacing through the dining room, Allison observed sixteen place settings.

Standing back, she admired her mama's work, typical of a Templeton-Miller dinner party: golden candles placed centrally into crystal candelabras, fresh holly garlands curling around black diamante table runners, Montgomery crystal flutes and wine glasses.

Allison heard Gabriel and his staff hurrying to the main entrance door. Walking towards the rear of the dining hall, she exited through the kitchen and used the staff staircase to gain access to her room. Yawning and rubbing her eyes, it wasn't long before she was asleep in bed.

Happy snoozing, Allison was awoken by a prod. Feeling groggy, she grunted, "What?"

Annie was sitting at the bottom of her bed. "Mama wants you to partake in lunch in the conservatory."

"Oh, are we not having lunch in the small dining room?" Allison said.

"Afraid not. There are fifteen places set and babies. You must change, Alice." Annie grinned at Ricky sitting next to her, stroking her hand.

"People are always telling me I must change," Allison muffled, struggling to sit up. "Oh, when did you come in?"

"With your sister, we all knew you'd be napping!" Ricky laughed.

"So, who's here?" Allison mumbled, rubbing her eyes.

"Everyone who showed up. And three of Mama's and Papa's friends," Annie replied. "Allison you must get dressed. Ricky, you must leave."

Ricky kissed Annie and departed from Allison's bedroom, while Annie was helping her sister to regain consciousness. Walking her into the bathroom, she flicked the light switch and turned on the hot water faucet. "Quick wash to wake you up. I'll do your makeup and hair."

"Are we lunching with the President?" Allison splashing water in her face. Grabbing a towel, gently tapping her face dry, she walked from the bathroom and noticed Annie. "Wow! You look lovely."

"I have chosen a Sylvester bandeau dress in blue with the matching bolero jacket," Annie shouted from the walking wardrobe. "Is that okay?"

"Why are you shouting? I'm standing right here!"

"Navy blue underwear, Alice?" Annie was holding a Sylvester silk bra and lace panties up for Allison's approval.

"Yes, black stockings with the lace tops, please."

Annie completed Allison's makeup and hair, leaving her dark natural curls to entwine over her shoulders. Supporting the elegant navy-blue two-piece, Allison and Annie made their way towards the conservatory.

The conservatory was filled with fresh flowers and glorious table wear. Family and guests stood around the room, chatting, and laughing over vintage wines.

Annie entered the room first, dragging her sister.

"Annie, Alice, my darlings," Eleanor came straight over to greet her daughters, kissing both on their cheeks. "You both look beautiful," she said to the pair. "Alice, there is someone I like you to meet."

Eleanor took hold of Allison's hand and walked her across the great room. Alice stopped before a couple who were in their early fifties. The handsome man devoured style, and the beautiful woman showed class of a sovereign.

"Maria and Giuseppe Mancini," Eleanor said. "Maria and Giuseppe, this is my infamous daughter, Allison Templeton-Miller."

Pale, nervous, and confused, Allison reached out her hand and greeted each one with a handshake. "Hello. Are you related to Romano?"

"They are," a voice echoed from behind.

"Romano!" Allison screamed, running over, and landing straight into his strong arms.

He kissed her, trying not to spill his drink. "Surprise!"

"Are you staying for Christmas?" Allison said, not realising that the room had gone silent.

"If Santa is," Romano held his arm out towards Maria and Giuseppe. "My parents are staying for the holidays, too!"

Allison turned around and smiled at the Mancinis. Theo-James and Eleanor now stood alongside Maria and Giuseppe Mancini, and the four of them gave Romano a little nod.

Romano bent down on one knee and held Allison's left hand. The pianist stopped.

"Allison Templeton-Miller, I love you with all my heart; you are my world, my life, and I want to seal this love forever."

A waitress spilled an Earl Grey in shock.

Romano opened a velvet box containing a ten-ounce amethyst ring. "Will you marry me?"

"Purple, my favourite colour," she murmured. Drowning within his deep brown eyes, she shouted, "Yes!"

Romano stood up, wearing the largest grin that mankind had ever produced, and placed the amethyst ring onto her third finger, left hand. Pulling her into his arms, he kissed her so deeply that the conservatory windows nearly steamed up.

Everyone clapped and cheered. Romano's parents were crying, Eleanor wiped tears of joy, Sebastian smiled, Oliver wept like a baby, Ricky whistled, Henry clapped, and the staff all gathered and applauded. Somewhere, Craig's hand was on his gun.

The pianist resumed playing: Tchaikovsky's *Romeo and Juliet*. Annie, Ami, and Rene ran over to the couple for congratulations. Showing the girls her rock, Allison was overwhelmed. Annie noticed that her sister was becoming paler and brought her a flute of champagne. Knocking the champagne back, Allison regained her colour.

Theo-James clinked his champagne glass with a knife. "Lunch will be served in fifteen minutes. Please take your seats. There is a place name card for every guest. But first, I would like to congratulate my daughter and her fiancé on their engagement." Theo raised his glass, "To Allison and Romano."

After the toasts concluded, Romano gripped Allison's hand and walked her over to the table.

"I never thought this would happen today," Allison said. "You were just filming in Italy, and now you're here!"

"I am so sick and tired of being away from you, Alice. It was breaking my heart. So, I arranged to see your parents and asked them for your hand. Don't worry, I checked with Sebastian first."

"You were all in on it!" Allison laughed.

Sebastian approached. "And the planning was exceptional. I did expect Eleanor to give it away in the trailer."

"I was excited," Eleanor said, taking her seat next to Allison.

"I'm penning the cover story for *Conception Magazine* after we hit the slopes. I have a photographer, hairstylist, and makeup artist flying in on the 26th." Oliver wiped his eyes.

"Oh!" Allison gave Oliver a handkerchief.

"We nearly panicked when you were asleep, though," piped in Ricky.

Maria and Giuseppe sat across from the happy couple. They were chatting in very good English, learning about their future daughter-in-law. Allison really liked them and felt at home in their company.

A three-tier cake had been wheeled into the conservatory and placed upon a vintage console table. Romano and Allison posed for photographs while cutting into their engagement cake.

The party continued into the late afternoon. Dinner was being served at eight o'clock, and cocktails were being served at seven-thirty. It gave the family and guests sufficient time to relax and change into their evening garments.

Templeton staff relocated Romano's luggage into Allison's room, where the couple spent the next few hours seizing precious time that had been previously lost.

****

Templeton House - Zurich - Switzerland
25th December 1977 - 4.00 p.m.

Eleanor kissed Theo-James, accepting his Christmas gift wrapped in gold paper.

Struggling to comprehend what she had seen, she gasped. "Oh, my darling Theo. It is so beautiful…"

"What is it, Mama?" Annie asked, perching on the edge of a luxurious fabric sofa.

"A pink adamus," Eleanor whispered, ogling the flawless sixty carat diamond ring.

Sebastian nearly fainted. Oliver squeezed Sebastian's hand and dabbed his brow with his handkerchief.

"You okay, Sebastian?" Allison called out. "You look awfully peaky."

"Fine, my dearest Alice. Just in shock, like your poor Mama," he smiled.

Theo slid the ring onto Eleanor's hand and kissed his wife on her cheek.

"Thank you, my darling," she said, peering into his deep blue eyes.

Everyone sat in comfort by the open fire exchanging their gifts. Red berry garlands hung from the rustic reclaimed mantel, while green candles flickered in brass sconces. The sound of St Barnabas Cathedral Choir played in the background.

The Templeton-Millers presented their Christmas gift to the Mancinis: exquisite Charles Montgomery jewellery for him and her. In return, Maria and Giuseppe had organised a shipment of vintage wine from their vineyard and an exclusive trip to Tuscany. Theo-James grinned from ear to ear with his Italian gift.

Sebastian and Oliver showered the Templeton-Millers with assorted gifts from the Sylvester collection. Oliver flaunted his 24-carat gold ring from Sebastian, and Sebastian revealed his white topaz cuff links from Oliver.

The Templeton-Millers ordered Oliver and Sebastian a Porsche 911. On returning to New York, both had to select their colour and any additional extras at the showroom.

Allison received jewellery from her parents, spa treatments from her brothers, and an exclusive shopping trip in Paris from Annie and Ricky. Romano had already given her the Montgomery snake bracelet before he left for Italy, but he had hidden another gift from her.

Reaching inside his jacket pocket, he produced a white envelope.

"What is this?" she said, surprised. Allison opened the envelope and slowly pulled out an official document:

The Marriage of

Romano Matteo Mancini and Allison Marie Templeton-Miller.

Venue: St Barnabas Cathedral, New York.

Date: 1st June 1980.

Time: 1.00 p.m.

"Oh," she whispered. "It's our wedding."

Annie, Rene, and Ami ran across to the sofa. "When are you getting married?" Annie demanded, trying to snatch the document.

"June 1st, 1980." Allison smiled.

"Two years?" Annie cried out.

"There is a waiting list, and even the rich can't pay their way to God," said Romano. He gripped Allison's hand and placed it to his lips.

Sebastian chipped in, "That is a very acceptable date, Romano. I can schedule 1980 around the wedding, keep it light." Looking over at Allison, he added, "You will be busy with wedding preparations, my dear!"

"The authorities registered the date because it will take at least six months to arrange security. Some of the avenues are being sealed off." Romano gestured with his hand.

"Is the Marianna arranged?" Theo-James said from his fireside chair.

"Yes. Five hundred guests in the day and a thousand in the evening." Romano had successfully achieved his goal.

"Wow! When did you arrange all this?" Allison was amazed by Romano's organisation. She had only been engaged a day, and her wedding was already planned.

"Alice, I have something else." Romano once again dipped into his suit pocket and passed her another envelope.

Allison opened it and muttered, "Collect an A4 file on the table by the window?" Confused, she stood up and walked over to a small table by the French windows. Glimpsing at a buff folder, she picked it up and carried it back to the sofa.

Romano inched closer as Allison sat down next to him. Placing the file on her lap, she opened it. Reading the contents, she squealed. "What? A house!"

"Our house," he said. "Once we're married. And not before."

Inside the file were plans and photographs. "New Jersey? I love New Jersey," she screamed in delight.

"You will be living near Fay and Lucinda."

"Neighbours?" Allison looked to Romano for an answer.

"Neighbours," he laughed.

Annie cut in, "It's a really expensive area where Fay and Lucinda live."

Theo-James looked at Annie, "My baby is accustomed to the high life, like all of you." Sweeping his hand towards his other children.

"Anyway, Annie, how can you say that? You live in the Hamptons!" Allison glared at her sister.

Interrupting the sibling's argument, Romano stepped in. "The house is currently twelve bedrooms. I am having the alterations completed now, and it will become a twenty-bedroom house. You, Alice, will not see the house until it is completed in February 1979. This is your wedding present from me."

Maria glanced at Romano. "Are you planning a large family, Romano?"

"Mama, there will be lots of Mancinis running around the house!" he replied.

Eleanor's eyes welled up and Oliver passed her his handkerchief. Theo-James stood up from his chair and walked over and tapped his future son-in-law on the back, indicating his approval.

Allison was so moved by all of Romano's work that she broke down.

"You buy a girl a thirty-million-dollar house, and she cries!" Romano joked.

The crowd laughed. Craig Welling completed his checks with Templeton's security and set his sights on Allison.

The Templeton-Millers presented him with a Christmas gift: an exclusive wristwatch by Vir. Overjoyed with his gift, he toasted Eleanor and Theo-James. The family and their guests dispersed into the dining room and enjoyed a splendid evening.

****

St. Moritz - Switzerland - 27th December 1977

A platoon of affluent vehicles travelled across the snowy landscape: Silver Ghost Rolls-Royces, four Range Rovers, and Theo-James's Christmas gift from Eleanor, an Aston Martin V8.

Templeton-Miller security had joined the party of sixteen. Eleanor had taken her seat in the Rolls-Royce with Allison and Craig Welling. Theo-James let Romano take the Aston Martin for a spin.

Eleanor touched Allison's hand. "You have been looking peaky over the past few days, darling."

Remaining silent, Allison glanced out of the steamy window of the Rolls. "I'm tired, Mama."

"Are you worried about the magazine?"

"No, I love journals. I hate journalists."

"I know that feeling. Make the most of the quiet time you have." Eleanor patted Allison's knee. "We all worry about you, especially Romano."

"Mama, after the interview, I need to talk with you, alone."

"A mother always knows when something is wrong."

****

Surrounded by spectacular forest views, Templeton-Lodge awaited the arrival of the family and their guests. Staff prepared thirty spacious bedrooms, arranging scatter cushions, pillows, towels, and fresh geraniums to formulate an intimate atmosphere.

Conception Magazine writers relaxed amongst antique furnishings, wood panelling, and beautiful landscape canvases. The aromas of Swiss cheese tarts coasted through the kitchen area as chefs and kitchen staff prepared dinner. A steward directed personal maids and valets onto the large wooden balcony.

The first car arrived, Craig Welling jumped out of the vehicle and walked over to the steps. Motioning the steward forward, Craig summoned the driver to open the rear passenger door.

Eleanor stepped out in a full faux brown fur coat, black leather gloves, and insulated snow boots, all designed by Charles Montgomery. Allison followed in a one-piece Sylvester jumpsuit, padded bomber jacket, and swathed in a woollen heritage scarf set.

"Madame," the steward bowed as he approached Eleanor.

"Jean! How lovely to see you again. Is everything up to standard?" She asked, removing her gloves.

"Oui, Madame," the steward said, clicking his fingers for the valets to assist with the luggage. "*Les gens du magazine sont arrives.*"

"Excellent, Jean. How are Conception fitting in?" she inquired, walking up the steps.

"Parfait," nodded Jean behind her.

Allison stood with her hands in her jacket pockets and shrugged at Craig. "I'll show you to your room. Mama has given us all a map to where our guests are sleeping, and you are next door to me!"

Craig laughed. "I know. I brought my earplugs."

"Oh!" Allison blushed so brightly that the snow turned red from her reflection. "Can you hear…"

"Not when I'm wearing the plugs," Craig winked.

After Allison introduced Craig to the lodge's staff and Jean apologised for his rudeness, she met the individuals from *Conception Magazine*.

"Alice, we are taking the photographs today. Oliver insists that the magazine publishes the engagement in a couple of days." Freddie said.

Freddie Gill was a petite but very athletic, clean-cut man, whose headshots were exceptional. This is the reason why Oliver Dupont poached him from *Capillus*.

Working alongside Freddie were hairstylist Jonathan Cig and make-up artist Marty Hug.

When Allison entered the lounge, both Jonathan and Marty went into fame shock. Freddie and Allison had already been acquainted when he photographed Templeton's first album cover and promotional posters for *Heavenly Body*.

"Romano should be arriving soon; he's with Papa! I'll go and change."

"Alice, are you wearing the agreed Sylvester two-piece trouser suit?" Freddie's fingers crossed.

"A deal is a deal," she said, disappearing up the staircase. Starstruck, Jonathan, and Marty followed her with their equipment trolleys.

As agreed, Allison changed into her Sylvester two-piece black tweed trouser suit. Both Jonathan and Marty tackled the beauty without any aggravation. Staring into the mirror while Jonathan curled her dark hair, she noticed Romano standing at the door.

"Mr Mancini!" Marty yelped.

Giggling at the mirror, Allison said, "Romano, meet your biggest fans, Jonathan and Marty."

"Will I have to endure a facial?" Romano looked worried, walking in from the doorway.

"Only a touch-up, sir." Marty gaped.

"Call me Romano! You guys are sleeping here tonight, right?"

"We fly back to the states tomorrow," Jonathan cut in, still entranced by the curling tongs.

"We'll all get to know one another." Romano winked.

Marty nearly collapsed and missed his footing colliding with his trolly. Allison burst into fits of laughter as Jonathan stood behind holding his tongs until she calmed down.

Romano shook his head. "Where am I getting changed, my dearest?"

"The bathroom, or Craig's room next door."

"Where did you change, Alice?"

"Craig's," she smiled.

"I hope he wasn't in there with you," Romano said, raising an eyebrow.

"Of course not; he waited outside," she said, wiping her eyes and still giggling.

Jonathan, Marty, and Romano all looked at one another and shrugged. Collecting his garments which were laid out on the bed, Romano escaped into Craig's room. Minutes passed, and he re-entered their bedroom wearing black jeans, a crisp white shirt, and a tailored black jacket.

"Romano, I must say, you look quite dashing." Marty smiled. "Can you sit here so I can complete my last appointment?"

"Appointment?"

"Yes, you!" Marty chuckled.

When the couple completed their makeovers, everyone moved downstairs. Family and guests relocated to the dining room to preserve their privacy. The lounge had transformed into an exclusive studio: cameras, tripods, light modifiers, and backdrop.

Oliver Dupont chatted with Freddie; turning around, he welcomed Romano and Allison into the world of *Conception.*

Sitting the couple down on a luxury leather Victorian sofa, Oliver positioned himself across from the pair, holding his portfolio notebook and pen.

Oliver interviewed Allison and Romano using his rehearsed questions. The true love affair, the perfect romance, and the fairy tale wedding to be, he scribbled.

Freddie snapped the couple in the middle of their interrogation by Oliver. The official photos portrayed Allison cuddling Romano against the backdrop, exhibiting her amethyst stone ring towards the camera, while Romano placed both his hands around her succulent slim waist, resting his head against her neck.

The hour-long interview concluded with some multi-million-dollar snapshots. Oliver ran over towards Theo-James's office and faxed the notes over to the New York nerve centre.

"Success! HQ have the notes. Freddie, you have an early flight, right?" Oliver shouted, strolling out of Theo's office.

"Six in the morning, boss!"

"We'll have the prints tomorrow night." Oliver clapped in delight.

"The January issue, boss?"

"On January 2nd, 1978, our mag will bless the stands!" Oliver gave his partner a high-five. "Excellent photography, Fred!"

Romano and Allison joined the family for drinks in the dining room. Freddie and his team dismantled their equipment and relaxed on the balcony drinking bottled beers. While Oliver indulged himself with champagne and Sebastian in the bedroom. In which order nobody will ever know.

****

Morning surprised the Templeton-Millers. Eleanor, Maria, and Giuseppe decided to avoid the slopes and elected to visit the shopping mall. Allison and Romano were the first couple to depart. Craig Welling and Tony Rosso chaperoned the loved-up couple.

Sebastian and Oliver withdrew to their ski lesson with Jacques. Dreaming of being educated into the world of the ski by an attractive male model ski instructor, poor Oliver was so disappointed when the only available ski instructor was a woman.

Theo-James embraced the warm air and bright sunshine, preparing his two sons for the downhill challenge. Every year was a new competition, and Theo-James always won.

Ami, Rene, and baby Ann opted to relax at the Gourmet Cuisine restaurant bar situated on the slopes. The boys would rendezvous with them after their downhill event.

Annie and Ricky lingered in bed after a long night of vomiting. Staff remained on service to assist the couple. The pregnancy did not agree with her, and Ricky worried she would miscarry.

Succeeding skiing down the advanced slopes, Romano, Allison, Craig, and Tony relaxed at one of the bars on the nursery slope. Admiring the fearless infants zooming past without sticks, Allison fell into a howl of laughter. The three guys accompanying her looked over their hot chocolates and then at one another.

"What's so funny, Alice?" Romano said, surveying the situation with his mirrored sunglasses.

"Look, over there!" she sniggered, pointing towards the slopes.

Sebastian and Oliver were snow ploughing, holding onto the instructor's ski poles, while children under seven bolted past them. Oliver was stiff as a board, and Sebastian crumpled into something from the prehistoric age.

Reaching the bottom of the slope, the instructor steered them to a rope tow. Grabbing the plastic handle, Sebastian juddered uphill.

Oliver grabbed the handle and slipped. The ski instructor struggled to pull him up. Both of Oliver's knees had collided together and became a pyramid shape. A passing skier stopped to help the instructor pull Oliver up. Once Oliver was mobile again, the lesson continued.

By now, Allison was literally crying with laughter.

"I have never known anyone to laugh as much as your fiancée. In the public eye, she seems so timid, and underneath, she's like this!" Craig commented.

"She's changing, Craig! Watch her win the five awards next month; I can feel a monster brewing," Romano said, leaning forward for a kiss.

Allison tapped him on his knee for being cheeky. "You guys, look!" She pointed to Sebastian descending the slope alone. Wanting to clap and cheer, she thought better of it. Sebastian would lose his concentration and fall.

Though Sebastian was her manager, he was her adored friend. Impressed by his efforts today, she arranged a treat for Oliver and Sebastian: an extravagant meal and fine wines.

****

New Year's Eve snuck up on Allison. Eleanor hosted a dinner party for the family. Theo-James affixed himself to his wife all evening, chatting, living life to the full.

Annie remained in bed, suffering with her sickness. Ricky refused to leave her, but she insisted he join the New Year's Eve celebrations downstairs.

Henry and Rene wished baby Ann good night in the nursery. Rene glowed around Henry and the couple were inseparable.

Richard and Ami became a foursome, clustered together with his brother and sister-in-law. They were all now best friends forever.

Sebastian, Oliver, Romano, and Allison mingled among guests and spoke with Maria and Giuseppe. Allison made the most of it. Tomorrow everyone would be leaving the lodge and carrying on with their own lives.

Opening the piano keyboard lid, sitting on the duet bench, she played *Heavenly Body*. The room fell silent, and the family and guests circled around the grand, clutching their drinks.

When the last note of the song was played, Allison dropped her head. Romano took a seat beside her on the stool and put an arm around her shoulder. A tear escaped from the corner of her eye.

Romano pulled her close to his chest. "I love you, Alice," he whispered.

"I love you too," she whimpered. "I will always remember this Christmas forever."

Romano gently caressed her cheek. "Happy New Year, baby."

1978 had arrived, and Romano and Allison welcomed it with open arms. It was another step closer to their wedding, and the pair of them couldn't wait!

CHAPTER 19

The Plasma Conference Park - Los Angeles

19th January 1978

The prestigious ceremony spotlights projected powerful rays of light into the night sky. The iconic red carpet showcased the spectacular grand entrance and a fashion placement arena attracted TV crews, photographers, and journalists.

Allison, clad in a crystal-beaded princess dress positioned herself against a backdrop of advertising, posing desirably.

Wearing their stylish Sylvester tuxedos, Templeton signed autographs in the fashion placement arena. The band members then scattered amongst the press.

Miranda Love strolled past Allison Templeton-Miller and elbowed her in the back. Not turning around, Allison flinched but continued chatting to the chat show host of *Morning Clock-in*.

The press bombarded Allison with questions. Flaunting her large amethyst stone ring, she replied politely until a reporter mentioned Eva Moulin.

Seeing Miranda Love standing next to her, Allison stepped back onto her extensive lace train. Stabbing her stiletto heel into the lace in an imperceptible manner, Allison responded to the Eva Moulin question.

"Eva was my advisor at The Kellie School of Performing Arts. I wish her family comfort during this dark time."

"Did you know that Madam Moulin was exploiting young talent for money?" A journalist said.

Glaring at the reporter, Allison responded, "I'm not aware of any such incident."

"My dress!" Miranda cried out. "It's ruined!"

Miranda's management ran over, bending down to rescue the ripped lace train.

Allison gave Miranda a wicked glare and continued to chat with other TV hosts. Allison laughed extra loud with a presenter of a daytime television show.

"Oh, no!" the presenter gasped. "M-Love's dress!"

"Train derailment," Allison joked, to thunderous applause.

The presenter raised her microphone. "You and M-Love are in competition for the Best Female Artist Award. Do you think you'll win?"

"I think the best girl will win. Thank you."

Allison got ushered away towards the entrance of the auditorium. Reuniting with her management team, including Belinda and Annie (who was now showing in her pregnancy). Allison searched for Romano.

Romano stood chatting with the band members from Templeton. Allison grabbed his arm.

"At last, I have found you. Come on we will be late."
Allison stared at Donny. "You are in so much trouble."

Donny pointed towards himself. "Me!"

"Belinda is on the war path." Allison said, pulling
Romano away from the band.

"Okay, I will go and find her." Donny scoffed.

"I walk through the valley of the shadow of death" Josh
joked.

Donny glared at Josh and ran towards the auditorium
doors.

Extending into the audience, a thrust stage surrounded
the performers. A variety of lighting created the tone of the
scene. An orchestra played film symphonies behind red
velvet drapes. At the corner of the stage stood a golden
podium checkmated by microphones and TV cameras.

Templeton and their partners sat in row A. Behind them
sat Sebastian, Oliver, Marshall Rusk, and Craig Welling.

Romano leaned into Allison's ear. "What happened out
there?"

"Miranda's big head ripped her dress," she said, facing
forward.

"You didn't have anything thing to do with it! I saw her
elbow you in the back earlier," he whispered.

"Me?" she laughed in bewilderment.

The organisers collected Templeton. Tonight, they were performing *Heavenly Body* for thousands of fans. Kissing Romano, Allison followed her band members into the dressing rooms.

Behind the scenes were total chaos; people were running around with earphones, microphones, and walkie-talkies. Rock groups were shouting. Singers were practising their scales. Dancers were arguing with one another.

Allison made her way into room twelve; following her were Sebastian Dupont and Craig Welling. Templeton and Marshall Rusk were assigned to room ten.

"You, my girl, have been a little devil tonight," said Sebastian, leaning against the dressing table.

"She had it coming. I suppose you didn't see the elbow go into my back." Allison stood still behind a screen as assistants stripped her purple gown.

"No, I didn't. What happened?"

"It hurt! I didn't flinch because I was on camera."

"Good girl. What a bitch!"

"So, I got revenge and stood on her dress!" Allison giggled.

Stepping out from behind the screen. Allison grinned wearing her black hotpants and leather peplum jacket.

"You look gorgeous, darling," Sebastian smiled. "Breath-taking, absolutely breath-taking."

Craig eyed her up and down, fidgeting with dickie bow.

A Sylvester dresser bent down and laced her black leather Victorian boots.

"Ready, guys?" she said. "Wait, I need lip gloss."

Marty Hug applied red lip gloss onto her heart-shaped lips.

"Alice let me do a final spray." Jonathan said, holding a can of hair lacquer.

Allison covered her face while Jonathan sprayed wildly.

Standing outside room ten, Donny, Ricky, Jack, and Josh talked between themselves. Sporting black mandarin shirts and leather trousers, the guys certainly looked the part.

"Who are we waiting for?" Marshall said, looking around the corridor.

"Marc!" Donny grinned.

"Where is he?"

The band pointed into the dressing room. Marshall walked over and opened the door. Excessive moans and groans flowed into the corridor.

Allison, Sebastian, and Craig stopped suddenly hearing the yelling from inside room ten.

"What's going on?" Allison asked Donny.

"Marc is screwing the hairstylists again," Ricky blurted.

"Hairstylists? Like, Joanna—"

"Yep," Josh piped in.

"When does he get the time?"

"Alice, please," Sebastian jumped in.

Marshall Rusk stormed out of the dressing room, red and angry. "You're on in five."

"What about Marc? We need a drummer," Josh yelled.

Marc Garcia strolled into the corridor, cool and collected. Brushing his hair back with his left hand and holding his drumsticks in the other, he said, "Ready!"

The guys from Templeton just collapsed into laughter. Marshall was having a heart attack. Organisers grabbed Dupont and Rusk, guiding the band into position behind a large black screen.

Donny, Ricky, and Jack picked up their guitars. Marc rested on his drum stool. Josh stood against his piano, and Allison positioned herself in between Ricky and Donny.

"Ladies and gentlemen, the greatest band in the building: Templeton."

The curtain rose. Spotlights blinded Allison as she sang the first few lines of *Heavenly Body* to raucous applause. Donny and Ricky stepped in on the third line of the song.

Romano, Belinda, Annie, and Miranda King sat huddled together, watching their partners' performances.

"She's good, Romano," Belinda whispered.

"Sorry about the engagement. Family thing."

"It's okay, she called us all from Switzerland. Fay, Lucinda, and I all know Christmas is for families. If we are all bridesmaids," she winked.

Romano laughed and winked back.

Allison owned the stage and theatre. Her powerful voice dominated the auditorium. The crowd watched in awe, and when the song ended, rows of people stood up from their seats and cheered as each member of Templeton bowed in recognition.

The curtain fell, parting the musicians from the audience. Sebastian ran out from the side of the stage and hugged Allison. Marshall smiled, standing back with his arms folded, speaking with the organisers. He ushered Templeton back to their dressing room to change into their tuxedos.

Allison accompanied Sebastian and Craig to room twelve. Sylvester staff clapped and offered her a glass of champagne. Removing the leather hot pants and jacket, she stepped into the purple princess dress, sipping the sparkling, effervescent liquid. "I can relax now!" Allison shouted over the screen to Sebastian.

"No, you can't!" Sebastian yelled back, sitting cross-legged on a sofa. "You have awards to win!"

Appearing from behind the screen again, she became the innocent princess dressed in purple, and the seductive black leather glad sorceress had disappeared.

"Miss Templeton-Miller, you'll always be my Best Female." Sebastian smiled while the organisers lingered outside the dressing room ready to escort them back to their seats.

Allison reunited with Romano as the presenter of the awards broadcasted his speech.

"Beautiful, Alice," Romano said, grabbing her hand and kissing her on her right cheek. "You are so beautiful."

"Our next category is Best Female. To present the award, actor Stephen-Paul Golding."

Violins played overtones as Mr Golding carried a gold envelope towards the podium. Dressed in a blue velvet tuxedo jacket and matching dickie bow, Stephen's colours radiated his sweeping blonde hair and blue eyes. The audience applauded and cheered whilst he dabbed the sweat from his brow. The presenter passed him the emerald music award.

Bending down into the microphone, he said, "The four nominees for best female are…"

Everyone fell into silence whilst Stephen read out the four nominees. "And the winner is…" Opening the envelope, he tried to rub away something in his eye. "Allison Templeton-Miller!"

Allison placed both hands over her mouth in shock. Sebastian and Oliver leaned over her chair and congratulated her. The band members jumped up and leaned in for a hug, with Belinda squashed in the middle. Romano kissed her the top of her head.

The violins resumed while Allison ascended onstage. Her sensuous purple gown overflowed onto the steps as she climbed up towards the podium. Stephen reached his hand out to help her. Presenting her with the Cantus Award, he kissed her on the lips. Allison looked at Romano in the audience.

Stepping in front of the microphone, gripping her award with trembling hands, she muttered, "Thank you to everyone who voted for me. I wouldn't be here tonight without my management team, Sebastian Dupont, my family, Green Records, and my fiancé Romano Mancini."

Romano blew a kiss. She waved to the audience and was escorted off stage by one of the officials, whilst Stephen followed behind, waving.

"What the hell was that?" Allison glared at him.

" A congratulation kiss." Stephen edged closer to her.

"On the lips, Golding?"

Stephen laughed. "I had to kiss something, Alice."

Holding the amethyst rock up to his face, she said, "Some of us are engaged, Stephen!"

An official broke up the conversation and explained that the awards are placed in a cabinet until the show was over.

All winners attended the press centre afterwards with their Cantus Awards.

Taking the award from Allison, another official escorted her back to her seat. Stephen walked off in the opposite direction. Reaching the front row and sitting next to Romano was bliss. Romano kissed her while an unknown actress announced the next category.

For Best Song, *Heavenly Body* and *My Heart is on Fire.* Allison gulped. The boys would never forgive her if her solo song won this category.

"*Heavenly Body*," the actress called out.

"Excellent," Allison sighed with relief.

Templeton and Allison made their way to the stage. Donny Davis announced the speeches, and the auditorium erupted into uproar.

In the next category, Best Music Video/Film, Allison once again climbed the steps onto the stage, made her speech, and followed an official. Templeton won Best Album for *Heavenly Body*, Best Composer, Josh Williams.

After the show had ended, the winners were positioned on a red carpet displaying their awards. Officials spirited Allison and Josh away so photographers could take million-dollar shots of the superstar holding her two awards and Josh with his Best Composer Award. Later the two of them rejoined Templeton.

Romano and the rest of the band's partners lingered behind a roped area.

"I'm ready for a drink!" Belinda called out.

"Me too," Miranda King said. "I hope Josh won't be long."

"I'm ready for bed," yawned a five-month pregnant Annie.

****

Event Spot - Los Angeles

19th January 1978 - 11.30 p.m.

Sebastian deposited himself and Oliver at a stylish caprice bar table. Uncorking a bottle of whiskey, the young waiter poured the drink into two glasses, removing the bottle he disappeared into the crowd of guests.

Tony walked over towards Sebastian. "Mr Dupont, everything is in check."

"Have the staff at Sylvester's gone?"

"Yes, sir. They have taken the dress with them."

"That was the arrangement. Good."

"She is on the dance floor with her girlfriends."

Oliver moved his head around and viewed the illuminated dance floor in the recessed section of the club.

"Where is Craig?" Sebastian said, sipping his whiskey.

"With the gang, sir," Tony replied.

"Good, I need him to stay there. You stay with us." Sebastian waved at a passing waiter. "My good man, I would like to order two more of these, and one orange juice. Thank you."

The young waiter appeared again with his tray and deposited Sabbatian's drinks.

"Dupont!"

Sebastian turned around and looked at a small, balding man wearing a tuxedo.

"Here we go," Sebastian snarled. "Bob! How the devil are we?"

"You thief!"

"Thief? You think I stole these good looks?"

"That girl of yours robbed us of our Cantus Award."

"Which one?"

"You know which one!" Bob said.

"What are we speaking about here?" Sebastian sipped his glass of whiskey.

"M-Love, your girl snatched the award from her!"

"How? I saw her walk onto the stage when her name was called."

"And she tore Miranda's dress!"

Sebastian laughed. "Malady didn't win the prize because of a dress?"

Bob Hinting pointed at the illuminated dance floor. "Her name is Miranda not Malady. She is not here tonight because of that little thief."

Sebastian stooped over and grabbed Hinting's collar. "That thief has achieved more number one hit singles and albums than Kingston. My girl breaks sales records. Your girl breaks up marriages. Shall I continue?"

M-Love's manager caught his balance and quickly scurried away like an animal escaping from a pen.

"I don't need bastards like him to spoil my whiskey," Sebastian said.

Oliver laughed. "You're spoiled enough."

"Alice is growing up. This is a dangerous industry. Someone needs to teach her how to defend herself," Sebastian said.

Tony received his glass of juice and quickly downed it. "Sir, if there's any more trouble, I will attend to it."

"No need. Darling, I can deal with that shrimp: grab him by the tail!"

Oliver choked on his drink.

"Cheers, my lovely." Sebastian slapped him on the back to stop the coughing.

The multicoloured dancefloor flashed while Allison strutted her stuff in a very short sequined cocktail dress. Belinda, Miranda King, Fay, and Lucinda gave a good performance as well.

"Sorry you couldn't come to the ceremony," she shouted to Fay.

"At least you got us tickets for here," Fay shouted back.

"Did the staff settle you in tonight?"

"Yep. Porta del Castello is a beautiful place."

"Which room have they put you in?"

"Michael and I are in the last room on the back, and Lucinda and Max are across from us."

269

"So, you are next door to Belinda and Donny?"

"Where's Annie and Ricky?"

"They are in the annexe outside for privacy. Ricky is worried. Her pregnancy is not good."

"I hope she is okay," Fay added.

Romano danced across the dance floor and put both hands around Allison's waist.

"Just going to borrow my fiancée," he smiled at the girls, sweeping her off the dance floor.

"Is something wrong?" Allison said, concerned.

"Yes, you! You're making my pants too tight!" Romano placed both hands on her backside and kissed her. Speaking with his mouth still on hers, he said, "Let's go to a private room."

"What's wrong with right here?" Allison said.

"That's why I like you. You're crazy."

Romano pulled her across to the private area. Opening the first door, "Sorry!" He closed it again when he witnessed a couple having sex on a sofa.

"Try number two!" Allison laughed.

Opening door number two, he pulled her inside and bolted it shut. Immobilising her against the white wall. Romano pulled up her dress and kissed her deeply, whilst pulling her black lace panties down.

She unbuckled his leather belt and unfastened the button of his trousers. Romano never wore underwear in a tuxedo and his erection sprung to life.

Lifting her up, he struggled to walk with his trousers around his ankles and suddenly threw her onto a sofa. Placing her forward facing, he felt the wetness of her sex. She was ready for him, and within seconds he entered her from behind.

Breathing deeply into the side of her neck, Romano thrusted into her, slowly caressing her breasts through the dress fabric.

Allison moaned, stretching both arms above her head. The peak of her sexual excitement discharged erotic tension, and within minutes she exploded into her tingling orgasm.

Still thrusting deeper, slower, faster, harder, crying out 'Alice,' Romano ejaculated. Eventually slowing down, Romano slumped into her, pressing his full body weight onto her back. Sagging against the back of the sofa, she groaned with pleasure.

Lifting himself from the top of her, Romano turned Allison around to face him. He shuffled to a tissues box sitting on a side table.

Tugging a handful of two-ply white tissues, he handed them to Allison. The couple cleaned themselves and deposited the soiled tissues into a bin beside the door.

"Yuk! How many dirty tissues are in there?" Allison pulled her face.

"Alice, please, we have just made love, and you are talking about dirty tissues." Romano moaned pulling his trousers up.

Leaving the room, Romano kissed Allison so passionately that she thought they might need the room again. No one would know any different apart from the red flushes painted on their faces. They joined the rest of the couples sitting at the bar.

"Waiter! Five bottles of your best." Romano balanced Allison on his knee. "And ask the others if they want a drink, too."

The party continued until the early hours, and two limousines waited outside the club for the clique.

Craig, Max, Lucinda, Fay, Michael, Belinda, Donny, Romano, and a tipsy Allison climbed into the first car. Sebastian, Oliver, Tony, Josh, Miranda, Marc, Jack, and two drunk blondes climbed into the second.

The first car headed back to Porta Del Castello, where Allison asked if anyone wanted to play a game of Twister. Romano refused, planning to get his exercise in the bedroom.

The second car drove to the Green Records Apartments, where Sebastian had plans for Oliver and his malt whiskey.

CHAPTER 20

Watch Films Studios - Bombay - India

19th February 1978

Located on the Arabian Sea, the city contained tranquil forests, valleys, and lakes of flowering plants, exquisite bird varieties, and other wildlife. Miles of golden beaches stretched against crystal green water.

A Hindustan Ambassador parked outside Karma International Airport. Allison, Stephen-Paul Golding, and Stewart Gloss walked out of the double doors into the sunshine. Craig Welling shadowed Allison, wearing white jeans and a striped short-sleeved shirt over his loaded nine millimetre.

The temperature in Bombay was pleasantly warm at 87-degree Celsius. A driver bowed and offered his car to Allison and Craig.

Climbing into the car, they both watched their luggage being squeezed into the trunk. Stephen and Stewart climbed into the auto behind.

The driver was under strict instructions to take his passengers to The Sapphire Palace Hotel. Travelling through small villages of small steak houses with small wooden porches. The smell of rotting garbage drifted into the back of the car. Trees of greenery surrounded most of the buildings until they hit the coastal road.

Allison noticed a green calming sea glistening against the sunlight. Beaches of golden sand appeared untouched by the breeze wafting against the metal of the car.

Suddenly the silence ceased. Car horns echoed in all directions. Royal Enfields, Jugaads, and buses zoomed past. Allison covered her eyes when a scooter nearly hit them.

"This is fun!" Craig laughed.

"I can't look!"

The car slid into the centre lane of the expressway. Cars, motorbikes, and scooters sped past.

Allison couldn't bear to look. "Oh!"

"You damn kids and your abbreviations," Craig said. "Oh?"

The vehicle veered right into a newly cemented road surrounded by sandalwood. Turning left through huge metal gates, the car pulled around a beautiful fountain of crystal blue water in front of a prestigious building. Erect flagpoles boasted world flags.

The fifteen-floored marble building was impossible to miss. Red mosaic tiles at the grand entrance swept inside the building. Ceiling fans cooled hotel porters pushing trolleys in their cotton Kurta sets. A beautiful young woman waited behind the reception desk wearing a green Saree, taking calls.

A doorman in a crimson turban and matching Nehru jacket opened the car door. Stepping outside, Allison couldn't believe the beautiful architecture. Craig stepped out of the car before her, scratching his back with his sidearm.

The second car pulled up, and another doorman reached the handle and opened the rear passenger door.

"Bloody studio should have sent us Mercs, not these toy cars. Your bloody back killing you too, Craig?" Stewart said.

"Sure, is Stewart," Craig said, groaning.

"How the hell did they fit all our luggage in?" Stephen said.

"They didn't. Third car!" Stewart pointed. "Wait until I see Greg Wizen; he's a dead man."

"What is Greg…" Allison said.

"Fired!" Stewart yelled.

"Boss of Watch Productions," explained Stephen.

Four chaperones aligned in the foyer, gesturing with their palms together, fingertips facing forward. Ira introduced herself to Allison, and she escorted the singer to her private chambers. Whilst Craig was escorted by Arjun to an adjoining room next door. Stephen and Stewart followed, grumbling.

The spacious suite featured a king-sized bed, a stand-alone bathtub, a walk-in wardrobe, and a lounge. A private balcony connected Craig's room to Allison's. Walking out onto the balcony, she noticed Welling puffing on a cigarette, flicking his ash into an ashtray.

"I love it here," she sighed, taking a seat next to him.

"Yeah. Magical," he replied between puffs. "I only go outside to smoke."

"Afraid you'll set off the fire alarm?"

"No. Afraid I'll give you cancer. It's my job, protecting you."

"Can I try?" Alice asked.

"Try what?"

"A smoke."

"No," Craig said. "You'll ruin your voice."

"Then this would all end, wouldn't it?" she mused, staring at the sun. "We'd be free."

"You'd be free." Craig stamped out his cigarette. "I'd need another job."

****

After dinner, Allison retired around ten; it had been an exhausting day, and she had to ring Romano. The Italian film star was on a film set in Rome, which meant Bombay was three hours ahead. Both Romano and Allison had agreed ten o'clock would be a good time to chat.

After waiting to be connected, Allison heard Romano's voice. "Hi, baby. You had a good journey?"

"I made it," she replied, swinging her legs.

"How is Mr Golding? Keeping his hands off you?"

"Yes!"

"Good…Craig will shoot if Stephen makes a move," smirked Romano.

"Romano, please. I can look after myself."

"Hmm…"

"I haven't told you the whole story."

"What whole story, Alice?"

"I am not playing his lover! I'm playing his sister." She rolled over on the bed.

"Go on…"

The Crystal Cage's script had to be adjusted, or I was out."

"Don't be silly," he said. "You, demanding, never."

"The adventure is about a brother and sister who follow a treasure map. They hunt down a magic crystal, which turns out to be a lost book, which is worth millions. I play Lilly, a strong, independent wo—"

"Yeah, yeah," Romano jumped in.

"Anyway, I have stunt personnel teaching me all the moves."

"Anything that you can use in bed?"

"Elbow strikes, throat punch, nutcracker choke, eye gouge, groin stomp."

"Let's skip that last one."

"I demanded the rewrites because I don't want to do any sex scenes with Stephen. We have a new actress playing his lover."

"Who is that?"

"Francesca S. Conti." Silence hit the airwaves.

"Romano?"

"Yeah."

"Do you know her from auditions, or from your bedpost?"

"Yes," Romano chuckled.

Allison laughed. "Well, this will be interesting at the film premiere."

"Are you upset?"

"No. It's in the past."

"I have an extra doing all of my sex scenes!" Romano blurted, trying to conceal his guilt.

"In case Miss Karate kicks you in the preverbal!" Allison cried with laughter and rolled onto her side.

Both chatted for another hour until Allison ended the call. Already jet-lagged, she struggled to keep her eyes open and collapsed into a deep sleep.

****

A sharp silver blade lunged into his chest.

278

"Cut!" Stewart Gloss screamed. "Nice slice, Alice."

"Cool," she said, sheathing a Malacca sword.

The vanquished villain sat up in the sand and clapped his hands together, removing the excess grit from his fingers. Film assistants ran over and helped him stand. Two assistants escorted Allison into a tent full of portable vanity tables and directors' chairs.

"Champagne, Alice?" Stephen-Paul Golding grinned, passing over a glass flute from his named director's chair.

"Thank you," she said, accepting the flute from his pampered hand. "When does Fran fly in?"

"Already here."

"Oh, I've not seen her!" she muttered, taking a well-deserved sip.

"She's staying at the Palace of Bondi," he grinned.

"Is that where you disappeared to last night?" she grinned back.

"Maybe. Jealous?" Stephen smiled, leaning closer.

"Don't touch me!" Allison shoved him forcefully back onto his chair. "Craig keeps his safety off, you know."

"Let him shoot. I still have time to snatch you from the Italian," he remarked, looking towards the sickly ocean.

"I love Romano, and nothing will ever change that."

"Not even his past romps with Fran?"

Allison looked directly into his handsome face. "I know all about it!"

"1974, I was headhunted for a role to star in one of the greatest movies to be ever made, and your fiancé stole it from under my nose!"

"How could he snatch it from under you? Your agent should have sorted the deal."

"He slept with the director's daughter!" Stephen snarled.

"Oh," she said, turning away.

"*Presto*! Romano Mancini, the leading man."

"He didn't do it on purpose." She shifted in her chair. "Right?"

"The relationship ended after the wrap."

A male of great proportion stood behind Stephen, pulling up a chair. "Joanna Starky dropped Romano. She was having an affair with the family gardener."

Stephen and Allison looked at him in amazement.

"Who are you?" Stephen inquisitively asked.

"I was Thomas Starky's film producer, and friend."

"What are you doing here in Bombay?" Allison asked, engrossed in the conversation. "Did you get lost?"

"I work for Watch Films."

"Are you still a producer?" Stephen inquired further.

"A producer? I'm your producer." He offered a handshake. "My name is Ivan Freidman."

Allison froze. "Are you related to Paul Freidman?"

"By blood. Paul is my younger sibling. I haven't seen him in years."

"I have," she said, shivering.

"Paul is a great businessman. If his projects make money, all well and good, and if the project is no longer feasible, he burns it all down."

"Tell us about Thomas Starky," Stephen stepped in.

"I worked as an editor for Movie World Productions. Thomas was a screenwriter. We became very good friends, and Thomas had an eye for the camera. Over a couple years, we produced and co-directed art films, low budget stuff. Suddenly someone sent us a great script the major studios had passed on. We took the chance."

"I have a bad feeling about this," Alice said.

Ivan stroked his stubble. "Thomas became a respectable film director and me a respectable film producer. He had a weak link, a daughter. Joanna squandered money, took drugs, lived with depression, and she ran off with the gardener. Thomas had high hopes for Romano, thought he would rescue Joanna. Nobody could rescue that girl."

"There were others?" Allison butted in.

"She was pregnant, but nobody knew the father." Ivan continued. "You are going to ask me how I know. I took her to the clinic. Joanna was six weeks pregnant. Romano was on location for about eight weeks, so that rules him out. The gardener had to return home, and Thomas had to temporary employ another worker. That only leaves one. She was in no state to raise a child…"

"Termination," Allison mumbled.

"Yes. When the gardener left, Joanna went with him."

"Where?" Stephen asked.

"Texas. She'd changed her identity. Thomas lost it."

"What happened to Thomas?" Allison said.

"Overdose. They said it was an accident, but we all knew. His wife had left him years ago, and he had to raise Joanna by himself. Poor bastard."

"The press never ran the story?" Stephen said.

"MW covered it up by announcing his retirement due to ill health. The funeral was private, and everyone involved got paid off."

"So, you moved out here." Stephen looked at the sea. It seemed a little darker than a few minutes ago.

"Romano got chosen for the role because the writer demanded a dark-haired actor rather than a blonde. If not for those demands, you were our first choice."

"I've heard that before," Stephen said.

****

Three weeks into filming, Allison met Francesca S. Conti. The beautiful five-foot six-inch-tall blonde appeared out of the blue. Fran had to delay filming due to another project.

"Allison Templeton-Miller?" Conti exclaimed.

Turning around, staring at a goddess like herself, Allison responded with delight. "Fran!"

"You are my favourite singer in the solar system. Could I have your autograph?" Fran squealed, hugging Allison.

"Sure." Allison choked. "Fran, I can't breathe."

"Sorry." Fran let her go.

Stephen approached both women and smiled. "A brunette and a blonde, which one do I choose?" he laughed. Grabbing Fran and pulling her into his arms, he kissed her passionately.

"Golding, put her down!" Stewart yelled through a megaphone. "Make-up!"

Stephen dropped Fran to the ground.

"Are you two…" Allison said, pointing her finger.

"Yeah," Fran sighed, gazing at Stephen.

"Marvellous news. You and Golding look like Aphrodite and, uh, you know, the guy," coughed Allison.

"Hephaestus," Craig called from off screen.

"You and Romano are the perfect couple. Gosh, I read the magazines all the time about you guys," Fran said. "When are you getting married?"

"Not yet. We are too busy," Allison replied, going off the subject.

Allison and Fran walked towards the make-up chairs that were ready for them. Sitting next to one another, Fran said, "Romano and myself had a quick fling years ago. Nothing like your relationship. Sex, lots of it."

Allison laughed. "Wait, what?"

"I'm four years older than you and just look at your career." Fran sighed changing the subject. "I'm not even married yet."

"You'll get married before me, I guarantee it. Stephen is twenty-eight, same age as Romano. You're twenty-six, the perfect age." Allison smiled.

"You're so lovely, inside, and out. We're gonna be best buddies." Fran smiled, gripping Allison's hand.

"Best buddies, Miss Conti," agreed Allison.

****

Synopsis April - August 1978

During a romantic moonlit night in Bombay, Stephen proposed to Fran. Media coverage of the engagement disseminated around the world. Allison ordered for the lovers' silk green sherwani and sarees, symbolising a new beginning, harvest, and happiness. Stewart Gloss continued ripping his hair out with frustration always trying to break the pair up from their constant osculating.

Leaving behind her beloved Bombay in mid-April, Romano and Allison had decided to organise their honeymoon with the guidance of the management team of The Sapphire Palace Hotel. Excited about the singer's return, the hotel offered the couple an exquisite honeymoon suite and indulgent treatments at the Sapphire Spa.

****

May produced an exciting month for Allison: four weeks of frequent recording schedules at the Green Records studio, producing her first solo chart-topping album.

****

June experienced another red-carpet film premiere, *The Crystal Cage.* Allison was overwhelmed by the critical reception regarding her character. She had taken prime leadership in this adventure film, tabloids, TV magazine shows, and radio; there was a huge demand for her. She believed that Stephen-Paul Golding and Francesca S. Conti might snatch the glory. Oh, how wrong was she!

Stewart Gloss wanted Allison to play Lilly again in his next solo adventure. Allison refused Stewart's suggestion and would only work on the project if Stephen and Fran were involved. The director would think long and hard about it.

****

July provided Allison and Romano with a much-deserved break. Residing in their New York apartment, the couple made the most of their time together: making love, watching movies, studying scripts, and writing songs.

Allison organised her luggage for Templeton's European tour. An English band called Cosmic Stars were supporting them and she had no idea how it would turn out. Romano prepared himself for his latest action hero film in Brazil.

The couple would not meet until the 5th of December at a television award ceremony in LA. Allison was presenting the Best Drama Award.

CHAPTER 21

Milan - Italy - 1st August 1978

Flashing cameras dazzled the members of Templeton's profiles. Allison leaned against a high glossed conference table. Five microphones, jugs of iced water, and ashtrays obstructed her space.

"Allison! When are you and Mr Mancini getting married?" A female reporter shouted, standing up from her seat.

"We'd do it right now, but you're not ordained," Allison answered to applause.

Another reporter stood up against the crowd of busybodies. "Question for Ricky. What does it feel like being a father?"

Ricky leaned into his microphone and answered, "It feels like I have a kid!"

"Is Annie returning to the studios?" a reporter from the back of the conference room yelled.

"She is, when baby Amile is six months old."

"Will you be a stay-at-home dad?"

"I wish. Both my wife and I are busy musicians, and Amile will travel with us."

"A question for Marc Garcia. When will you be settling down?"

"Never! I like my fun too much." Marc grinned, turning towards his band members.

"For Josh: Will you be writing more songs for the new album?"

"Already done!" Josh smiled triumphantly.

"Josh, when are you and Miranda settling down?" A cream-skirted reporter asked.

"That's classified!" Josh gave no clues away, but he had mentioned to Allison that Christmas was a good time to propose.

"A question for Jack Evens. When will you settle down?"

"Never!" Jack replied. He was already married, and only the band members knew of his secret.

Gillian Terrance and Jack Evens were childhood sweethearts from New York. Gillian moved to London to pursue her career in banking. Jack attended the Kellie School of Performing Arts and became Templeton's bass guitarist.

The couple owned a five-bedroom cottage on prestigious gated grounds, an ideal retreat for them to enjoy their private life away from the press.

The band members continued to endure the severity of the press. Jack avoided most of the questions especially from the cream suited female.

"A question for Donny: when are you and Belinda marrying?" The creamy skirt reporter repeated.

"Can you ask questions about our music instead of our private lives?" Donny snapped. "I refuse to answer."

Sebastian Dupont appeared elegantly and placed himself in front of the band holding one hand in the air. "No more questions."

The room carried moans and groans into its atmosphere. Sebastian smiled, dressed in his traditional grey designer suit and pink cravat. Templeton acknowledged Sebastian's instructions and dispersed from the conference room.

Congregating in the bar area, Marc Garcia was already chatting to the barmaid. Donny, ordering four bottle beers and a glass of red merlot, slammed a two hundred lira note onto the counter. "I detest the press!"?" he growled, guzzling back his bottle of beer.

Allison laughed. "You stressed, Donny?"

Donny could have killed her with his looks. "Hmm."

"Belinda!" Allison smirked.

"Why is that woman always buzzing around? Don't you women get PMT?"

"Weddings?" Allison giggled.

"Yup, from morning until night. Fuzzing around with magazines and samples."

"Well, you'll have to marry her."

"I'm trying. But I have this tour; she's now filming in the Bronx. Early this year, she was in France filming."

"Instead of doing it big, just do it!" Allison said, pulling him to one side.

"Alice, I want to give her everything. I really do. But my schedule, her schedule."

"Christmas, you're both off. Do it then," Allison whispered, still gripping his arm.

"I will sort something out. You will be first to know."

Marshall Rusk interrupted the chatting. "Guys! I want to introduce you to Cosmic Stars."

Templeton looked over their shoulder towards a smart four-membered band: a drummer with long whisking designer hair just riding above his shoulders, a tall guitarist with dark brown hair, a keyboard player with the same style of hair in medium brown, and the lead singer, tall with curling blonde hair.

"Meet Templeton: Donny Davis is our lead singer and guitarist. Donny, this is Craig Johns, lead singer, Dave Holly, keyboard. Stan Bigs, drummer, and Alfie Crook, guitarist."

Marshall introduced each band member of the English band to Templeton. When Cosmic Stars reached Allison, the room went silent. "Allison Templeton-Miller," whispered Craig Johns.

Allison reached out her hand and laughed. "Call me Alice; some of these guys call me Ali."

"Alice it is," he smiled, shaking her hand.

Alfie and Dave followed Craig, in awe of her presence. Stan was the last band member to greet Allison, and as soon as he touched her hand, a weird negative sensation ran up her arm and down into her stomach.

"Hi, I'm Stan," he extracted a predatory grin.

"Call me Alice." She pulled her hand away from his.

"You're more beautiful than your pics," he flirted, still trying to touch her.

"Thanks!" she said, wiping her hand with a tissue.

"We're all going to have lots of fun on this trip!" Stan raised both eyebrows.

"Fun," panicked Allison.

Craig Welling walked over and stood between Stan and Allison, hand on his holster.

"We need to talk," she whispered.

"Sorry, gentlemen," Craig said. "It's Alice's naptime."

"See you later, Stan," she said.

Craig and Allison strolled into the reception area of the hotel.

"Is it that drummer from Cosmic?" Welling checked the coast was clear.

"Naptime? Really?"

"Never was a good liar," he said.

"I have got a bad feeling about that guy."

Craig laughed. "Singer, actress, now a psychic too?"

"Shut up! He was trying to come onto me."

"He would have to dodge a few bullets first."

"Thanks, Craig."

"Anything for my little girl."

Later that afternoon, Cosmic Stars had attended their rehearsal and went back to the hotel. Templeton rehearsed for the next two hours. Unfortunately for Templeton, they had to suffer more interviews and photoshoots inside the stadium.

Miranda King (Josh's partner) and her crew were the assigned make-up team for the band.

"Are you going to join Josh and me for a coffee?" she bellowed.

"Miranda!" Alice yelled, jumping off the stage for a bear hug.

"I brought Earl Grey!"

"We've met," Allison joked. "You look great."

"You look even better with your four Cantus Awards."

"Miss Cantus misses her man."

"Where is he now?"

"Brazil. A superhero movie."

Miranda laughed. "I can't see Romano in tights."

"He looks good in mine," Allison chuckled.

Arriving at the dining area, which was more of a five-star *á la carte* restaurant, Josh greeted Miranda with a warm embrace.

Sebastian made his presence known. "Darling Alice! I brought you a surprise!" Smiling with pride, holding his arm out towards the door, he said, "Marty Hug and Jonathan Cig."

The two gays rushed past Sebastian and picked Allison up into the air.

"These cheeky chappies are now in my employment."

"Doing what?" Allison said, looking at the pair of starstruck males.

"I had an arrangement with Oliver, and he kindly allowed me to poach them from *Conception*. At a price!"

"In other words, you had lots of pillow talk," she laughed.

"Allison-Templeton-Miller!" Sebastian shrieked.

Marty Hug and Jonathan Cig joined Miranda, Josh, and Allison for breakfast.

"I love your trolly cases." Miranda pointed out.

Josh noticed the new signage on their cases.

"Yeah, we are officially stylists to Allison Templeton-Miller." Marty proudly announced.

"Yep, splattered all over your cases." Josh laughed.

Allison sank into a deep pink pudding sofa. Gripping a small china cup and saucer she suddenly asked, "Does anyone think that Stan Bigs is strange?"

Josh looked at Miranda. "He seems okay."

Allison remained confused. "I just get a strange feeling about him."

Marty and Jonathan had not met Cosmic Stars, so they couldn't comment on the matter.

"Getting bad vibes, Alice?" Miranda asked.

"I don't like how he undresses me with his eyes."

"He's a man, Alice." Josh piped in.

"I hope you don't undress woman with your eyes, Josh!" Miranda peered at him.

"No, I use my hands. Look at Marc!" Josh laughed.

"He's a drummer too," Allison butted in.

"Blame the drums." Miranda giggled.

Later that evening, while Cosmic Stars were performing their greatest hits, Templeton struggled dressing into their costumes. Allison sported a Sylvester design swing dress and the guys in double-breasted pinstripe suits. The colour theme: black and white.

Marty and Jonathan completed their masterpieces, glittering Allison's hair, and make-up.

The Italian officials ordered Templeton to make haste towards the stage. Finally arriving and assembling by the side of the stage, Allison grabbed Josh's hand and gripped it tight. Templeton watched Cosmic Stars bowing to the screaming crowd.

Alfie, Dave, and Craig walked off-stage in the opposite direction to Stan.

Passing Allison, Stan leaned in. "See you at the party, gorgeous."

Josh glared. "You okay, Alice?"

"Yep, he so gives me the creeps!"

"I see what you mean!"

An Italian official wearing a headset shouted, *"Pronto,"* counting down with his fingers, *"Andare, Andare, Andare!"*

Ricky shouted, "What?"

"Go, go, go!" Donny yelled.

Templeton made their entrance onto the stage, submerged by flashing multicoloured lights. All five members stood in a line together and bowed to the crowd. Screams and cheers engulfed the stadium as the members took their places.

After a successful performance, Templeton walked around the stage to fiery applause. Officials ushered the band to their dressing rooms. Donny moaned at the speed he left the stage.

"Hurry, the backstage pass holders are waiting!" Sebastian cried out.

"I hate signing autographs." Marc replied, pacing along the corridor.

Persisting fans waited in the VIP lounge. Donny, Ricky, and Allison were the first to greet them. Marc tried to turn in the opposite direction when a security guard stopped him.

"Garcia!" Marshall shouted.

Josh and Jack collapsed laughing at the drummer.

An hour after the stadium had emptied, Templeton evacuated the building and attended their hotel after-party.

Flashes bolted from cameras while the band struggled to get inside. Fans were forced back by security, but the press broke through the line. Each member waved and smiled at the paparazzi.

Inside the hotel's gothic-styled ballroom, disco lights flashed onto a barren dance floor, as technical personnel and their teams crowded the bar. Marc Garcia escorted a brunette, gripping her butt.

Donny, Ricky, and Josh chatted with Marshall, while Allison lingered close to Craig and Sebastian. The Cosmic Stars entered the party dragging along hot groupies.

"You ever had a threesome?" Stan whispered in Allison's ear.

Allison turned around and noticed his arm around a beautiful Italian woman approximately her age.

"Where did you come from?"

The young woman squealed, "Allison-Templeton-Miller! *Mio Doi! sei bello!*"

Allison replied sympathetically, "*Grazie.*"

Marty leaned into her and said, "What is she saying?"

"I'm beautiful!"

"You are, baby," winked Stan, walking off with his bed buddy.

Sebastian walked across, offering Allison a glass of red wine. "Good work tonight. Breakfast is at eight o'clock. The car will collect you and Craig at ten. Okay?"

"Yes, sir!" Allison grinned, taking the glass from his hand.

Craig positioned himself next to her and offered Miranda a glass of vodka and cola. Marty and Jonathan ordered bottled beers from passing waiters.

Miranda, pointed towards Stan, "Craig, you have to stay near Alice; that freak over there is a sex pest."

"Which one?" Welling joked.

Josh joined Miranda, placing his arm around her waist while clutching his bottle of beer. "Craig, it's true. Stan has a thing for Alice."

"Everybody has a thing for Alice." Craig looked over at the striking figure mauling the Italian groupie.

The party continued into the early hours. Craig escorted Allison back to her room. With a partition door in between his and Allison's room, Craig could provide extra protection.

Allison hit the goose down pillows without any hesitation; the warm lubrication of hot water from her shower and the chilled red wine operated her snooze button.

Next morning, Sebastian trudged into Allison's suite. Gold-striped curtains hid the Italian sunlight. Sebastian stepped on a damp towel thrown on the bedroom floor.

The king-sized bed exhibited a hump in its centre. Tugging the eiderdown duvet, Sebastian revealed a twenty-two-year-old curled up in a ball. Dressed in white satin Sylvester pyjamas and a matching sleep mask, Allison groaned.

"Wakey, wakey!" Sebastian shouted.

"What time is it?" she grunted.

"6:45."

"Morning or night?"

"Shower and get dressed! Marty and Jonathan will be here in twenty."

"Twenty what?"

"Just get up."

Moaning under her breath, she lifted her mask and hung it on the headboard. The adjoining door opened, and Craig Welling appeared wearing his usual dark grey suit and open-neck white shirt.

"Morning, Craig. Can I borrow your gun?" Sebastian pointed at the fatigued superstar.

"I told you to take a nap, Alice!" Craig laughed.

"Okay, I'm going! In the shower," she winced.

"We will be in Craig's room. Call us when you get dressed." Sebastian walked over into the adjoining room and left the door ajar.

He made himself comfortable in Craig's lavish green chair while the latter sat on the side of the king-sized.

"We have a problem, boss."

Sebastian looked over the top of his glasses at Craig, hands overlapping atop his crossed legs. "What's the problem, my dear man?"

"Stan, Cosmic Stars drummer," Craig said. "Apparently, he's concocting sexual gestures towards Alice."

Sebastian altered his position in the exclusive chair. "Any witnesses?"

"Miranda King and Josh." Craig started to pace around.

"We'll have to keep a close eye on this one. I can fly Tony across."

"Rome? Good idea, boss." Craig grinned, looking out of the window.

"If I disclose some information to you, it must stay in this room between us. Understand?"

Craig nodded at Sebastian and took his place again on the king size.

"They have been many reports of sexual assault regarding this drummer, but nothing is proven. Cosmic Stars management are Australian even though the band are British and, I must say, very professional. I believe Stan, real name Martyn Wardle-Stanley, is a predator. His management team share the same interpretation."

"I'll make the call," Craig answered.

"Good man. I will converse with Cosmic's manager, Jeff." Sebastian asserted.

A knock sounded from inside Allison's room. Sebastian stood and prepared himself to walk into the next room when he heard Allison answering the door. "Morning, you two."

"Morning, Alice. Boy, we need to do some work here," laughed Jonathan, plucking pieces of her hair."

"Rough night!" she said, dressed in black tweed trousers and a white three-quarter length sleeved blouse.

"Sebastian. Good morning," grinned Marty.

"Little Miss Sleepy here couldn't get out of bed this morning," smiled Sebastian, taking his place in Allison's chair.

The two stylists finished a fantastic job on the superstar. Pulling on her tweed jacket and black riding boots, she was ready for breakfast.

Sebastian, Craig, Allison, and her stylists positioned themselves at a centre round table. The restaurant became the focal point in the hotel.

Waiters served spectacular gourmet breakfasts and provided outstanding service within the establishment. Sebastian ordered two Earl Grey teas in china teapots and crockery to match. Craig, Jonathan, and Marty opted for cappuccinos.

Warm croissants took centre stage in breakfast baskets placed on the table. Allison's breakfast overwhelmed her stylists.

"Wow, for someone so little, you can really put it away!" Marty laughed.

"I'm famished," she mumbled, eating another bread roll obscured with lashings of creamy butter.

At the next table, Marshall, and the male members of Templeton, apart from Miranda, took their places waving at the gang of five.

"Good morning, guys and doll!" Sebastian waved back.

"Morning, Sebastian," they all said simultaneously.

"Where's Marc?" Allison shouted over.

All eyes averted up towards the ceiling, and Ricky made a sexual gesture with his index finger sliding through a hole.

"I get it! You think he would settle down before his thingy drops off!" she said, swallowing a strawberry.

"Allison Templeton-Miller!" Sebastian cried out.

"What has she done now?" Marshall leaned over from the next table.

Two members from Cosmic Stars entered the restaurant, dressed in black jeans, crisp white shirts, and striped boating jackets. Their management team and security accompanied them, selecting two tables at the very far side.

"I must say, Cosmic Stars dress very smart, on and off stage," Jonathan remarked.

"Even their security is smart!" Allison chipped in.

"And I'm not?" Craig glared.

Tapping his arm, Allison smiled. "You are always prestigious, Craig. Charles Montgomery suits. Designer guy or what?"

Blushing, Craig drowned himself in his cappuccino.

When breakfast was over, Allison and her table dispersed from the restaurant and headed for the elevators. The Sylvester team were still in Allison's suite, packing luggage for her lunchtime flight to Rome.

302

The elevator door opened and a tall, scantily dressed Italian female looked down at the floor. Raising her head, she ran out of the elevator and disappeared.

"She was in a hurry," Craig said, guiding everyone into the elevator.

Allison looked over her shoulder. "I think that was the girl from last night. Stan's date! Did you see the bruising on her arms?"

Sebastian glared at Craig and changed the subject. "Your car will be ready in half an hour, Alice. You two are accompanying her, so be ready."

Marty and Jonathan replied, "Sebastian, are you travelling separately?"

"I'm afraid so. I have pressing issues to deal with. Craig will be accompanying you."

The elevator doors opened onto the twelfth floor. Sebastian stayed put while the remaining four left for their rooms. The doors closed, and he disappeared.

"What was that all about?" Allison quizzed Craig.

"Business," Craig said.

"My business?"

"Your business is my business."

****

Sebastian Dupont relaxed in a scarlet armchair as a waitress set down a china tea set in front of him. Nodding his appreciation, he greeted his guest.

"Jeff! Please, take a seat…"

Jeff Taylor, the Australian manager of Cosmic Stars, unbuttoned his pin-striped suit jacket and sat down. Jeff's fetching auburn hair and piercing blue eyes, impressed Sebastian.

"Tea?" Sebastian slid a cup and saucer towards Jeff.

"I will decline. I'm a coffee man, myself."

"We have a problem."

"The kind that can be solved with money?" Jeff asked. "Or the kind that doesn't matter?"

"Stan!"

"I see…" Scratching the bottom of his chin, Jeff knew what the next line was going to be.

"Sexual predator!" Sebastian did not mince his words.

"Security is keeping an eye on him."

"Not a very good one!" Sebastian remarked between sips.

"What's happened now?"

"A groupie found her way into his bed last night. This morning it was evident that the sex from him, shall we say, was irregular?"

"How do you know this?"

"My people. In the elevator this morning. She ran past us wearing the same clothing she had on the night before. Apparently covered in bruises."

"How do you know she stayed with Stan?"

"So obvious. A groupie! Sex and the prospect of love afterwards. She was seen with him."

"I see…" Jeff massaged his temples. "What do we do about this? I have no other drummer."

"Any idiot can bang on some bongos." Sebastian clicked his fingers. "But we need to deal with this situation, now! Allison Templeton-Miller is his next prize, and I am stepping up security."

"Who did you contract?" Jeff said, sweating. He felt a cold hand grab his shoulder.

"Mr Welling!" Sebastian said. "How kind of you to join us."

****

Rome, Italy - 3rd August 1978

Templeton disembarked from Green Record's private jet. Six black Range Rovers waited with running engines on the tarmac. Photographers snapped shots as the group posed for pictures. Climbing into their vehicles, the members of Templeton left the airport, passing swarming crowds of fans waving cardboard signs and posters of Allison Templeton-Miller.

The cars maintained their positions following behind one another—a pair of police cars placed themselves at the front and the back with Range Rovers in the middle. Sebastian had met Tony on a US commercial flight and travelled with him in an executive Mercedes explaining the Stan situation.

One hour later, the vehicles arrived at the luxury hotel, and multitudes of people had gathered behind temporary plastic barriers. One by one, the Range Rovers indicated towards an entrance guarded by Gendarmerie and slowly drove to the rear of the hotel.

Allison, Craig, and her personal stylists greeted the hotel management. The second car carried Josh, Miranda, and Marc, followed by Donny, Ricky, and Jack. The remaining three vehicles carried the Sylvester team, hairstylists, and make-up artists. Equipment and technicians had flown in the day before.

Lush suites were issued to Templeton on the tenth floor and double rooms on the fourth floor to Cosmic Stars and their staff. Like usual, Craig had an adjoining room to Allison on the right, while Tony Rosso had adjoining room on the left.

"A security sandwich," Allison said.

"You're not salami, Alice," Craig advised.

A press interview was scheduled at ten o'clock in the morning, and rehearsals were all day. Templeton made the most of their time by relaxing in the bar. Allison stayed in her room speaking to Romano. Brazil was five hours behind Rome, and he only had thirty minutes to chat because of his filming break.

Cosmic Stars had arrived just after Templeton and joined them in the bar. Stan, on the other hand, thought he would check out Allison and sneaked away to floor ten.

Stan walked down the corridor and listened at each door. He finally heard what he was searching for: suite fifteen. Peering over his shoulder, he walked in the direction of the stairs, rubbing both his hands together. This was going to be his lucky night, he buzzed.

Templeton later gathered in a remote private bar attached to the hotel. The trendy, bright, friendly establishment served alcoholic beverages and hot snacks. Sebastian paid a large sum of money to compensate for the loss of business and the bar closed its doors to the public for a few hours.

Allison accompanied Craig and Tony, telling them that Romano was lovesick in Brazil.

"That would be another great song," Allison laughed.

"Are you talking to yourself again, Alice?" Welling asked.

"Only if you stop listening."

Taking their places inside a booth. Craig, Tony, and Allison watched bottle beers, whiskey, and orange juice flowing around the other tables.

"Agenda!" Sebastian sounded above the chatting. "10:00: press conference, thirty minutes. Sylvester people! Stadium dressing room setup: a bus will be collecting you all at 9:00. Lunch at 12:00. Cars collect at 13:30, and no straddling. Rehearsals are at 15:00. Photoshoots from 17:00, then food. You're on stage at 20:00, after Cosmic! Any questions?"

Everyone nodded.

"Security will be tight from now on," Marshall butted in. "No groupies!"

Marc moaned.

"Get yourself a wife!" Ricky laughed.

"I prefer other men's!" Marc replied.

"Gentleman, please. We have security issues, and I must stress this is serious," bellowed Sebastian.

Everyone went silent. "You!" Jack whispered at Allison. "The security thing is about you!"

Jack Evens had sneaked into the booth and sat by Allison's side.

Allison whispered back, "How do you know it's me?"

"You're the most famous. It's got to be you!"

The meeting continued over more drinks and snacks as they memorised the timetable. Sebastian issued signed posters to all the staff and approved the photographs to be taken with the band.

Leaving the bar through the side exit, Templeton made their way towards the hotel restaurant. Stan hustled into a dark alcove and stepped out in time to catch a glimpse of Allison.

Allison noticed him blowing her kisses and she flinched grabbing hold of Craig's arm. Stan shuttled away from the restaurant towards the restrooms.

A young, naive Italian waitress besotted by the handsome drummer bumped into him. Stan held out his arms and rested them upon her shoulders. Glancing into his beautiful face, she blushed.

"You work in the bar?" he asked.

She shook her head. "*Si.* "

"English?"

"*Piccolo, si…*" She nodded while her heart pounded.

"*Bueno!*" he said, pulling her into the male restroom and kissed her against the tiled wall. The bronzed, soft-skinned waitress fell into his embrace. He locked the door and ripped her panties down and caressed her sex.

Moaning wildly, the waitress yanked the zip open of his jeans and tugged at the bulge that lay dormant. Picking her up and sitting her on top of the vanity unit, he let go of his button and forced his jeans down. Opening her wide Stan slid himself inside. With no respect he pounded hard against the unit, fondling her breast with force. It was seconds before he ejaculated.

He quickly removed himself from inside the waitress and placed both hands on top of the vanity unit. Staring uncontrollably into the mirror he noticed the waitress looking disappointed at the quick session.

"I need you to do a job for me," he said, panting. "*Trabajo?*"

"*Si.*"

Yanking up his jeans he produced a plastic package from his pocket containing white powder.

"You. Put this," shaking the bag of white powder towards her face. "In Allison Templeton-Miller's wine. *Vino!* Yes?"

"*Si.*" The waitress grabbed the bag. "*I...poot...n. Allison... vino...si!*"

"Yes!" he grinned.

"*Te da?*"

"Yes, now. If you're a good girl, I'll give you some more of this!" Stan said, gripping his bulge.

****

Allison enjoyed the familial company of Sebastian, Craig, and Tony at the sumptuous dining table. Nibbling spiced chicken sticks, she ordered another glass of red merlot from the waitress.

"Alice, darling, you must cut down on your eating. You never know when the next photoshoot will be nude," gestured Sebastian, tasting his cool glass of champagne.

"I'm only on my second course."

"Of what, the hour?"

"Sebastian, how many have you ordered?"

"Three."

"I'm the youngest, and I require energy as a superstar!" she spat.

"Youngest? You will be the fattest," Craig scoffed.

The waitress carried the merlot on a silver tray and interrupted the laughter by placing the glass on the table in front of Allison. "*Eccoti,*" she said with a bow.

Allison smiled and nodded. Taking a sip, she scowled. "This tastes different."

"Darling, they're called spices. You've probably never noticed them before with your Caucasian tastebuds," advised Sebastian.

Crockery clattered and assorted aromas wafted through the restaurant. Contemporary golden lights twinkled above the structure, silhouetting solid, featureless shapes.

Drowsiness conquered Allison halfway through her third course of gnocchi.

Sebastian, Craig, and Tony glanced at one another.

"You tired, Alice?" Craig said, tapping her right hand.

"Hmm?" she replied, dropping her fork.

Sebastian glanced at his pocket watch. It was early: eight o'clock. "You must be jet-lagged! Strange, it was only a three-hour flight."

"Tony, Craig can you escort Alice to her room." Sebastian choired.

"Sure thing, boss!" Craig nodded back at Sebastian.

Trying not to arouse any attention, Tony and Craig accompanied Allison to suite fifteen. Once inside, Allison collapsed. Craig dropped to his feet to check her pulse. Tony walked in and witnessed the horror.

"What's happened?" he shouted.

"Her heartbeat is shallow! Get Sebastian!" Craig growled.

Tony rushed out of the room and ran down the stairwell. A ping came from the elevator, and the doors opened. Stan walked out and turned left towards Allison's suite.

Craig lifted Allison onto the bed and tried to make her comfortable. The door handle turned; Craig knew that Tony would have rushed back into the room. Flicking the light switch, he drew his semi-automatic and clicked the safety off.

"Alley cat, I'm here," a voice whispered from the door.

"Freeze!" Craig screamed, kicking door closed and pointing his pistol at the intruder's head.

Stan froze on the spot with both hands in the air.

"On the floor!" Craig yelled.

"Okay, okay," Stan said, kneeling.

"You're lucky there are too many witnesses, or I'd paint the bathtub with your brains."

Tony ran into the room, slamming the door shut in Sebastian's face. "What the f—"

"Hold this." Craig tossed the sidearm to Tony.

Pulling out a ball of cable ties, Craig kicked Stan in the back, so he fell face-forward into the carpet. Welling tied Stan's hands behind his back.

Sebastian, still clutching his forehead from walking into the door, felt Allison's to get her temperature. Picking up the telephone receiver, he called management and demanded a doctor.

"Flip him over, Tony." Craig threw him a roll of electrical tape from his bag.

Tony hurled the villain onto a wicker chair and duct-taped his legs. "What did you give her?" Sebastian screamed.

"Zolpidem," Stan spat. "Crushed, not stirred."

The hotel manager unlocked the door with a master key. Craig shook the doctor's hand. Standing in shock, the manager couldn't believe what he was witnessing. The doctor ran over to the bed carrying a leather case.

"Zolpidem! Thirty milligrams." Sebastian said.

"A sedative. That's triple the dosage." Listening to her heart and pulse, he remained silent. "My team will pump her stomach. She should survive."

Sebastian cringed. "How long until she wakes up?"

"Eight to ten hours. She will be very ill. I recommend a bowl for the sickness and keep the bathroom ready. I'll write you a script for Sulfamethoxazole." The doctor passed a prescription into Sebastian's hand. "Keep her hydrated."

Sebastian thanked the doctor as he returned to his post. "Allison's incident cannot leave the room. And have hospitality clean up this piece of dirt," he said, kicking Stan's feet.

The hotel manager agreed. "I will contact the *Polizia Stradale*. They'll be discreet."

"Thank you…"

While the manager called the authorities on the telephone in Craig's room, Sebastian realised Allison would not be performing in tomorrow night's show.

"Craig, we must submit Alice's apologies at the press conference in the morning, stomach bug. Also, we need a meeting with Marshall and Jeff." Sebastian turned to Stan and pointed, "You're fired!"

Two police officers booked Stan for sexual assault. They escorted him down the stairwell and slipped out the rear

314

entrance. The hotel manager accompanied the authorities and ensured staff were kept out of sight.

Craig left the shambled room and ordered Sylvester staff to dress Allison into her nightwear and watch her for the night.

Sebastian and Tony met with Marshall and Jeff in a concealed meeting room near reception. Ordering tea and coffee, Sebastian commenced the meeting.

"Marshall, plan B!"

"Oh, is Alice not performing tomorrow?" he said surprisingly.

"Stomach bug and attempted rape." Sebastian announced.

"What!" Jeff shouted.

"Your predator spiked her drink, then tried to break into her room with a stolen keycard!"

"How do you know it was him?"

"Don't ask me. Ask the jury."

Jeff shook his head in defeat.

"So, what's the plan?" Marshall piped in.

"Marc will play for Cosmic and Templeton. Ricky and Donny take the lead: Plan B."

"Got it!" Marshall agreed.

"You are talking about my band without my say so." Jeff cut in.

"You couldn't manage a kindergarten, never mind a world tour," Sebastian lashed out. "If anyone mentions this to the press, I will sue until your estate is worth less than a bag of donuts. Understand?"

Jeff held his head in his hands. "I can't get a drummer on notice this short."

"That's your problem, not mine!" Sebastian shoved his cold tea to one side and stormed out of the room.

****

Rome, Italy - 4th August 1978 - 7.00 a.m.

The morning sunlight cast a rosy hue across the bedroom. Allison slept beneath an alluring duvet without eye movement or muscle activity, unresponsive.

Craig opened the adjoining door and walked into Allison's suite. Noticing a Sylvester dresser asleep in a chair, Craig approached the snoozing female and gently coughed.

"Alice all right?" he whispered.

Opening her eyes, the dresser squinted. "Hasn't moved since yesterday."

"Coffee, miss…"

"Adele. Adele Blacken," she yawned, rubbing both eyes.

"Blacken? So, no creamer?"

"First man to make that joke all day," she replied.

Craig tackled the coffee machine and returned with two mugs, handing one to Adele.

Adele giggled, seeing him sit on a child's stool. "You want to swap with me?"

"It's all right; I'm a kid at heart," he said sipping a bit of his hot coffee.

"Do the ladies call you Craig or Mr Welling?"

"They don't call me at all," he answered. "I have noticed you for a while now…Never knew your name."

"You're an American," she said. "Not knowing things is your national pastime."

"That's enough out of you, cheeky," Craig blushed and looked down into his mug again. "Do you like bodyguards?"

"Only when they're protecting me." She dipped her head down again.

Craig was just about to ask her out on a date when a stirring sound echoed from behind.

"She's waking up!" Adele jumped from the chair.

Rushing over to the bed, Craig and Adele observed moaning and grunting. Allison propped up her head on the pillow. Stomach-wrenching retching flooded the king-sized. Adele placed a stainless-steel bowl on top of the duvet. Craig ran to the other side of the bed and grabbed her arm.

"Help me sit her up," he said.

Adele grabbed the other arm and pulled her up with Craig. Allison's head floppy, eyes clenched closed, she continued to vomit. Adele repositioned the bowl in front of her.

"Poor thing," whispered Adele.

Craig couldn't watch. Like a volcanic reaction, all the toxins erupted from Allison's stomach.

"So much for the doctor's stomach pump," Craig said.

"We need another bowl!" Adele cried.

Craig rang the reception for an entire set of mixing bowls. After a few minutes, a blunt knock came from the door. Craig ran over to take the fresh crockery from two maids.

Sebastian entered the room while the maids collected the soiled bowl. Covering his nose and mouth with a silk handkerchief, Sebastian gasped. "My goodness, that smells!"

Craig mopped his brow with the back of his hand. "This is bad, boss!"

"She'll require lots of water." Sebastian stared in horror at the helpless creature.

"I need a drink too!" Craig butted in.

"Adele, my darling, would you be so kind enough to nurse Alice today?" Sebastian asked.

"Of course…Could I take a minute to freshen up?"

"Take as long as you need."

"Thank you," she walked towards the door and disappeared down the corridor.

Allison was now awake, choking up another bowl of vomit. White as snow and dripping sweat from her forehead, she couldn't care if the room caught on fire.

"My poor Alice, you look like a sitcom during a writer's strike. I'm afraid you won't be performing today. We arranged for Adele to look after you." Sebastian muffled instructions into his handkerchief.

"But the band needs me…"

"The band needs you to get better," Craig smiled.

"Can we get some more air fresheners?" asked Sebastian.

Planning his next move – Marc Garcia and Marshall. It was going to be a fun morning.

****

Marc Garcia perched against a table; arms folded. Wearing skinny jeans and a Templeton t-shirt, he looked casual. Marshall Rusk, on the other hand, paced the carpeted floor.

"Stan resigned last night," Rusk said.

"Couldn't get his own way?" asked Marc.

"You could say that."

"So, you're going to suggest I take the drums for Cosmic."

"No. I'm going to demand it."

"That will never happen," Marc bit a fingernail.

"Why?" Marshall stopped in his tracks.

"Their management team are useless!"

"If managers weren't useless, they wouldn't be managers." Marshall looked over at Marc. "Are you okay taking the drums for Cosmic and Templeton?"

"All right, but I'm not changing outfits!"

"Deal. Now go and rehearse. Get a feel for their songs."

"Must do my best," Marc winked and walked out of the side entrance. "You owe me."

Hotel staff entered the room, organising and arranging tables and chairs. Jugs of iced water blotted out tables; microphone stands were unsheathed.

Donny Davis rushed in. "Plan B…Alice is ill, vomiting!"

"Darling, you didn't have to experience the smell!" Sebastian answered.

"Sebastian, Donny…Marc has agreed to proceed with both bands." Marshall said.

"I knew he'd come through for us," Sebastian grinned. "Good man."

"So, the show will continue with Cosmic?" Donny butted in.

"Continue? The show must go on!" Sebastian smiled at a waitress scurrying past. "Hang on, madam! *Aspetta Li*!" shouted Sebastian.

The waitress stopped but didn't turn around.

"*Messo I sonniferi nel vino*!" Sebastian shouted.

Still unresponsive, she remained in the same position. Sebastian clicked his fingers and ordered the hotel manager to attend the room.

Sebastian whispered to Marshall and Donny, "We need a moment."

Both acknowledged Sebastian and removed themselves from the conference room. The day manager attended to Sebastian's request amid the clattering of equipment.

"You hear about the incident last night?" Sebastian said.

"Yes?" the manager nodded.

"That young lady was the waitress who served Alice her last drink."

The manager listened and walked towards her. Sofia started sobbing as he escorted her into a staff area. The door behind them clicked closed.

Sebastian ordered tea in the lounge area of the hotel and made himself comfortable. Sporting a navy-blue suit, pink cravat, and matching handkerchief, he thought long and hard about purchasing a cane to support his style.

The police stepped into the foyer, weapons at the ready.

"Staff area," Sebastian pointed with a silver spoon.

"What's that smell?" the detective said. "Earl Grey?"

He shuffled back into his chair and hid around the groves. Sipping his piping hot tea, Sebastian enjoyed the moment.

****

Adele approached the king-sized bed and removed the stainless-steel bowl away from Allison.

"How are you feeling?" she asked.

"Oh!" Allison replied, leaning into her pillow.

"Would you like a bath? Revitalise your strength!"

"Sure," she said. "Just close your eyes."

"Certainly." Adele removed the duvet from Allison. "I'll go and run your bath. Lavender?"

Splattering above the water and gasping for air, Allison emerged from the foam. Brushing away the soap from her eyes, she noticed Adele standing in the doorway speaking with Craig. Whispers and giggles pierced the steam as Allison tried to eavesdrop.

Closing the door behind her, Adele sat on the toilet seat and gripped a dove-soft bath sheet.

"Craig!" Allison's eyebrows danced.

"Craig who?" blushed Adele, gripping the towel even tighter.

"He likes you!"

"I'm not entirely sure on that."

"Rubbish!" Allison splashed her hand above the water. "Never ignore love."

"It wouldn't work!"

"Why?"

"He's your security. I work for Phillippe."

"When does your contract with Sylvester end?"

"I'm not sure, two years?"

"Good, you will be my personal assistant, I'm promoting you." Allison coughed.

Adele was speechless.

"I'll pay you double. Triple if you bring me a fresh bowl to throw up in."

"What should I say to Phillippe?"

"Nothing. Carry on and do not sign Phillippe's new contract," Allison sputtered, wiping the soap from her face.

"I don't know…"

"Yes…You say yes! To Craig and me."

Allison escaped the tub. Cushioned in between a huge soft towel and furry slippers, she headed towards the bedroom. Adele exchanged her wet, soggy towel for pink satin pyjamas. When she was fully presentable, Allison lay at the top of the bed drinking iced cold water.

"I'm starved! Can you arrange food, Adele?" Allison asked.

Adele discarded the dirty laundry and nodded in admission. She disappeared, leaving Allison relaxing on her pillow.

"Are you decent?" Craig yelled from next door.

"Only at singing!" Allison yelled back.

"Boy, you look a lot better."

"I feel it…I'm starved!"

"You need food? I'll get your something."

"No! Adele is sorting me a club sandwich."

"Good."

"You should ask her out!"

"Wow! Get straight to the point, Alice."

"So…"

"I nearly did." Craig grinned while he sat at the bottom of the king-sized. "Before you threw up."

"So do it after lunch. Tony can take over tonight."

"Allison Templeton-Miller, back from the dead!" Craig laughed.

"Not until Jonathan fixes my hair."

"You think she would?"

"You two are made for one another, and she will always be my assistant, Sylvester or no Sylvester."

The two of them laughed and talked until Adele interrupted them with a club sandwich. Leaving Allison on her own, Craig and Adele escaped into his room. The lovers arranged a date in the restaurant that evening.

Allison enjoyed the company of Jonathan and Marty. Tony arrived to confirm the security change. He smiled at Jonathan and Marty's creation – Allison Templeton-Miller back from the dead.

The concert in Rome was a great success, and the band paid tribute to Allison by sending flowers, cards, and gifts to suite fifteen.

The next few days were hectic for the band. Templeton and Allison flew to Belgium. Back to full health, Allison attended interviews and thanked her fans for all the gifts she had received.

Martyn Wardle-Stanley was charged with attempted rape and held in custody until his hearing. The waitress Sofia Rus was also charged as an accomplice and was released on bail until the trial.

Sofia grassed on Martyn and in her defence had been a victim of lust, lured in by a predator. The Italian authority's affirmation of the case was sealed confidential, so no media would apprehend the story.

Sebastian organised Burrows and Burrows Lawyers in New York to attend the trial on Allison's behalf.

After eight weeks of a gruelling and successful sell-out tour in Europe, Sebastian declared himself the most desirable, matchless manager in the world and treated himself to a Russian Faberge cane. Reuniting with Oliver and shaking on more business deals for Templeton, he relaxed in his New York apartment and bade goodbye to an extraordinary year.

Allison attended the Television Awards in LA with her beloved fiancé. Dressed in a black and red Spanish-styled evening gown, she presented the best TV Drama Award.

Leaving the ceremony early, Romano and Allison headed home to Porta del Castello. The couple had a lot of making up to do.

Romano, Templeton, and other associated personnel were still not aware of the incident in Rome. Green Records wanted it to remain that way.

Before the trip to Belgium, Adele, Craig, Tony, Sebastian, Marshall, and Jeff Taylor signed a non-disclosure agreement. Allison didn't read it but signed it anyway.

EPILOGUE

Tuscany - Italy - 31st December 1978

Allison sighed. "I love it here," she said, admiring the beautiful hilly landscapes overlooking the medieval historic town below.

"I love you." Romano lovingly touched her hand from across the small metal table.

"I don't want to do this anymore." She refilled her wineglass and stared at the cloudless sky.

Romano froze. "Us?"

"No." Turning her head around, she looked into his Latin eyes. "Music, films, fame? I want to be a mother, a wife, a family!"

"My love…I want that too." Romano stood up and pulled her into him. "This was my dream: to propose here, where I grew up."

Allison looked up at him and sighed, "Our world, we sacrifice everything to achieve fame! Let's be normal."

Romano bent down on one knee, holding both of her delicate hands in his. "Allison Templeton-Miller nothing about you is normal. Will you marry me?"

Allison stammered, as she tried to form her words. Romano swept her off her feet and kissed her heart-shaped lips.

Welcome to the family – Allison Templeton-Mancini.

The Heavenly Body - Book 2

Matrimonium

A cultural universal

An institution

A wedding ceremony

1st June 1980

Romano Matteo Mancini and Allison Marie Templeton-Miller

PROLOGUE

Las Vegas - 15th March 1979

Mountain ranges, desert vegetation, and rocky landscapes surrounded a pool within the Mojave Desert. Sprawling, glitzy illuminations cascaded into the darkness. Congested intersections of the Las Vegas Boulevard flowed freely through the city of shopping, fine dining, and high-stakes gambling.

Nirvana International Hotel hosted a panoramic city viewpoint gracing the dazzling skyline. The jewel of Vegas, with world-class butler service, accommodated the Templeton's Three Nights in Vegas Tour.

Opening the button-tufted suiting fabric door, Allison strolled into Donny and Belinda's suite. High-quality furnishings embellished the room with opulent, expensive touches.

A voice screeched, making its debut. "Turn around and don't look."

Allison closed her eyes and turned around, smiling. Belinda shouted, "Surprise!"

"Oh my God!" Allison opened her eyes in bewilderment.

Flaunting flawlessly, Belinda exhibited a pink cowgirl outfit. "What do you think?"

"Hmm…Good!"

"Better than good. It's show biz, baby." Belinda pointed into the prestige walk-in wardrobe. 'Yours is hung up in there'.

"Why are we wearing fancy dress?" Allison walked into the dressing area.

"I'm getting married!" she squealed.

"Married, tonight?" Allison was in shock.

"Yes, and you are my maid of honour!" screamed Belinda, ecstatically bouncing up and down.

"I thought you wanted a white wedding. You've been canvassing every bridal magazine on the shelves for months."

"Well, I can't wait any longer, and we agreed it'll be fun!"

"What about Fay and Lucinda?"

"After tonight, the invitations will be posted".

"Invitations?"

"The girls have arranged our celebrations at the Marianna next month, two hundred guests…Alice! You know, a wedding reception!"

"Oh, do you have a dress?"

"Yes, designed by Charles Montgomery…All hush," Belinda beamed with pride. "Come on, let's get dressed, or we'll miss the ceremony".

"Where are we going?" Allison said, taking the outfit off the hanger.

"The little gingerbread house! Honeybee John is marrying us."

"For goodness sake, Belinda," Allison said, struggling into the skirt. "Will this be legal?"

"It's all legal and above board!"

Allison eagle-eyed herself in the mirror: a pink rhinestone-tasselled shirt, pink denim miniskirt, white cowgirl riding boots, and a pink Stetson. Belinda ran up to her and hugged her hard. As both nodded in approval, Belinda said, "Let's go and get married, girl!"

Lurking outside the suite, Craig Welling leaned against a carpeted wall surrounded by greenery, clutching Adele in his huge arms. Suddenly, the door swung open. Grasping a pink and white posy, Belinda bounded into the small foyer with Allison behind her.

"You as well?" Allison laughed.

"I'm afraid so…Still prepared, though!" Craig opened his white waistcoat to reveal his weapon.

Adele was dressed in the same pink attire as Belinda and Allison, while Craig was dressed in his white cowboy suit. Allison assumed that the groom and his merry men were all wearing white.

Craig escorted the girls towards the rear of the hotel where a white limousine was waiting, camouflaged in pink silk ribbons. Excited at the prospect of her long-awaited wedding, Belinda dived in first.

The stretch limo soon approached a multicoloured house enclosed by flowered picket fencing. Inside the stone building sat a nervous groom and an impersonator of the famous comedian Honeybee John.

Belinda screamed in delight, "We're here!"

"Don't we know it?" Allison said.

Craig and Adele expressed amusement towards the bride. The limo pulled up by a white entrance gate exhibiting a red carpet. The uniformed chauffeur opened the rear passenger door and stepped back in complete surprise as the bride leapt out. Allison followed, smiling apologetically towards the driver. Adele giggled at the comedy show.

Two white rhinestone cowboys waved, standing in the chapel foyer. Jack and Marc chatted between themselves, gesturing the bride forward.

"You guys as well?" Allison observed the Toscano pedestals of lavished white lilies and pink peony garlands.

"I think I look sexy," Marc replied.

Craig howled with laughter. "This is going to be a good night!"

"A good day…It's midnight!" Belinda marched towards another set of glass doors. "Come on, let's do this."

Josh shrugged at Marc, following her. Allison walked behind them, shaking her head in disarray. Glancing at the altar, she noticed Donny and his best man Ricky were also dressed in white cowboy suits. Sitting between the posy-covered pews was her friend Miranda dressed in pink, imaging all the cowgirls in the place.

Belinda screamed, "I'm here, husband!"

Standing by the altar, Donny seemed nervous, overlapping both his hands against himself. Ricky cried with laughter, trying to compose himself. A figure towered behind the groom and best man, sporting dark sunglasses and a black and orange suit.

"Oh no," Allison whispered, apprehending Honeybee, kneeling at her feet.

"Allison Templeton-Miller…It's an honour, honey," Honeybee said in his southern drawl.

Belinda arrived at the altar and stood against Donny. Everyone else filed into the pews. Opening the ceremony, Honeybee began to sing '*Bee cause I love you forever*'.

Allison cringed and sank further into her seat. Turning her head in confusion, she noticed everyone else was in hysterics. Not amused by the show, she zoned out, playing with her shirt tassels. The booming voice snapped her attention back, making her jump.

"We are gathered here today to witness the vows between Donald Alfred Davis and Belinda Jane Ross-Belling. Today, we will join Donald Alfred and Belinda Jane in holy matrimony. If there are any dis – bee - lievers, speak now or go away! Good…Please repeat after me. I, Belinda Jane Ross-Belling, take thee, Donald Alfred Davis, my buzzy bee, to love you, baby, all my life."

Belinda repeated her vows. Now it was Donny's turn.

"I, Donald Alfred Davis, who is your honey bunny, take thee, Belinda Ross-Belling, to love you, baby, all my life." Honeybee declared.

Donny gazed into Belinda's eyes, gripping both of her delicate hands, and repeated his vows.

Honeybee cut in, "The rings, Ricky".

Ricky passed two diamond wedding rings over to the mimic.

"Please take this moment to exchange your gifts of love". Honeybee said.

Ricky collapsed into the pew, teary-eyed from laughter and exhaustion.

Donny placed the ring onto Belinda's third finger left hand, repeating after Honeybee, "Baby, you got me all buzzed up".

"Belinda, repeat after me: I will love you honey," she repeated, whilst placing Donny's wedding ring onto his third finger.

"By the powers vested in me, I now pronounce you husband and wife". Honeybee took a step back. "You may kiss the bride".

Applause, cheering, and whistling consumed the entire gingerbread house. Allison, highly delighted that the ceremony was over, stood with Adele and Craig. Josh rushed around with his camera, taking snaps of the bridal party.

The bride and groom posed for official photographs and signed their marriage certificate to prove they were legal.

Honeybee made a play for Allison. Craig stepped in. "Could I have your autograph and photo, please?" A quiet western accent escaped from Honeybee.

"Sure!" Allison bobbed her head.

Craig stepped to one side and allowed Honeybee to walk forward with a pen and paper.

"What is your name?"

"Andrew...Please sign it, 'To Andy'." Smiling, he handed his pen over to Allison.

Allison shouted at Josh to snap Honeybee and herself. "You are funny...I never thought you were ordained".

"Night school."

"Wow. You passed?"

"The third time." Looking down at her, he smiled while posing for the instant camera. Within five minutes, Josh developed the print by shaking it around in the air. The image of Honeybee and Allison slowly emerged.

"I am so honoured. I'll keep this forever," Honeybee said.

"Are you a Templeton fan?" Allison asked.

"Huge…I got all your records. God's truth, I just bought your second solo album."

"Is it okay if I send one of my people tomorrow with two VIP tickets?"

"Really?"

"Yes, you made my friends very happy tonight. Or should I say this morning'. Allison grabbed his hand. 'I want to thank you personally. Tomorrow is our last night, and I would like you and a chosen guest to attend."

"I don't know what to say."

"Andy, I mean, Honeybee says, 'Buzzing Las Vegas!'" she laughed.

The impersonator bowed in awe before the Queen of Pop, accepting her gift.

Templeton, Craig, Miranda, and Adele crumpled into the limo, waving goodbye to the gingerbread house staff and Honeybee. Corks popped, disco lights flashed, music blasted. The limo engulfed the celebrations with an hour-long excursion along Las Vegas Boulevard.

Two o'clock in the morning and the city continued to party, from casinos to restaurants and clubs. The limo entered the rear entrance of the Nirvana International. Everyone embarked upon weariness when the car parked in the VIP slot. Belinda kissed Donny and asked the guys to wait outside, requesting a one-to-one with the girls.

The cowboys dispersed from the limo while the pink cowgirls remained seated inside.

"I want to thank you all, for all of this." Belinda began tearing up, wafting her hand around the limo.

"I couldn't ask for better from my friends. You guys have supported Donny and me," she sobbed.

"It's your wedding day." Alice hugged her. "Don't cry".

"I'm not crying."

"Go to your husband. It's your wedding night. Have lots of sex and make babies!" Allison giggled.

"Let me remind you, Allison Templeton-Miller: it's your turn next!" Belinda laughed.

Adele and Miranda joined in the conversation. "Allison Miller-Mancini!" they all bellowed at the same time.

"1st June 1980, fifteen months. Not long, girl!" Belinda smirked, wiping her eyes.

"Oh." Allison never said anything else after that.

The happy couple encountered their honeymoon suite. Allison sat alone in her room wearing black satin Sylvester pyjamas, pondering her extravagant wedding.

Sipping a cup of Earl Grey tea, admiring the scenic views of Vegas, she shuddered at the year ahead. Life would be changing dramatically. Would she be ready?

Ingram Content Group UK Ltd.
Milton Keynes UK
UKHW020801190723
425424UK00017B/365